Published by Grays Harbor Publishing.
graysharborpublishing.com

Cover design by Clayton Swim.

Aberdeen (Grays Harbor Series: Book 3) First Edition

ISBN: 978-1948714051

This book is dedicated to my sister, Danell, for pointing out my shortcomings before the world was allowed to see them.

By 'shortcomings', I meant professional, not personal. In that regard, I'm exceptionally well-adjusted and humble.

PROLOGUE
WESTPORT

Opening his bedroom door, seventeen-year-old Aaron Williams can hear the wind blowing through the front door as his father exits the house in search of his stepmother, Diane, who went missing earlier in the evening. He feels Amanda's hand reach out and hold onto his arm, pulling him closer, then she begins to whisper something to him. He wants more than anything to be out there with his dad, instead of searching the house yet again with his twelve-year-old sister — but as he bends down to listen to her, he can hear the fear in her voice, and he realizes how unfair it would be to her if she were to be left by herself in a house with no electricity, and no possible way to call for help.

"It'll be alright, sis..." he says soothingly. "Dad will find her, trust me."

"He won't find her — not out there."

"Why do you think that?" Aaron is bent down, with his ear right next to her mouth, and he can hear the excitement in her voice as she slowly pulls away from him.

"Because she's still in the house..."

He looks down at her and sees a glint of shimmering light coming from her hand, and by the time he realizes that it's a knife, she's already plunging it toward his chest. Barely missing, she swipes the blade down across his face, slicing the skin open on his left cheek — and then she thrusts it into his coat, missing the flesh on his waist by only a fraction of an inch. Desperate to get away, he pushes her

1

against the bedroom wall and runs out of the room, holding the door closed behind him.

"Dad!" he screams, hoping that his father, Paul, will hear him and come running. "Dad, you have to help me!"

"Aaron, open the door — I'm hurt," he hears Amanda say from the other side of the door.

"Just stay put until Dad gets here." Feeling the blood running down his face, he reaches up and wipes some of it from his chin, as it drips steadily onto the carpeted floor below. Looking down the corridor at the front door, seeing no sign of his dad anywhere, he feels the handle on the door beginning to twist — at first gently, but then more forcefully as he struggles to hold it shut.

"Check under their bed, Aaron," she says, rattling the door violently as she begins kicking it.

"Knock it off! Just stay calm!" Surprised at his sister's strength, he wonders whether he can hold her back for very long. Then he looks behind his shoulder at the door directly across the hall — a thick, solid wood panel that leads to the full basement underneath the house.

"She wanted to take us away from here, but I stopped her," she says, suddenly stopping her assault on the door.

He hears a tapping on the other side, like she's slowly jabbing the tip of the knife into the surface of the door. He holds onto the handle tightly with both hands, using the wall next to him as leverage with his body as he waits for her to continue her attack — and after several seconds of complete silence, he feels a sharp, piercing pain in his arm as the blade of her knife slides through the gap between the jam and the door. Letting go of the handle, he turns around and almost falls down onto the floor, his stomach feeling queasy as he opens the basement door and escapes into the dark space beyond. As he shuts the door behind him, his fingers search desperately for any sign of a

2

lock that might keep her from doing the same thing — and then he hears his bedroom door opening, and the delicate footsteps of his sister as she walks across the hallway and stands directly in front of him. He can feel his heart pounding as he holds on tightly to the handle, but instead of trying to open the door, she does something far worse — she locks it.

"Aaron... Amanda..." he hears from the living room, recognizing his father's voice. "Are you guys in here...?"

"Dad, help!" Aaron cries out, slamming his fists against the door as he hears the first gunshot, followed closely by another one. "Dad, can you hear me?" He beats on the solid door until his hands hurt, and then he listens closely as a slow, quiet set of footsteps echo faintly across the hardwood flooring in the living room. Soon the steps come closer, and he sees the shadows of shoes through the gap under the door.

"Aaron, are you there?" asks Amanda.

With his legs suddenly feeling wobbly, Aaron turns around and sits down on the steps, crying uncontrollably as he listens to Amanda giggling on the other side of the door.

"By the way, you left your flashlight out here. If you stay quiet and do what I say, I might give it back to you."

After hearing her walk away, he sits down on the stairs for a while, his mind racing in circles as he tries to comprehend what just happened. With his legs still feeling numb and unsteady, he stands up and tries the handle again, hoping that she might have unlocked it before leaving — but as he attempts to turn the handle and push helplessly against it, the sound of something being dragged across the floor in the master bedroom and into the hallway causes him to scramble down the stairs in fear, hiding in the corner of the dark room once he reaches the bottom. When the door opens and fills the room with light, he can see at least two rats scurrying back into the darkness in the opposite corner, and Amanda's silhouette holding a gun at the top of the stairs.

"Don't try anything stupid," he hears her say, as she turns around and pulls something onto the stair landing.

He steps out into the open, figuring that he might be able to plead with her. "Amanda, listen..." Before he gets a chance to say anything more, however, he looks up and sees something tumbling down the staircase, landing only inches from his feet. He glances up just as she exits the room, closing the door behind her once more — but the last thing he sees before the light disappears completely from the space around him, is the tortured look on his stepmother's face, staring back at him from the lifeless corpse that's now lying at the foot of the steps.

The last time he looked at his cell phone, right before the battery finally went dead, it said that he'd been trapped in the basement for nearly three days — and that was at least a day ago. Like clockwork, every evening around dinner time, Amanda shows up at the door with something to eat — and every time, just before leaving again, she spits on the food and then kicks the plate down the staircase. The fact that most of it lands on Diane's body doesn't really bother him much, since he has a hunch that the meal might be poisoned anyway. So far, his only source of food or liquid has been a jar of canned peaches that was probably forgotten on a shelf long ago, and because he's been rationing the contents carefully, he can start to feel himself becoming weaker.

His pleas for help have mostly gone unanswered, although one evening she did talk to him for a long time about what was going on in the neighborhood — a conversation that was entirely one-sided.

Amanda's mental state had never really been all that stable, especially after their last visit with their birth mother. She seemed to take her rejection out on everyone, except for the person who truly deserved it. Their mother was a drug addict and a drunk, and had disappointed both of her children more times than Aaron cared to remember — but while his attitude eventually turned indifferent and detached, Amanda's remained forever loyal to a parent that viewed her as nothing more than an unwanted responsibility. As much as he'd like to blame her latest behavior on the virus, which he can't even be certain that she has, his instinct tells him that her sudden turn toward violence is merely another progression in her psychological collapse — one that he'll be lucky to survive.

As he huddles into the corner beside the stairs, out of sight from the landing above — he can hear the rats somewhere in front of him, gnawing on either the food his sister has left for him, or on Diane herself. Annoyed at the sound of it, he stands up quickly and throws an empty glass jar across the room at them, shattering it into thousands of sharp pieces on the floor. For a minute he stays still, hoping that the noise didn't anger Amanda, but then he spots something on the other side of the room, a speck of light shining back at him from the far wall. Hearing nothing coming from upstairs, he stumbles across the floor until he reaches the source of the light, feeling around on the wall until he grabs onto a doorknob. He nearly drops to his knees as he remembers that the basement has an outside entrance, something his father said was once used to load coal into the basement — a discovery that would've been much more useful three or four days ago when he was still strong enough to break a door down. When his hand grips the knob and turns it, he's surprised when the door slowly swings open and reveals a set of double doors above him. He can see daylight coming through the spaces in the boards as he climbs up the steps ahead of him, and a single bolt latch that's locking the doors in place. As carefully as he can, with his hands shaking from low blood sugar, he manages to squeeze two fingers through the tight space between the doors, unlocking the latch and releasing the half-rotten wood that stands between him and freedom.

Unsure of what time of the day it is, he opens the doors quietly and steps out into the dim light of downtown Westport, breathing in the fresh air that's coming from the ocean only a short distance away. Although it's overcast, he can tell from the brightness over the harbor that it must be early morning. He turns around and closes the doors again, not wanting his sister to know that he's gone, then locks the latch again before walking north toward the shops of the retail district.

Once he's out of sight from the house, he stops on the sidewalk and sits down on a bench, his body tired and sore from the endless hours of sitting and sleeping on the concrete floor. He tries to focus his mind on where he can hide — someplace that preferably has a comfortable place to sleep, and a source of food and water that will get him by until he can think of something more permanent. Fantasizing about the apocalypse in the past, he always thought that the first place he would go would be the Peterson Bar & Grill — but unfortunately, he also told Amanda about it on numerous occasions. He decides instead to walk down the street to a small gas station that also doubles as a mini grocery store for the neighborhood.

It's raining lightly on his soiled jacket as he passes the intersection that leads to the public access road, and as he looks around at the houses lining the street, he's amazed at how empty and abandoned the town looks now. Amanda had mentioned to him that nearly everyone was gone, but looking at it now, he'd swear that there was nobody left at all. Smelling the wet pavement under his feet, and the fresh smell of pine trees that are blowing in the wind next to him, he walks up to the doorway of the gas station and pushes against the door — relieved when it swings open without any resistance.

"Is anybody here?" he asks quietly, hoping that he doesn't receive an answer. Looking behind him first, to make sure he wasn't followed, he reaches down and locks the door, then grabs a bag of spicy potato chips from a shelf next to the register. Walking down the main aisle, which is lined with mostly empty shelves, he grabs more snack items that were apparently unpopular with the panicking evacuees — then finds some equally undesirable sport drinks before sitting on the floor in the back. He's exhausted from not sleeping for days, and sick to his stomach from the sudden overindulgence of sugar-filled junk food, but he finds an office in the back of the store with a couch in it, and decides to lie down for a while until the nausea goes away — oblivious to the fact that someone is staring at him from the other side of the glass windows.

Aaron wakes up suddenly, startled by a loud noise that's coming from the back door beside him, and surprised at the relative darkness that's now filling the room. Someone is slamming their fist against the door, trying to twist the locked doorknob in an attempt to break in. With no window to the back of the building to see them, he gets up from the couch and sneaks quietly into the front of the store. It's almost nighttime by the looks of the faint daylight still visible, and as he approaches the windows along the entrance wall, he quickly drops to the floor and hides behind a magazine rack as he spots two men standing outside, their faces pressed up against the glass as they peer inside. He recognizes one of them as the owner of the store, and he doesn't know whether to be frightened or comforted when he sees him reach for the handle of the door — but any hope of comfort vanishes completely when he watches the man struggle with it, despite having a set of keys clearly hanging from his belt. The other man looks directly at Aaron, then starts hitting the glass with his elbow. Aaron moves across the floor and away from the window just as the guy arches his back and screams, then drops to the ground, grabbing desperately at his side.

Standing casually behind him, with a bloody knife in her hand, is Amanda. She turns toward the owner of the store and takes a few steps forward, then thrusts the blade deep into his stomach as he tries to back away from her. Once he's down on the ground, still scrambling to get away, she slices the blade furiously at his hands, then shoves it into what Aaron can only guess is the man's throat. Next, she calmly reaches down to his side, grabs the keys, and opens the front door.

Aaron is frozen with terror as he watches her wipe the blade onto her white dress, then walk up to the counter and take a package of black licorice from behind the counter. She starts to walk out, then turns around and slowly looks the store over. Afraid to even breathe, Aaron prays that she doesn't notice the wet shoe prints that are still visible from when he entered the building earlier — but instead, she opens the package of candy and leaves the store, not bothering to close the door behind her. He watches as she disappears into the fog in the distance, then he closes the door once again, knowing that when morning comes, he'll need to find another place to hide.

Grabbing another bag of chips, he heads into the back again and begins to close the office door for more privacy — and then he notices some movement outside. Through the fog and misty rain, he sees shadows moving through the night — and the longer he watches, the more of them appear.

He wonders how many of them out there are like Amanda, and how many people, innocent or otherwise, that she's already killed.

CHAPTER 1
ABERDEEN: MARCH 27TH

Larry glances over at Christine, who's sitting next to him in a plastic lawn chair behind the pharmacy window — then he stares out at the city of Aberdeen again, where a glimmer of sunlight is stretched out across the parking lot and nearby buildings, contrasting with the dark clouds that are still directly overhead. They're both trying to wrap their heads around a radio conversation they just had, talking to a man that claimed to be living at the hospital on the other side of town. He said that his name is Mike Garrett, and that he was a nurse before the viral outbreak began — but after that things became rather confusing. He never asked whether or not they were sick, or had any symptoms at all, or even where they'd been for the past several months — and he was also vague about any of his own personal details. Some privacy and skepticism on his part was fully expected, but he wouldn't even go so far as to tell them how old he is or what he looks like.

The strangest part of the entire conversation, however, was his invitation to a face-to-face meeting, despite knowing hardly anything about them. He seemed eager to meet them in person, and told them to arrive at the front entrance of the hospital shortly after daybreak the following morning. After a conversation in which almost no information was shared, it ended with an almost desperate plea for a visit, which left both of them questioning his possible motive.

"Do you still wanna go?" Larry asks Christine, who's been mostly quiet since the radio call ended.

"I don't know — what do you think?"

"It could be a trap, or it could answer a lot of questions — I don't really know what to think."

They'd been up for most of the night talking about whether or not they should be going, or even if the man would allow for a visit to take place, but neither of them thought that the invitation would come so quickly and easily.

"If he were anyone else, I would probably leave him behind — but the fact that he's a nurse kind of changes everything, doesn't it?"

"I guess someone like that could come in pretty handy. So, we're still going?"

"Yeah, I guess so — but we have to be careful."

Across the highway from them, sitting by itself in a large parking lot, is a building that still has thin wisps of smoke rising through its badly damaged roof. Other than the one structure though, this area of the city looks untouched from the inferno that destroyed nearly everything on the opposite side of the Wishkah river. Although his view to the west is mostly obscured by the glare coming off of the filthy windows, he can still make out the silhouettes of the surviving brick and stone buildings that are towering over the ash and rubble around them — a lasting testimony to the early builders of the city, who were from a time when buildings were supposed to last more than a single generation. Taking up much of the historic downtown district, even most of those relics from the past have been devastated by the fires as well. The wooden interior floors and roofs have been gutted by the intense heat from the flames, making everything appear more or less unaffected from the street level, but otherwise useless when you look beyond the outer walls.

The parking lot in front of the pharmacy is littered with trash, much like everywhere else. Before she was killed, Larry mentioned to his sister that the lasting impression of the human race will undoubtedly be the massive amounts of garbage that we've left behind — both below and above the ground. Still though, compared to the cities on the peninsula, the east end of Aberdeen appears to be relatively pristine. There are no broken windows or cars left in the middle of the road, and no doors that have been ripped off of their hinges by the hordes of infected that have ravaged many of the other towns in the state.

Sitting on one of the benches from the waiting area, which she's covered with electric blankets and plastic table cloths from the 'Household' department, Christine waits for Larry to return with tonight's dinner — a meal that he's preparing on a miniature camp stove that he found in an abandoned house somewhere on the other side of the harbor. Although they've known one another for only a short period of time since first meeting in Grayland, she already thinks of him as sort of a father figure or uncle — someone that makes her feel at least somewhat safer during dangerous or tense moments.

The sun is setting in the west, leaving the north-facing storefront already in the shaded darkness of nightfall. A propane lantern is on the floor nearby, quietly hissing in the background as it fills the back of the store with a crisp, white light.

"What'd I tell you, huh?" Larry says, holding up two cans as he walks up to the camp stove that's sitting on the pharmacy counter.

"What are they?"

"Beef and cheese ravioli. I never thought I'd have these again."

"Sounds delicious." she replies sarcastically.

"It'll be hot, and it'll keep us alive — that's the important thing. We're lucky to have anything at all."

"I know, I'm sorry. I'm just nervous about tomorrow."

"I know, me too," he says, emptying the contents of the cans into a new pot. "I thought it would take some arm twisting for him to see us."

"That's one of the things that worries me. It was too easy — we didn't even have to bring it up."

Larry leans in over the stove, taking in not only the smell of the canned ravioli, but also the heat from the burner. He thought that the weather would improve once they came in from the cold coastal winds of the beach, but the climate of the harbor felt different, even colder somehow — like the dampness of the fog was permeating every pore of his skin.

"Jake said he was a doctor," she says.

"Maybe it's a different guy."

"Either way, we have to be careful. We don't need him."

"Agreed." He takes the pot from the single burner and sets it onto the counter, then dishes the pasta into two foam bowls, handing one of them to Christine. "Still, it would be nice to get some answers, especially if this guy has talked to people outside of the area."

She takes a bite of the meal, nearly burning her lips in the process — but once it cools down she's reminded of how much she misses the taste of hot, semi-nutritious meals. "Do you ever think about home, and the way things used to be?"

"I try not to," he says, as he sits beside her in the makeshift campsite and begins eating. "Sometimes I can't help it though, like when I wake up in the middle of the night and I forget where I am for a minute — then it all suddenly comes back to me."

"I do that too sometimes. Did you get to say goodbye to any of your friends before the end?"

"No, I never really had any to be honest — not any of them worth saying goodbye to anyway."

"I did, I had a lot of them."

12

"Did you get to say goodbye?"

"Just one of them. My friend, Kelsie, who lived across the street from us. The last time I saw her was when she waved at me through the window, since neither of our parents would let us outside. She died a couple of days later."

"I had to watch my..." He cuts his sentence short, listening to a thumping sound coming from somewhere close. "Did you hear that?"

"Yeah."

They both stop eating and listen to the noise, coming from somewhere above them. Soon it turns into obvious footsteps, and then a rough dragging sound that moves steadily across the ceiling.

"Do you think it's Amanda?" Christine asks.

"She doesn't make any sound when she walks — it's like she's a ghost or something."

"Unless she wants us to hear her..."

Larry sets down his unfinished bowl and stands up, then pulls his gun out and starts to slowly make his way to the other side of the store where the sound is headed — careful to stay inside of the dark shadows.

Christine moves behind him, hearing another set of footsteps on the roof as well. "There's two of them," she whispers.

"I hear that too... They're in the other back corner."

Both of them freeze as they hear a loud banging noise, like a piece of steel being smashed with a hammer. After a minute or so of constant hits, the high-pitch creaking of a rusty hinge fills the empty store, echoing throughout the space — and then the footsteps continue, coming down a staircase somewhere in the back of the store.

Larry quickly heads back to their supplies and grabs a rifle and an extra pistol, handing the smaller gun to Christine — then the two of them position themselves behind an aisle that has a clear shot of the double doors that lead to the back.

"Whatever comes through those doors, we kill them, understood?" Larry asks her.

"Yeah, I understand."

Both of the intruders can be heard crashing down the stairs and into the area of offices and storerooms, and then they pause just on the other side, their breathing audible even from halfway across the store. When the doors slowly begin opening, Larry looks through the scope of the rifle that's already aimed in that direction, and then fires several shots the moment he sees both of them come through the doorway — hitting at least one of them with a direct head shot. With both of them now on the ground, he stands up and motions for Christine to follow him.

"The closest one is still moving, Larry," Christine warns him, as they carefully approach the two people.

Firing another round into each of their heads, Larry walks up to each of them and uses his foot to roll them over, revealing their faces. They're both younger men, probably in their twenties or thirties — both of them with horrible scars on their faces and arms. Even the clothing that they're wearing has areas that have either been burned or melted.

"Are they dead?" Christine asks.

"Yeah, they're both gone."

"However they got in, more could follow them."

"I know. I'll stay up and take watch until morning, and then we'll pack up some of this stuff and leave at daybreak."

"Are you just gonna leave them lying here?"

"I'll cover them with something. Go back and finish your dinner, even if you're not hungry — you're gonna need your strength for tomorrow."

As Christine walks back to the campsite, Larry feels the cold air

14

blowing in through the double doors that are now exposed to the outside air. He knows that more people might follow, but he's not really concerned about any of the infected. His only worry is that a young girl might find her way into the building, and that as quietly as she moves, she might already be inside.

CHAPTER 2
GRAYLAND: MARCH 27TH

Awaking in a strange room, and seeing the light gray clouds moving across the sky outside of the window, Curtis sits up in bed and smells the scent of something cooking in the other room. For a moment he almost forgets where he is and why they're here, and why he's lying down in someone else's bed. As he swings his legs over the side though, he sees the makeshift beds on the floor where Matt and Ben spent the night, and he remembers watching them fall asleep as he took the first shift, wondering whether he and Sarah would ever be able to sleep alone in the same room again. For the time being, however, he wouldn't have it any other way. They're all new to this area, and it was somewhere around here that Larry and Beth disappeared from radio contact — and last they heard, they still had Amanda with them.

He stands up, feeling the fatigue in his legs from the last few days setting in, then he walks to the window and looks out at the beach to the west. Fog is rolling in heavily from the surf, which is nothing unusual for the area, but he had plans to search some of the neighboring homes today for more supplies, and fog could make it more difficult to spot any people that might be lurking in the shadows around town.

Hearing the voices of his family downstairs, sounding relaxed for the first time in months, he goes across the hallway and enters another bedroom, this one with a much less picturesque view of the town. As much time as he spent on this coast as a kid, for some reason

16

they never really went to Grayland for anything, so his knowledge of the town is limited at best. It was always a place they simply passed through on their way to Cohassett to the north. He remembers seeing the cranberry bogs just off of the highway, the flooded fields overflowing with red berries ready for harvest in the fall. Other than that, his only real memory of the area was after his parents both died, and his Uncle Brian stopped at a local cafe to buy him a hamburger. It was also the last time as a child that he visited the Washington coast.

Looking out at the town now, he can see the building that used to be a cafe in the distance, although he's fairly certain that it became a laundromat in more recent years.

"Curtis, are you awake up there?" Sarah asks from the floor below.

"Yeah, I'll be down in a minute," he replies back, still looking at the highway that sits between the property and the beginning of town. The streets look empty, but he can see broken windows in several of the buildings, which he knows could be an indicator that they're not alone.

He walks down the stairs and sees Sarah in the kitchen, cooking something on the gas stove top as the boys sit in front of the living room window and look out at the ocean beyond.

"You slept a long time," Sarah says.

"What time is it?"

"Almost eight. Are you hungry?"

"Yeah, starving." He sits down in a bar stool on the opposite side of the counter from her, and she sets a bowl down in front of him and then comes around the corner and sits with him. "Is this from the cans we brought with us?" he asks, seeing a variety of soups that have been mixed together.

"No, I found these in the pantry, along with a few other things." She sips at the hot soup, looking out at the wall in the front yard that blocks the view of the town from the bottom floor. "Are you still

17

planning on going out today?"

"Yeah, I don't wanna get too low on food."

"Just you?"

"Unless you want to go..."

They've had this discussion several times in the past, but last night they came to an agreement that one of them would always be with the boys, and that Matt and Ben should never be separated from each other again. They also decided that it was probably safer for the entire family if Curtis were to hunt for supplies alone, instead of potentially risking all of their lives against an army of the infected — a problem that seems to be growing more dangerous as each day passes.

"No, we'll stay here. See if you can find a radio though — if we're gonna split up, we should at least have a way of reaching one another."

"Yeah, okay, I'll keep an eye out for a set. You guys might wanna gather up some firewood from the shed out back — it can get pretty cold at night when you're right on the beach like this."

"Hey dad," Matt says uneasily, as the two brothers approach their father. "We haven't seen anyone on the beach all morning."

"You say that like it's a bad thing..."

"There aren't any bodies either."

At first Curtis is confused at the observation, disturbed at the idea that his son is even noticing something like that — and then the full gravity of the situation hits him. Since last September, early in the days of the outbreak, they've seen bodies on every beach that they've come across. Most of them came in on the tide, washed up from who knows where, and some of them were more local, likely killed by the other infected and left on the beach. Sand dunes that are clear of the rotting corpses that litter the other beaches in the area could be an excellent sign, that this part of the coastline is truly deserted — or it could mean something else entirely, a sign that the town isn't as abandoned as it appears.

"Just keep watching, if anyone is around, they'll show up on the sand eventually."

Waiting for the boys to go back to the living room, Sarah leans in a whispers "They're worried about something else, they just don't want to say it."

"I know, I've been thinking about her too."

"Matt thinks that she killed Larry and Beth, and that she's still out there somewhere."

"He's probably right."

"I know, but we can't have them thinking that she's waiting around every corner..."

He stands up and sets the bowl in the non-functioning sink, then kisses his wife on the forehead. "It might not be her, but there probably *is* something around every corner."

Deciding that it's probably best to stay off of the highway until they get to know the town better, Curtis walks down a pathway along the edge of the dunes, winding past damaged beachfront homes that have been battered from the storms of the past few months, and some by years of neglect by the looks of them. In many ways, Grayland looks almost identical to Westport, at least from the ocean anyway. Both of them have mostly older homes that are surrounded by blackberry vines and other imported vegetation, all of them nuisances that constantly threaten to overtake and conceal the properties. One difference, however, is the spacing between the lots. Grayland doesn't really have a dedicated residential or commercial area, since it's not actually an incorporated city. Instead, the houses, businesses and small developments are widely scattered between the ancient dunes along the Pacific, and the wetland bogs that rest at the bottom of the coastal hills to the east.

As he approaches the neighboring home, which sits only a few hundred feet to the south, the first thing he notices about the older single-story house is the broken window next to the back door, and shards of glass that are still lying on the porch below it. Stepping onto the wooden planks of the porch, he sees that the door is actually open slightly, and when he pushes it with the baseball bat that he's carrying, the stench of the air nearly knocks him over. The kitchen on the other side of the door is a mess, with trash covering the floor and cabinets ripped from the walls and thrown haphazardly around the room. In the distance, he sees what he can only imagine are the former residents of the home, their bodies lined up in a perfect row across the floor of the living area.

He really doesn't want to go any further inside, but the most reliable source for weapons that they've found so far are in the homes where suicides have taken place — and as far he can tell, this certainly looks like one.

Careful not to step on anything overly disgusting, he makes his way through the kitchen and toward the source of the rotting smell, trying not to look directly at the people as he searches around them for any gun that might have been used. Seeing nothing that resembles a weapon of any kind, it suddenly occurs to him that there's something missing — blood. There's none on the carpet, or on their clothing for that matter — and although their bodies are too decomposed to tell for sure how they died, from the looks of their twisted limbs and the wounds on their torsos, it appears that at least a couple of them were horribly mutilated before they were placed here, as if pieces of their flesh were carved away from the bone.

Whatever this was, it was certainly no suicide.

Desperate to get out of the house, and for the smell of fresh air, Curtis leaves the house and looks back at their new, temporary home next door, and considers going back to his family before he ventures even further away. The bodies that he just found, however cruel their deaths might have been, obviously happened months ago though, and he left the .38 revolver with Sarah for protection. He closes his eyes and breathes in deeply, trying to shut out everything except for the sound of the ocean waves and the seagulls in the background, and reminds himself that his family are better off staying exactly where they are. With his nerves a little more calm, he keeps walking down the path toward another house, this one in shambles and covered in decades worth of brush and rusty wind chimes — the latter of which are filling the air with a hectic sound that's more chaotic than soothing.

The place is surrounded with a simple welded wire livestock fence, with one gate that's fastened with a padlock. The fencing looks as though someone has tried climbing on it, but Curtis can't tell for certain whether it's recent or not — or whether it was possibly an animal that did it.

Grabbing onto one of the metal posts, he steadies himself and climbs easily over the wire, then walks up to the front door slowly, careful not to make any noise as he makes his way up the half-rotten wooden steps. Through the windows, he can tell that this place is different than the last, with a relatively clean interior despite the wretched upkeep that the outside has received. The handle is locked, but with a gentle tap with the end of his bat, he breaks the built-in window in the door and exposes the small living room beyond. The inside of this house is musty, much like every other place they've been to recently, but it shares other similarities as well. There's virtually no food in sight, aside from a few open packages of dry pasta and stale cereal — and there's a body that's not much more than a skeleton, falling halfway out of the bed and onto the floor.

After thoroughly searching the rest of the house, finding only a few batteries and a can of potato soup, he finally looks through the utility room last — and on a shelf, sitting next to the back door, he sees a radio hanging from a hook on the wall.

Placing the bat on top of the dryer, he grabs the radio and turns it on, surprised to see that it's still mostly charged. "Is anybody out there? Larry, Beth?" he says into it, feeling somewhat foolish. After hearing nothing in return, he turns it off and sticks it into his pocket. Opening the door next to him, he steps into the backyard and looks out at the ocean that sits not very far from the house. The structure might not look like much, and the yard looks even worse, but the view of the dunes and surf beyond are breathtaking. He watches for moment, then sees a woman walking along the water toward the south. She's moving exactly like the others they've seen — slow and uncoordinated, wandering in a jagged line as if she were drunk. As she disappears from sight behind some pine trees, Curtis looks back to the beach and sees a man walking quickly in the same direction, carrying what appears to be a large walking stick. The man, who's much older and walks with a surprisingly upright posture and steady gait, suddenly stops in his tracks and stares straight ahead. Only a moment later, two more people can be seen coming into view, dragging the woman through the sand by her feet, then dropping her in front of the old man. As she tries to scramble away, he takes the wooden stick and begins hitting her over the head with it, and the other two men simply stand back and watch.

Not wanting to be seen, Curtis drops to the ground and looks away as he hears the woman crying for help in the distance, and in only a couple of minutes the beach becomes silent once again, with only the sound of screeching seagulls perceptible over the howling wind. Getting to his feet again, crouching behind some brush along the path, he sees the older man continuing his walk to the south, with the younger ones following closely behind him, dragging the body of the woman with them as they struggle through the loose sand of the dunes. It's only right before they vanish from his sight that he notices her hands clutching desperately at the ground, and he realizes that she's still alive.

Feeling scared for the first time since arriving here, he stands up and looks back toward their new home, suddenly aware of the fact that they must have passed right by Sarah and the boys.

"Matt, don't bother chopping anything, just grab whatever has already been cut," Sarah says quietly to Matt, as she heads back to the house with her arms full of firewood, with Ben right behind her.

"What if we run out?" he replies, still holding the ax in his hands.

"There's enough wood there for weeks, just do what I asked — please..." As she turns around to face the house again, she stops quickly after hearing something across the yard from them, causing Ben to nearly run into the back of her. "Ben, go back to the wood shed, and tell your brother to stay quiet."

"What is it?"

"Now!" she answers, quietly but firmly.

She hears it again as she slowly sets the firewood onto the ground and starts to back up toward the shed again — a rattling sound that she recognizes as the front gate into the yard. It could be Curtis, but she has no idea why he would make so much noise when they're so close to town, and when she knows that he has a key to the padlock. When she enters the shed and hides behind the stack of wood in the center of the building, Matt crouches down next to her and points across the property.

"There's some bushes over there where you can see through the gate..."

"That's too far away — we need to stay together."

"What if it's dad, and he can't get in?"

Thinking of everything that could possibly go wrong with his plan, she listens closely to the gate still rattling in the background, and decides that he's probably right — Curtis could be in danger if the town is full of the infected, and he's trapped outside of the walls with them.

"You have to promise me that you won't go any closer than those bushes over there..."

"I promise, I'll come right back as soon as I find out who it is. Should I have the gun?"

"Absolutely not." He stands up and starts to walk away, staying low to the ground. "Matt..."

"Yeah?"

"Give me a thumbs up if it's your dad."

"Okay, I will."

Around the perimeter of the yard, just inside of the wall, there's a thickly planted bed of perennials and small trees, providing enough cover for Matt to sneak most of the way around the side of the house without being seen by anybody — including Sarah. When he reappears, she can see him lying down on the thick mulch, with a large, leafless decorative maple tree towering over the top of him. Almost immediately after he lies down, she sees him give an enthusiastic thumbs down, and then she hears another noise coming from the other side of the yard, from the gate they originally entered when they found the place. She motions for Matt to stay down, then pushes Ben to the ground as she peeks over the pile of wood at the other gate.

"What is it?" Ben whispers.

"Someone is at the other gate too."

Hearing a slight rattle from the chain, she watches as Curtis emerges through the opening and locks the gate behind him, and she quickly motions for Matt to return before waving her arms to get Curtis' attention. He crouches down when he sees her, then quickly makes his way to meet them.

"What's wrong?" he asks Sarah, who looks at an out-of-breath Matt that just returned.

"There's a man at the front gate," Matt says, breathing hard.

"An old guy?"

"No, he's young."

"Did you see someone out there?" Sarah asks.

"Yeah, let's get back inside."

Winding their way around the corner of the house, careful not to be visible from either entrance into the yard, all four of them enter through the back door of the home, and into the brightly lit kitchen that's lined with windows that all face the front of the place. Seeing a brief glimpse of the guy, Curtis ducks down, then watches his family do the same as he sneaks up the staircase and into the spare bedroom.

"Boys, I want you to stay down on the floor — we don't know if this guy has a gun or not," Sarah says.

Standing on one side of the window, Curtis looks down and sees the man that's still trying to open the locked gate, and guesses that Matt is probably right, the man is probably barely out of high school. He's also seemingly unaware that there's a chain wrapped securely around the steel tubing and attached to the concrete wall next to it. It might be easy enough to climb, but there's little chance of actually breaking through the barricade.

"Curtis..." Sarah says from the other side of the window, pointing down toward the ground.

"Don't worry, he can't get in."

"I know, but look..."

He looks at the other side of the property, at the street just past the wall. Another two men are approaching the young man, both of them carrying iron pipes in their hands.

"Don't watch," he says, as he looks around at the rest of the town.

She sits down on the bed and looks up at him instead. "Why, what's going on?"

"I saw some men on the beach, hunting an infected woman."

"Are those the same men?"

"No, they're not — which means there's more of them around."

"Did they kill her?" Matt asks.

"No, she was still alive."

"What are they gonna do..."

"Enough, there's some things we don't need to know," Sarah says, cutting him off. Looking back up at Curtis, she recognizes the look in his eyes, a fear that she hasn't seen since that horrible night at the Regency Hotel in Westport. "What is it?"

"There's more people across town — a lot more."

CHAPTER 3
GRAYLAND: MARCH 28TH

After a nearly sleepless, but otherwise uneventful night, Sarah wakes up in an empty bed and sees Curtis staring through the window at the town of Grayland beyond. She feels exhausted, having gone through yet another roller coaster of emotions over the last twenty-four hours. This house felt perfect, like an actual home, a place she might have only fantasized about in her former life. The fantasy, however real as it seemed when they first arrived, was now being taken away by the same violent and repulsive people that they were running from just two days ago.

She stands up and stretches, thankful that they've decided to stay another night and rest their sore bodies before continuing to the south. If the timing were right, they would still push forward, sore or not — but neither of them thought that it was a good idea to be on the road with murderers wandering the streets around them.

"Where are the boys?" she asks, looking down at the vacant sidewalk in front of the house.

"In the other room. Did you sleep okay?"

"No — I kept waking up, thinking that I was hearing somebody breaking into the house." The longer she looks around, the more people she can see going in and out of the buildings across the highway. One of them is a fire station, and several of the others appear to be small houses or mobile homes that are clustered together in a park. "Have you counted them?"

"The people?"

"Yeah, any idea how many there are in town?"

"They come and go too much to keep track of them. I've seen maybe a dozen or so at once, but there's probably at least two or three times that many."

"Are they sick?"

"Not like any that we've seen, but they definitely have something wrong with them."

She looks across the road at the driveway to the trailer park, and sees two of them dragging something behind them, like a deer or small livestock animal.

"They're hunting," Curtis says in a somber tone.

"Hunting what?"

"I think anything that moves. They're going door to door, pulling the infected out and killing them, then taking their bodies down that road."

"They're armed?" she asks, frightened at the idea that there could be a militia looking for them.

"No, just primitive things. Pipes and pieces of lumber, that sort of stuff." He points to the southeast, where there's a woman walking down the street with a shovel in her grasp. "See that woman, walking this way? Watch her for a minute."

Almost immediately, the woman drops the shovel and then bends down to pick something up. As she begins walking, she suddenly stops and turns around, then swaps the two items once again. Finally settling on the shovel, she continues her journey to the north, stopping occasionally to swing the shovel at figures that aren't there.

"She's crazy," Sarah says.

"They all are, they all do shit like that if you watch them for long enough."

Sarah sits down on the bed and tries to wipe the sleepiness from her eyes, hearing the sound of the ocean outside as the breakers crash into the outgoing tide. It's normally something soothing, a natural rhythm that induces sleep even when you're well rested — but her body is tense with anxiety, and the never-ending roar from the sea is beginning to eat away at her sanity.

"We never really talked about where we're going from here — we only agreed on going south," she says, her voice tired and defeated.

"We can't really say for sure, it depends on what we find when we get there."

"I know, but it would be nice to have some sort of a goal or a destination, even if we don't end up staying there."

"North Cove is the closest town, but I think we can pretty much assume that it won't be all that different. We need to go east, and find some abandoned farm or something."

"Why are we going south then?"

"Directly east of here is nothing but swamps and forests — we'd starve to death out there."

She stands up again and heads for the door, peeking into the other bedroom where Matt and Ben are watching the beach from the comfort of the king-sized master bed.

"Where are you going?" Curtis asks.

"I'm gonna get our bags ready. I figured I would raid the house of anything useful."

Stepping inside the bedroom just long enough to grab a plastic grocery bag, she walks into the hallway bathroom and opens the door all of the way, trying to let as much light in as possible. She starts with the basics, like new bars of soap and toilet paper, but when she opens the medicine cabinet above the sink, she sees something unusual looking on the top shelf. Pushed to one side is a small stuffed animal, and attached to it is a single key with something written on it. Curious, she takes the key and the bag and goes back into the spare bedroom and stands in front of the window next to Curtis.

29

"What is that?" he asks.

She holds it up, showing him the label. "According to the tag, it's the key to the basement."

Curtis turns the key and hears the deadbolt unlock, then looks back at Sarah and the two boys. Matt and Ben have been told to stay upstairs while they search the room below, and after a bit of complaining at first, both of them shut up as soon as the stench of the basement air reaches their noses. The air is damp and mildewed, but there's something else wrong with it, a strange staleness that doesn't smell right. Curtis leads the way, holding both a flashlight and the revolver as he slowly descends down the staircase. He thinks it's likely a concrete slab covering the floor below them, but whatever is there has been littered with a mountain of miscellaneous items.

"It looks like a bunch of random crap," Curtis says, scanning the numerous piles scattered across the room, all of them filled with common household items like toasters and remote controls — but also various other things, like power tools and garden hoses.

"Was this guy the town thief or something?" Sarah asks, reaching down to pick up another flashlight that's lying on top of the closest heap.

"Why don't you ask him..."

She looks up and sees someone on the other side of the room, a rope wrapped tightly around his neck and hanging from the floor joists overhead. "That's not funny, Curtis."

"Well, it's not like he's gonna get offended, is he? Does your light work?"

She switches it on, illuminating the room even more than his does. "Look at all of this... We need to go through it all before we leave."

30

"I don't see any weapons though." He sifts through some of the stuff with his shoes, not wanting to touch anything that might be contaminated — then a thought occurs to him. "This guy wasn't the last one in here."

"Why do you say that?"

"Because the door was locked from the outside — there's no way to lock it from in here." He shines the light onto the staircase behind them, seeing the two boys looking back at him from the other side of the door. Then he sees a worn track down the middle of each step, the wood stained red with blood. As he follows the bloody pathway onto the floor and across the room, he stops when the light hits a neatly stacked pile against the far wall.

"Is that what I think it is?" Sarah asks, covering her mouth with her forearm.

"Yeah, it's bodies — it looks like dozens of them."

CHAPTER 4
ABERDEEN: MARCH 28TH

With their bags filled with a wide variety of food and medications, Christine looks back across the parking lot at the pharmacy, its normally white exterior walls now glowing orange in the light of the sunrise to the east. Larry insisted on keeping watch the night before, and she's concerned that he might be starting to show the first signs of sleep deprivation. There were moments this morning when he would blank out, or sometimes even nod off while she was talking to him, but she's not the least bit concerned that it's the virus — those are all late-stage symptoms of the disease, and Larry hasn't shown any early signs of it. A sharp mind and a rested body would still be nice though, especially on a day like this.

As they cross back over the Wishkah river and into the heart of Aberdeen, she looks ahead at the remains of the city, where the fog has settled over most of the downtown buildings, giving the impression that many of them are still smoldering from the fire. According to Larry, the harbor to the south looks pretty much the same as it ever has, with only a few missing ships from the numerous docks along the shore.

The city itself, however, feels different.

It feels dead.

Compared to every other city along the coastline of the Pacific Northwest, one might say that Aberdeen's history is rather colorful — with illegal gambling and prostitution attracting more attention from people around the region than even the harbor has. Even in the very early days, when its convenient proximity to calm waters along the ocean made it an important port for the logging and fishing industries, the burgeoning young town quickly developed a reputation for an immoral and oftentimes illegal nightlife. Known by many as 'The Hellhole of the Pacific', its name became synonymous with murder and debauchery to those living on the western side of the Cascade mountains.

Although the whorehouses have disappeared in more modern times, along with the underground casinos and serial killers that used to infect the city — much of its former reputation has stayed intact through the decades. Larry made the comment as they were leaving that he's never seen Aberdeen so peaceful, but he couldn't give her a single example of what's been wrong with the city in his lifetime. 'It's just an easy city to pick on', was the answer he gave her.

Regardless of whether Aberdeen still deserves its infamous notoriety or not, what Christine sees in front of her today makes her feel sorry for the place. She remembers learning about the bombed out cities throughout Europe and Asia after World War II, and she can only imagine that walking through them must have felt at least somewhat similar. As the wind blows in across the water, each gust seems to tear the buildings apart even more, sending more pieces of rubble onto the street beside them, the large chunks of burned brick and stone disintegrating into fine powder the instant they hit the pavement. Skeletons and badly decomposed corpses can be seen as well, their charred remains visible for several blocks in front of them.

"Eerie, isn't it?" Larry says, his eyes wandering around the ruins the same as hers, not sure of whether to take in the destruction or look for infected people that might still be lurking behind the fog-shrouded walls.

"Have you ever seen anything like this?"

"Nobody has — except maybe this guy we're supposedly meeting."

"You don't trust him?"

"The only person in this world that I trust right now is you — and we both have to be careful not to put ourselves in any kind of vulnerable position."

"What if he wants us to put our guns down?" she asks.

"Then we put them down — the visible ones anyway."

He places his hand in front of her, motioning for her to stop — then he points down one of the side streets that leads up to the hills. She can see a dog on the next block, eating the cooked meat from the bones of one of the infected.

"You want a dog?" she asks.

"No, not the dog — look just past it."

On the corner of the intersection is a small sporting goods store, advertising guns for sale in large, red letters — along with camping supplies and clothing.

"It's probably burned out, like everything else," she replies.

"Still worth checking out later though, just in case."

Although the location of the hospital is clearly marked on the few undamaged signs along the highway, Larry decides to follow some of the smaller streets that parallel the bottom of the hill instead, mostly out of the concern of being ambushed on the more obvious path. Unfortunately, there's only one road that leads to the hospital itself, and can be seen from virtually every floor of the main building.

"The houses aren't that bad up ahead," Christine points out, nodding toward a neighborhood beside the medical district that appears to be entirely undamaged from the fire.

"That makes it even more dangerous then," he responds, gasping for breath and grabbing at his hip as he grimaces in pain. "If they survived the flames, that means the bastards living in them did too."

Moving slowly, they finally reach the entrance to the hospital, where Larry sits down on a bench that overlooks the nearly empty parking lot. It also has a partial view of both Aberdeen and Cosmopolis to the south — the latter of which has smoke rising from several spots.

"*Are you hurt?*" comes a voice from the radio.

Reaching into his pocket and pulling the radio out, Larry turns around and looks at the hospital behind him, but there's too many windows to tell where they're coming from. "I'm not sick, if that's what you're asking," he says into the handheld.

"*Maybe I can take a look at it for you.*"

"Yeah, that'd be great. Where to now?"

"*The neighborhood is relatively quiet, so I leave the main entrance unlocked during the day. Follow the stairs up to the sixth floor — I'll be waiting for you there.*"

"Okay, we'll see you in a few minutes."

"*Oh, and don't get off on the second floor, no matter what you hear on the other side of the door. There's someone down there that you really don't want to mess with.*"

"Alright, got it." Larry looks up at the windows on the sixth floor, and can see someone looking out one of them, waving their hand at him. Giving a slight wave back, Larry stands up and grabs his bags again, then pushes his way through the glass doors and enters the cold, dark main lobby, which looks even creepier than either of them expected it to be.

"I suppose it looked better before," Christine says, careful not to step in the pools of dried blood on the floor.

"I would hope so..." He points across the room to the right, next to an information desk that's been trashed by either vandals or the infected. "That looks like the door to the staircase over there..."

He pulls a sanitation wipe from a container on the desk, and then uses it to open the door handle, which is also covered in blood, then holds it for Christine to enter after making sure the area is clear.

35

"He said he leaves the entrance open during the day, right?" Christine says.

"Yeah, why?"

"That implies that he closes it at night. Why is the handle still filthy?"

"That's a good question."

Once inside the narrow shaft, they both turn their flashlights on and start walking up the stairs, their steps echoing loudly in the otherwise complete silence of the place. When they reach the second floor, Larry points at the door, which has a window in it that shows nothing but darkness. He aims his light at the glass, seeing a long, empty hallway with rooms on both sides of it. Then he spots something about halfway down, a person coming out of a room and staring in his direction. In an instant, they begin running at full speed toward the door, screaming at the top of their lungs as they crash against the heavy steel. Larry jumps back and pulls his gun out, aiming it at the woman's face that's now pressed against the window. She has bruises covering her head, and her hands are bleeding at she slams them into the door.

"Larry, come on, she obviously can't get through..." Christine says from behind him, motioning for him to continue up the steps.

The sounds of her screams fade away as they climb further, until they finally disappear altogether as they reach the sixth floor landing. Larry holds onto his flashlight with one hand, but he keeps his other wrapped around a revolver inside of his coat pocket.

"Go ahead and open the door, then back away," he tells her.

"He'll know that you have a gun in there..."

"Good, I hope he does."

The door opens with a deafening creaking sound, and when it stops all Larry can hear is a subtle humming noise. It takes him a few seconds to realize that it's coming from a fan overhead, and from computers that are turned on and running on one side of the room. The sight of electricity, with bright lights and warm air, it all causes him to momentarily forget the potentially dangerous situation that they're in — and it's only when Christine pulls her gun out and aims it across the room that his mind comes back into focus again.

"Whoa, I'm not gonna hurt you, I just have it for protection!" a man says from across the room, holding a semi-automatic pistol in his hand. He looks to be in his late forties or maybe early fifties, and is wearing a pair of clean scrubs.

Larry pulls his own gun out of his pocket and keeps it aimed at the floor, then gestures for Christine to lower hers. "It's okay, Christine." He tenses up when he realizes that her finger is actually on the trigger, despite the fact that her hands are trembling uncontrollably — but then she holds it out for Larry to take. "No, you keep it — just stick it in your pocket for now." He glances back at the man in front of them, who looks even more relieved than Larry. "I assume you're Mike?"

"Yeah, you must be Larry — and Christina..."

"Christine," she answers back, correcting him.

"Right, sorry. Listen, I'm not really sure how we're supposed to do this — I don't think any of us are very trusting right now."

"That's probably an understatement," Larry says. "How about we just sit down and talk, and then see where that takes us...?"

From the signs hanging on the wall, this area appears to be the old ICU and CCU units, with multiple glass-faced rooms encircling a central area filled with desks. Mike points to some office chairs sitting next to a workstation, then sits down in one of them, placing his gun into his pocket as he spins the chair around and faces them.

"You were a nurse here?" Larry asks, as he takes a seat across from him. Christine stays back and leans against the wall in the hallway, her eyes still deeply suspicious.

"Yeah, thirty years this August. Born and raised here in the city."

"Neither one of us is from around here, I guess it must be..."

"Why did you lie about locking the doors at night?" Christine interrupts, causing Larry to squirm in his seat.

"I didn't lie, the doors are locked just before sunset every night," Mike answers calmly, with a slight smile on his face.

"Sorry, she's just really nervous," Larry tries to explain.

"It's alright, I appreciate bluntness — it can save a lot of time."

"The doorknobs downstairs are covered in blood... You didn't bother to clean them?" Christine asks, her tone bordering on rude.

"No, I rarely leave this floor. The door locks are all automatic, which I can control from up here. Before the fire, we used to get a lot of people wandering in after dark, so we started locking everything up to keep them from crowding the staircase."

"We? There were more of you?" Larry asks.

"There were eleven of us at first. We stayed behind after the evacuation to look after the patients."

"What happened to the others?"

"Five died from the virus, two were killed by the infected patients, and the other three took off when the fire started to get worse. I'm not sure if they're still alive or not."

"Are any of the patients still alive?" Christine asks, her tone softening.

"I think a few of them are still downstairs, including the woman on the second floor. She's been here since the beginning." He stands up and starts walking, flipping a light switch on as he passes by it, which illuminates the hallway in front of him. "Come on, I want to show you something..."

Grabbing onto the desk next to him for support, Larry stands up and slowly begins to hobble after him, but first he leans in close to Christine and whispers... "Is it me, or is he really fidgety all of the sudden?"

"It's not you, I noticed it too. He's sweating like crazy."

Larry tries to look into each room as he passes by them down the hall, but they're so dark that he can't really make out any details. "I take it you have a generator?"

"Yeah, but I have no idea how much fuel I have left, so I try to keep things to a minimum. It's been a lifesaver though."

The temperature begins to drop as they walk further down the corridor, and by the time they finally reach the waiting room at the end, the air feels cold and damp. The entire southern wall of the waiting area is filled with clear windows, overlooking the city below and harbor beyond. Once they get close enough, Larry looks down onto the rooftop of another part of the hospital and sees several bodies scattered across the flat roof.

"Who were they?" he asks, pointing down to the remains.

"I don't know, they just showed up one at a time — but that's not what I wanted to show you." He nods his head to the southeast, in the direction of the Highway 101 bridge that leads into the city from Westport and Cosmopolis. "That's where they're getting in from. Everything to the west, the entire city of Hoquiam, has been completely destroyed — including the bridges over the river."

"You mean the infected?" Larry asks.

"Or whatever you wanna call them — I guess infected works as well as anything. The area to the east doesn't seem to be very active, so I haven't seen much come over from there — but Cosmopolis must be crawling with them."

"Westport and Grayland too, and the peninsula."

"And everything south of there," Christine adds.

Larry sits down in one of the chairs to rest his sore hip, and discovers that the cushions on these seats are far more comfortable than the ones in the ICU. He also notices that Mike is still sweating, even in the frigid temperatures on this end of the building. "So you're proposing that we stay?"

"This place is ideal when you think about it. There's plenty of room, food, water, electricity," Mike argues.

"Until the fuel runs out..."

"We still have the other stuff — and the security."

"Yeah, and all of that will last longer if you're alone."

Mike sits down next to him and sighs, then takes a small syringe out of his pocket and holds it up. "This is why I need you."

"What is that?" Larry asks, feeling suddenly nervous.

"It's insulin. I'm on the last bottle."

"You're diabetic?"

"Yep, type one. I've been trying to stretch it out, but it's running pretty low."

"I'd think a hospital would have more of it on hand..."

"We did, there was an incident a few months back, and it ended up being destroyed."

"What kind of an incident?"

Looking suddenly pale, Mike stands up and puts the syringe back into his pocket. "I'm sorry, but I'm feeling a little off, I'm just gonna go check my glucose level real quick..."

"Yeah, no problem," Larry replies. "Do what you need to do."

Mike gets about halfway across the room, then stops and turns around to face them again. "Look, I'm not asking you to do much, I just need you to watch over things while I'm gone, and unlock the door to this level when I get back."

"How far do you have to go to find more?"

"Just down to the bottom of the hill, to a medical supply center in the city. Hopefully they'll have more of it."

Christine watches for him to leave the room, then she sits down next to Larry. "Is he infected? He's acting really manic or something..."

"No, I don't think he's infected. My mother-in-law was diabetic,

40

and she had the same symptoms when her insulin would get out of control. He's probably scared to death."

"He said he still had some."

"That's not the problem. He could have gallons of it back there, and in a few months none of it will do him any good. It all expires eventually."

CHAPTER 5
GRAYLAND: MARCH 28TH

"Curtis... wake up..."

Opening his eyes to an almost completely dark room, Curtis sees Sarah standing over him with the gun in her hand, offering it to him. Matt and Ben are right behind her. "What's wrong?" he asks her.

"Someone just broke into the house — they're still downstairs..."

Taking the gun from her, he stands up and walks to the closed bedroom door, then after listening for a moment he opens the door to the walk-in closet. "Everybody inside... Grab all of our bags too."

"There's no way out of there!" Sarah protests in a whisper.

"There's a hatchway into the attic in the ceiling. Come on, let's go before he comes up the stairs," he says, as he picks up his own bags and throws them into the back of the closet.

Curtis can hear the creaking of the wooden steps outside the bedroom door as they load the last of their supplies in, and just as the handle starts to turn, he reaches over and grabs the baseball bat that was leaned up in the corner of the room, then quietly shuts the closet door. They can hear what sounds like a man enter the bedroom and stumble around for a few minutes, knocking things over and mumbling random cuss words — but he never tries to open the closet. Instead, they hear the springs on the mattress squeaking as they climb onto the bed, then a loud snore as they quickly fall asleep.

"They sound like they're drunk..." Sarah whispers in his ear.

"You have duct tape in one of your bags don't you?"

"Yeah, why?"

"Find it, but be quiet — we don't want him waking up."

He can hear rustling behind him as she searches through the bag, and he hopes that the man's snoring provides enough noise to cover it up. Then he feels a tapping on his shoulder.

"Here... Now what are you going to do with it?"

"I'm gonna tie him up — shooting him would make too much noise."

With the gun in his pocket, he holds the baseball bat in one hand while he opens the closet door as slowly as he can, seeing a massive silhouette stretched out over the top of the bed. He tries to creep as silently as possible across the floor, but the solid hardwood planks groan with almost every step. When he gets to within striking distance, he looks back at the closet and sees only Matt's face staring back at him, and then Sarah pulls him back inside. He lifts the bat into the air, takes a deep breath, then swings it straight down against the man's skull, feeling the jarring impact in his forearms.

For a minute he just stands there, listening for any sign that the guy is still alive — and then after what seems like an eternity, he hears the raspy sound of congestion coming from him. "Sarah, give me the light..."

She comes out and hands him a flashlight, then turns her own on as well, seeing a trail of blood running from man's head. "Is he alive?"

"Yeah, but I'm not sure for how long. I hit him pretty hard." He takes the tape from her, then pulls his arms across his back to bring his wrists together, then begins wrapping tape around them. "Of course he had to be the biggest guy in town..."

"Do you want me to tie his feet together?"

"That's probably a good idea."

As she winds the tape around his ankles, she sees Matt and Ben approach the bed, both of them staring at the intruder. "What are you planning on doing with him?" she asks Curtis, who takes the tape back

43

and places a piece of it onto his mouth.

"I'm gonna take him outside, then figure out how to patch the door downstairs." Confident that he can't get loose, Curtis grabs the man by his feet and pulls him off of the bed, hitting his head against the floor hard enough to hear a cracking sound.

"Curtis!" Sarah cries out. "At least pretend to be careful..."

"Then grab a pillow and put it under his head — the stairs aren't gonna be much better."

Struggling with the man's weight the entire way down the staircase, Curtis searches the first floor carefully when they get to the bottom, then tells the others to stay inside while he takes the guy outside.

"I might be several minutes, I'm gonna try to find where he got in."

"Don't wander out of earshot."

"I won't, I promise."

He drags the man across the yard, stopping in the corner where there's almost no grass — where it looks like the sand dunes below have worked their way up to the surface. Leaving him there, he runs over to the shed and picks up a shovel that's leaned up against the building, then returns to the corner and starts to dig a hole in the soft, wet soil — an act which requires almost no effort in what appears to be almost pure sand. When he's done, he starts to push the man toward the hole, then finally uses the shovel when he begins to struggle against him — confirming Curtis' fear that the man is still very much alive. As his body drops down into the shallow grave, Curtis walks around to the other side and begins to quickly pull the loose sand over the top of him, then looks up and sees Sarah staring back at him from across the yard. When she turns around and heads back to the house, he finishes the job and packs the ground down tightly with his feet, then throws the shovel down and follows her.

When he walks through the door, he has no idea what to expect — since what he just did seems horrifying to him as well. "Listen, I don't..."

"You don't have to say anything," Sarah interrupts. "I would've done the same thing."

Curtis walks over to the couch and nearly collapses onto it, overcome with emotion, and then he looks up and sees Ben staring out the window on the south side of the room, looking back in the direction of town.

"Dad, I can see lights over there..."

After covering the front door with a partial piece of plywood, the entire Lockwood family sits in front of the upstairs bedroom window, watching as the once peaceful town of Grayland descends into chaos. At first they weren't going to let the boys see what was happening outside, but they've passed the point of being able to shelter them by now, and knowing the cruel realities of the world around them is probably more important than ever.

The lights that Ben had seen earlier turned out to be bonfires, most of which seem to be concentrated behind the trailer park, near a cranberry bog if Curtis' memory is correct. They can see the outlines of people passing in front of the fires, but it's impossible to estimate how many are out there. They've also seen groups of them on the highway directly in front of the house, usually dragging something behind them, most likely another person or animal from what they witnessed earlier in the day — but what they do to them is mystery, a mystery that none of them really want the answer to.

"We'll leave first thing in the morning, as soon as the town looks empty again," Curtis says.

"Will we walk on the beach, like before?" Matt asks.

"I don't know, son, I saw several of them on the beach the other

45

day, and it was broad daylight. It might be best to stick to the dunes."

"You know," Sarah says, still staring out the window. "After Larry and Beth left the cabin, I used to blame all of our problems on Amanda, thinking that she ruined whatever life we'd carved out for ourselves — but looking at this, everything was bound to fall apart eventually, wasn't it?"

"We'll find someplace..." Curtis tells her.

"I know, I think we will too, but it won't be anywhere around Westport or Grayland."

CHAPTER 6
GRAYLAND: MARCH 28TH

Huddled in the dark, listening carefully to every sound coming from outside the house, Rachel can't help the thoughts of regret from entering her mind. In the very beginning, after the virus had sent everyone around them into isolation, she remembers telling Bill that she wanted to stay in their home on the west end of Olympia. For an urban setting, the house was somewhat secluded compared to many of the neighboring communities — and by the time they left, she was fairly certain that they were the only living souls in the entire area.

As much as she wanted to stay in familiar surroundings, however, Bill felt just the opposite. To him, living in a dead, abandoned city was giving up on any kind of future, and he was determined that if there was any small pocket of humanity left, he was going to find it — with or without her and their son, Travis.

Foolishly, she made the decision to follow him on his search, regretting that choice almost immediately after leaving the city and entering the town of McCleary. It was there that they saw the first signs of the infected — and when Travis first developed the early symptoms of the virus. Whether he had it when they left home or not she couldn't tell for certain, but part of her still blamed the trip for sickening her only child, and Bill for instigating it.

It was several days ago that she made the second worst decision of her life — and that was when she listened to Bill yet again, and left Larry, Beth and Christine behind in that house. Whatever happened to the three of them is a mystery to her, but it couldn't be much worse

47

than the horrors she encountered soon after exiting the home that night. After dragging Rachel's family into a large building, the hunters pulled Bill aside and began torturing him mercilessly, leaving her with mental images and sounds that will haunt her for the rest of her life. It was only after the hunters became distracted that it left an opportunity for her and Travis to escape through the rear of the building, leaving Bill behind, his body so badly mutilated that he would've only been a hindrance to them anyway.

Since that night, they've watched the hunters go door to door in search of people, forcing her and Travis to move three times already. As of this morning though, moving is no longer an option — not after Travis woke up to a coughing fit, soaking the washcloth with fresh blood from his lungs.

They both knew what it meant — he wouldn't be here for more than a day or two at the most.

She can see people in the distance, going from one house to another, pulling everything from furniture to people out into the street, and then executing them without any hesitation. Eventually they'll come to their house too, but for now she can still hear Travis behind her, his breathing weak and shallow, but at least he's still breathing.

"Mom?" Travis says, his voice weak and congested.

"Yes, I'm here, honey." She watches him struggle to get off of the couch that he's been sleeping on. "You need your rest, you shouldn't be getting up..."

He stands up, then stumbles into the chair next to her and looks out at the scene through the window. "They're getting closer..."

"They won't find us, we'll hide."

"Mom, promise me something..."

"Sure, honey, anything."

"Promise me that you won't leave the house, no matter what."

48

She doesn't really know how to answer him, and she's more than a bit confused by it — wondering if the virus has finally begun to affect his mind. "Of course I won't leave..."

"Promise me, no matter what."

"I promise, no matter what. Where is this coming from?"

Holding onto the arms of the chair, he pulls himself up, but instead of returning to the couch, he grabs the doorknob on the front entrance and turns the handle. "Lock the door behind me..."

Before Rachel can say anything, he opens the door and steps out into the night, slamming it shut again before trudging through the muddy ground in front of the house. She rushes to the door and starts to open it, but then looks out and sees several people surrounding her son — all of them armed with something. As they close in on him, she sees him take something out of his coat, then place it next to his head. Just as she realizes what it is, she sees the muzzle flash, then hears the gunshot as it echos off of the neighboring buildings. The people, none of whom she can see all that well, all look in her direction for a moment, and then most of them turn and walk the other way, while the two remaining people stay behind and each grab one of Travis' arms. As they drag him off into the darkness, Rachel feels her legs give out from under her, and she drops to the floor in tears — stopping only momentarily to lock the door.

Dark thoughts are no stranger to Rachel's mind — having grown up in a broken, dysfunctional family where abuse seemed more like a tradition than a crime, she'd felt completely alone more than once in her life.

This, however, was very different.

In some remote corner of her mind, she's telling herself to escape this godforsaken place, and to return to her home in Olympia, where the absence of life seems preferable to whatever inhabits this place — but another part, a much more dominant fragment of her consciousness, is telling her to follow Travis' example, and to simply give in to the grief and heartache.

As she looks across the room at the knife lying on the kitchen counter, she imagines both scenarios in her head — and then she thinks about the sacrifice that Travis just made for her, all so that she could live through this somehow. She gets up, taking another look through the window at the empty street beyond, then she walks into the kitchen and picks up the knife, staring at the surface of the blade, which is still stained with the blood of someone that she killed only two days before. Taking in a few deep breaths, she places the knife into a bag she found in the bedroom closet, and then packs the rest of the space with extra clothes and a few items of food.

She knows the hunters won't stay away for long, but she also knows that there's no possible way that she can wander around at night without being seen. Picking up the bag, she walks into the hallway and opens up the attic door, which is slightly recessed into the ceiling and difficult to spot unless you happen to be looking for it. Once she climbs the narrow, rickety steps and into the low-ceilinged space above, she barely has time to reach down and pull the stairs back up before she hears somebody banging on the front door. In a matter of a few minutes she can hear them inside, throwing things around and fighting with each other. She very quietly tugs on the string that's hanging from the attic door, then pulls it back up and ties it to a nearby rafter. Still listening to them, she rests her back against some insulation and closes her eyes, drifting off to sleep for the first time in days.

CHAPTER 7
ABERDEEN: MARCH 29TH

Watching Christine step into an old patient room, Larry waits until he hears the door lock before he turns and walks back down the corridor and into the main ICU area. As grateful as he is for Mike's hospitality, they've also only known one another for less than a day, and for much of that he's been sleeping in the same room while Christine sat quietly and watched over him.

As he enters the reception area, he sees Mike sitting at one of the computers playing a game of solitaire.

"Do you ever turn the generator off to save fuel?" Larry asks him, sitting down at a desk next to him.

"I did once, and almost didn't get it started again — so now I just run it all the time."

"So, about this plan of yours... Have you been outside of the hospital since the outbreak started?"

"Honestly... no, I haven't."

"I've been to several cities now, and whatever horrible image you have in your head — believe me, it's a lot worse."

"I'm still going."

"I know, but I'm going with you. Christine can stay behind and let us in."

"You trust her not to fall asleep or something?"

"You have no idea what she's been through — she can handle it."

Looking relieved, Mike rolls back his sleeves and holds out his arms so that Larry can see them. "Do you mind doing the same?"

51

With some hesitation, Larry takes off his coat and displays his own arms, which seems to please Mike. "Looking for bruising?"

"Yeah, you can never be too careful."

"So when did you wanna take off?" Larry asks.

"How does tomorrow morning sound?" Mike points to the wall, where there's a clock hanging on the wall. "It's two o'clock in the afternoon, it's getting a little late to do it today."

"Shit, I didn't realize I was out for that long..." As Mike smiles and goes back to his game, Larry looks around at the emptiness around him, and feels bored for the first time since being trapped on the boat in Sequim. "Have you looked around the hospital for insulin?"

"I've looked through most of it."

"But not all of it...?"

"Not the second floor — for obvious reasons."

"Did you know that woman?"

"Just as a patient, nothing personal."

"Do you mind if Christine and I take a look later tonight?"

"Be my guest... I'd appreciate it, but I really wouldn't recommend it."

Curious as to what the city looks like at sundown from the waiting area, Larry gets up and stretches his sore leg out, then begins walking toward the hallway. "I'm heading to the other side for a bit."

"The lights are turned off on that end."

"That's okay, I have a flashlight. By the way, who was that guy you were talking to in Shelton? The one on the radio..."

"His name is Frank, and his wife's name is Mary, or Marie, I can't remember which."

"Is he okay? He sounded like he was in trouble."

"He's more than in trouble — Frank is infected, he has been since almost the beginning. I started talking to his wife early on, and I still hear from him occasionally."

"Is his wife sick too?"

"No, Frank killed her months ago."

After watching the city of Aberdeen from six floors up for a couple of hours, Larry is more convinced than ever that the city isn't nearly as dead as they assumed it would be. Whether the people have come in from across the southern bridge, or have been in the city this entire time, it's hard to tell for sure — but he can definitely see movement in and around some of the buildings, mostly down next to the edge of the harbor. Although most of the activity seems to be confined to the shadows, or during periods when the cloud cover is particularly dark, he can also see some of them walking around in the open, unencumbered from the daylight.

"Seen anything exciting?" Christine asks, walking up behind him.

Larry smiles as he stands up and grabs his light. "A few months ago this would've been mind-boggling — but no, I haven't seen anything out of the ordinary." When he turns around and faces her, he can tell there's something different, and when she finally walks into the light from the windows he can see what it is — she's cut her hair extremely short, making her look even younger than she really is.

"I got tired of dealing with the mats, so I just cut it off."

"It looks good."

"No it doesn't, it looks like crap — I'm definitely not a hairdresser."

"Well, on the plus side, nobody gives a shit anymore." After a quick check to make sure he has an extra light and plenty of ammunition, they start walking back down the hallway toward the stairs. Mike, for whatever reason, is nowhere to be seen.

"Where are we going again?"

"The second floor, down to a supply room that might have extra insulin. He drew us a map," Larry says, handing her a piece of paper with a crudely drawn outline of the floor.

"What are we gonna do about the woman?"

"Hopefully she won't even know we're there. Mike said he's gonna turn the lights on for us, so at least we won't be going in blind."

As they open the door to the staircase and start their descent, the lights suddenly come on overhead, and they hear the radio begin to crackle.

"*Do you have lights now?*"

"Yeah, thanks. We should stay off of these though, they might attract too much attention down there," Larry replies into the radio.

"Do you trust him?" Christine asks.

"I don't distrust him."

"I keep remembering when Jake bragged to me about killing him."

"It might not be a good idea to bring that up, especially the part about me being his brother-in-law."

"I know, I won't say anything."

When they reach the platform for the second floor, Larry peeks through the window in the door and sees that the overhead lights down the corridor are all brightly lit, along with most of the rooms — but almost all of the doors are shut. Mike told him that this was the maternity ward before the outbreak, but it's been virtually unused since the virus was first reported.

"Do you see her?" Christine asks.

"No, I don't see anything."

"It says the supply room is all the way down on the other side, then to the left."

Larry takes a key out of his pocket and quietly inserts it into the lock, but despite his best effort, the door makes an incredible amount of noise when he opens it. He stands there without moving for a minute, only halfway through the doorway while he waits for

54

someone to run toward them — but the place stays eerily quiet. When he steps into the cold hallway with his pistol held firmly in his hand, he can feel warm air blowing across his face from the ventilation system above — but the air smells putrid, like rotting flesh.

"That smell is horrible..." Christine whispers to him.

"Do you need to stay here?"

"No, I'm fine — let's just get this over with."

Looking into each of the lighted rooms as he passes by them, Larry can see bodies lying on the beds and even the countertops in most of them. A little over halfway down, the lights over them start to dim, then blink a couple of times, making the two of them exchange worried looks as they continue their search. With his gun still in his grip, Larry takes a flashlight out of his pocket and turns it on, then stops in his tracks as he stares into one of the rooms.

"What is it?" Christine asks.

"That's the woman I saw through the door..."

Christine takes a look for herself, and sees an old woman lying on an exam table. "She looks dead..."

"Good, that'll make this a little easier."

Only a moment after they begin moving again, the lights flicker, and they hear some commotion from one of the rooms behind them. Larry turns and faces the one with the woman, but Christine tugs on his sleeve and points to the other side of the hallway, where he can see some faint movement coming from inside the darkened room.

"We should get out of here..." Christine says, still backing up further away from the staircase door.

Larry aims his gun at the door just as it starts to open, and a half-dressed man wearing only a pair of unbuttoned pants comes stumbling out into the hall, looking at the two of them with a confused look on his face.

"Does that map have another exit listed?" Larry asks.

"No, it just has the path from the stairs to the supply room."

They keep backing up, watchful of any activity in the rooms that are still behind them, and then they see somebody else enter the hallway and stand next to the shirtless man. Larry recognizes her as the woman that he saw the day before, the woman that was just lying down and motionless only moments before. As they move away from them, the man pushes the woman out of the way and begins walking toward Larry, glaring at him with an intense look on his face.

"Just shoot him, Larry..." Christine says, hiding behind him.

"How many of the others that we passed by are still alive? I don't wanna wake them all up." When they get to the end of the corridor, he motions for Christine to head left toward the supply room, but sees another silhouette about forty feet away from them, obscured by darkness where the lights are out on that end.

"Larry..."

"I know, I see them. The supply room is this side of them, see the sign on the wall?"

"What if they come closer?"

"I'll shoot them, but let's hope that doesn't happen, okay?"

While they've been stopped, the man following them has kept creeping forward, inching his way in their direction one painfully slow step at a time.

"Just keep moving, slow and steady," Larry tells her calmly. "We don't want them riled up."

Christine keeps her eye on the person down the hall, but they don't move a muscle until she opens the supply room door, and then she sees them glance behind themselves, where she can hear another door open somewhere in the darkness.

"Get inside, quick!" Larry says, nudging her through the doorway.

He locks the door behind them, then shines his light around at the unlit storeroom — a room that's already been trashed from the looks

56

of it. Spilled medication bottles cover the floor, along with crushed tablets and capsules that have obviously been walked on repeatedly.

"How are we gonna find anything in this mess?" Christine complains

"Just look for any clear bottles, I'm pretty sure that's what it's kept in."

He starts sifting through the clutter on one of the shelves, when he hears a knocking on the door next to him. Aiming the light at the window, he sees two faces looking in at them, the shirtless man, and another man that has a deep cut all the way down the right side of his face. It's severe enough that Larry is pretty sure that the eye is gone.

"Larry, I think I found them..."

In her hand is a broken bottle, with a label that says 'Human Insulin rDNA Suspension'. She points onto the floor, where there's several boxes, all of them smashed.

"Shit..." Larry says under his breath. He grabs the radio and pushes the button down, then looks back at the men outside the door, who are still glaring at them. "Mike, are you there?"

"*Yeah, I'm here. Did you find any?*"

"It's all smashed, there's nothing left down here. You'll probably hear a bunch of gunshots in a few minutes — it's just us getting out of here."

"*Did you need any help?*"

"I don't think so, just stay by the radio just in case."

"*Okay, I will.*"

Placing the radio back in his pocket, he turns to Christine. "You have two .38 pistols on you, right?"

"Yeah, and four of those quick load things."

"You still have that little .32 I gave you?"

"Yeah, it's in my sock just like you showed me."

Larry can hear the fear in her voice, and as much as he regrets bringing her along, he also can't imagine leaving her alone upstairs. "Okay, you just stay behind me, and let me do all the shooting, okay?"

She simply nods, her jaw visibly trembling even in the dim light.

"And if for whatever reason you have to shoot somebody?"

"I take them down with a body shot, then shoot them in the head — I've got it."

"Okay, good. Step back and cover your ears, this is gonna be really loud."

Larry takes in a deep breath, then aims his semi-automatic pistol at the head of the shirtless man, who doesn't even react to it. He fires one bullet directly into his forehead, then does the same to the other man, dropping both of them instantly. Figuring that Christine won't be able to hear him anyway, he points at her flashlight, then at the door, prompting her to provide him with light. Once she does, he opens the door and fires another round at the first woman he saw, and then shines his own light down the darkened hallway — but doesn't see anybody there.

"Can you hear me?" he yells.

"Yeah."

"Keep an eye behind us, we still don't know what came out of that other door."

They move more quickly this time, and then hear the door at the end of the corridor open again as they begin to turn the corner. Standing right in front of the staircase door is another man with gray hair, who's wearing a hospital gown and facing the stairs.

"Are the people behind us coming?" Larry asks.

"No, not yet."

He keeps moving, then stops about fifteen feet from the man, who's still facing away from him. Aiming his gun at the man's head, and feeling guilty about firing at someone who isn't posing an immediate threat to them, he pulls the trigger and kills the man —

breaking the glass in the door in front of him at the same time. He opens the door and looks the staircase shaft over closely, then pulls Christine out of the corridor and locks the door. When he turns around and faces her, she's already sitting down on the steps and crying, her entire body shaking from the stress.

He sits down next to her and starts to put his arm around her shoulders, but he stops when he notices the bright red spots of blood that's now covering his arms and hands. "Listen, we're both still alive." He grabs the radio out of his pocket, intending to give Mike an update, then he puts it away again. "Why don't we just leave this place..."

"And go where?"

"We'll go back to the other side of the river and find a nice house. We didn't see a single infected asshole over there."

"This is the only place I've been able to sleep — I mean truly sleep."

"Mike wants my help tomorrow — are you okay being here alone?"

"I'll be fine, as long as I stay on the sixth floor."

CHAPTER 8
GRAYLAND: MARCH 29TH

As peaceful, beautiful, and relaxing as the ocean appears in the evening, when the last rays of saturated sunlight are displayed over the water, the mornings can oftentimes be just the opposite. It's quite unusual for the coastline this far north to have anything resembling sunshine in the early hours of the day, and the overcast skies only add to the cold, gloomy look that the water takes on. There was a time when Curtis hated mornings like this, when the rain showers from the dark gray clouds overhead would start as a gentle misting, and then go on to last for the rest of the day.

This particular morning, however, is different.

It's not the weather that's changed, since the sky looks exactly the same as it normally does — but for the first few hours of nearly every day, most of the infected are nowhere to be found, giving his family their best and perhaps only shot at making it out of this place alive. Looking out at the beach in front of him, this morning appears to be no different.

With all of their supplies packed up, the family prepares for a long journey south, unsure of just how long it will take them to reach someplace safer than this. It's barely daybreak as Curtis leads them down the same path that he found a couple of days prior, winding through pine trees and tall grass that provide decent cover from the local residents. Although the wind is blowing in the trees above them, concealing the noise their footsteps make in the soft sand, they still walk in silence, all of them well-aware of the dangers that surround them.

As they pass behind a house, only a few doors down from where they left, Curtis stops and listens when he hears somebody struggling from beyond the solid board fence next to them. Motioning his family toward a small shed, the four of them move quickly down the trail, then up onto a mostly rotten wood porch that's covered with moss and algae, making it slippery to move over. He can hear a gate opening behind them as he pushes the door open and lets his wife and kids inside the dark building, then sees two men coming out of the enclosed yard and onto the trail.

"Curtis," Sarah whispers, pulling him next to her. "There's somebody in here with us."

Hearing something move in the far corner, he pulls the gun out of his pocket and then turns his flashlight on, hoping that the light doesn't attract too much attention from the outside — then steps in front of his family when he sees a woman covered in blood standing against the opposite wall, holding a knife that's shaking in her hands.

""Don't come any closer!" she screams at them.

"Keep your voice down," Curtis tells her, speaking in a volume barely more than a whisper. "There's two men outside, and they're sick."

"And you're not?" she responds, speaking much quieter now.

"No, none of us are." He hears footsteps outside, but when he turns around he discovers that there's no lock on the door, just a small rope attached to it that he grabs onto and wraps around a nearby hook on the wall. Ignoring the woman for now, he hands his flashlight to Sarah, then braces himself against the crudely made door made out of old boards, and watches as it almost falls to pieces when one of the men throws himself into it. By the third hit, one of the boards in the middle finally comes off, exposing the man's torso on the other side — but he apparently hasn't noticed it, because he continues his assault

61

by slamming his forearm just beside the missing piece. Holding the door with his shoulder, Curtis takes a kitchen knife from one his bags and then thrusts it into the man's chest — but Curtis loses his grip on it as the guy pulls back, and the knife stays lodged inside of him.

Curtis starts to position himself in front of the door again to brace it, but before he gets his footing set, the second man kicks the door in and tears the hinges from the wall, sending his overweight body and what's left of the door directly on top of Curtis. He can feel the back of his head get slammed into the wooden planks of the floor as the man grabs him by the hair with both hands, violently yanking on his head as he tries to dislocate it from his spine — and then everything slowly begins to fade away, including the screams that seem to come from all around him.

"He'll be fine, honey, he just needs to rest for a few minutes, that's all..."

The voice sounds far away, scared, and slightly muffled, but Curtis recognizes it as his wife. When he opens his eyes and feels the splitting headache start to develop, he reaches up and taps Sarah on her knee.

"Oh, thank God..." she cries out, still trying to keep her voice as quiet as possible. "How do you feel?"

"I think the bastard hit me in the same place that Jake did." He sits up a little and looks around, but most of the building is too dark to see much of anything. "What happened to those guys?"

"You killed the first guy, and Rachel killed the other one."

"Who?"

Sarah motions for Rachel to come closer, and Curtis sees the woman that was hiding come into view and sheepishly wave to him.

"Do you think you can walk, babe?"

"I think so..." With a little help from both women, Curtis gets up onto his feet and then sits down on an old toolbox that's lying next to him. "Could you get me some painkillers? There's part of a bottle in my bag." He sees his sons both standing by the missing front door, each of them looking around at different parts of the rain-soaked forest outside. Feeling a nudge against his shoulder, he looks up at Sarah and sees her holding out two pills, but not the ones he was talking about. "I meant the hydrocodone..."

"I know you did, but these are gonna have to do for now — we need you alert for the rest of the day. Rachel said we have to get east of Westport by sundown."

"We're going south, Westport is north of here."

"We can't go south, Curtis — it's not safe down there." She picks up his bags and hands them to him, then grabs her own while Rachel does the same with hers. "Is it clear, Matt?"

"I think so, I don't see anybody."

"Okay, both of you grab your bags. Matt, just keep the gun where you can reach it, okay?"

"Maybe I should take it," Curtis says, staggering momentarily as he stands up and takes a few steps.

"No, he'll be fine. Just get your legs back under you."

The group, which now has five members, all step out onto the crumbling porch and into the wilderness again, their muscles feeling tired and sore from the constant stress and almost complete lack of sleep. None of them are looking forward to walking into Westport, not after the horrors they've already witnessed there — but the desolate wasteland of Olympia, which apparently suffered greatly from the virus according to Rachel, sounds peaceful and quiet compared to the towns along the coast, and the only way to get there is to pass through an area they know to be infected.

"We can't go through town, there's too many of them," Rachel tells them, as they walk down through the dunes and onto the beach where there's fewer houses that could be occupied.

"Well, we can't stay on the beach like this, we're sitting ducks," Sarah replies.

"We can take the old farm roads, but they're on the other side of town." Curtis says.

"I didn't see anything like that on the map," Rachel says, as she pulls out an old road map that's falling apart and glances over it.

"They're probably not on there — but they exists, I've been on them before."

"Are there houses on them?"

"Not very many, just a few farms."

"As long as we stay north of Grayland, it's fine with me."

Curtis' head is still throbbing, but the pain finally starts to subside by the time they turn and head up the beach access road. As they cut through the fire station parking lot and into a large field behind it, he notices Rachel's reluctance to look back at the trailer park or cranberry bog next to it — but chooses to say nothing. They know relatively little about her, but the fact that she's traveling alone in a town like this speaks volumes about what she's likely been through.

The yard that they're walking through runs right next to a cranberry bog, just like most of the properties on this side of town, although it looks as though this one hasn't been used in several years. As they get closer to the house, Sarah tells the boys not to look into the field or the small yard surrounding the home itself — but they do it anyway. The livestock that used to live here, which were probably either cows or horses judging from the size, are now lying in stacked up piles of bones that are scattered around the place — and the former residents, two adults and several children by the looks of it, are hanging from a large tree in the middle of the pasture. He tells

64

himself that they were probably killed by the virus, and their bodies mutilated afterward by the lunatics in town, but he knows deep down that's not likely what happened.

Beth once told him a theory that Jake had come up with, one that sounded too dark and grim for him to believe at the time — but he's starting to wonder if it might actually be true. According to him, the only possible way that he could see a single organism wiping out an entire species, especially one as diverse as the human race, is for people to deliberately engineer one — a doomsday parasite built with the sole purpose of killing every man, woman and child on earth. The only thing he was unsure of was whether or not these infected survivors were part of the plan. They could be an unforeseen glitch, or they could be part of the overall design — to finish eliminating whatever remains of humanity.

Whether or not any of this conspiracy theory is true, it's hard not to think the worst of mankind when you see houses like this one ripped to pieces and spread across the land for no apparent reason, and children murdered and propped up like decorations. More than ever, Curtis is determined to stay away from any signs of people, and he hopes that walking through the forests and swamps on the eastern service road will provide them with as little contact as possible.

"Mom, my feet really hurt," Ben says, lagging behind the rest of them a bit. "Can we stop for a while?"

Sarah stops, along with the rest of the group, then she kneels down and takes Ben's right shoe off. "Is this one hurting?"

"Yeah, they both are."

She holds his shoe up for Curtis to see, showing him the holes developing in the sides, and the sole that's beginning to separate from the rest of it. "He needs new shoes."

"We'll probably find something in Aberdeen, if there's anything that hasn't burned up."

"Is that far?" Ben asks.

Sarah glares up at Curtis as she places another pair of socks over his existing ones, giving him more cushion.

"There's nothing I can do right here, it's not like we have a lot of choices available," he says to his wife. Once they begin walking again, he pats Ben on the shoulder and takes one of the bags from him, lightening the strain on his feet. "We should be there tomorrow — you're gonna have to tough it out until then, okay?"

"Okay, Dad."

"Have you guys walked very far before now?" Rachel asks.

"We took our first long one in September, and haven't really stopped since then."

"We left Olympia about the same time, but we stayed in a couple of places along the way."

"You and your husband?" Sarah asks her.

"And our son, Travis," she answers, getting choked up as she says his name.

"I'm sorry, Rachel, I really am."

Sarah looks back at Curtis and holds her hand up, motioning for him and the boys to back off and give them some privacy. "Listen, if you ever want to talk about it, I'm always here for you... Curtis and I still have a daughter in California, who we haven't heard from since the outbreak started."

"What's her name?"

"Annie — she was going to school down there. We just weren't able to get her home in time."

"My niece was about that age, she lived just north of Seattle with my sister — but they're both gone now too."

They both walk in silence for a while, looking out at the fog-covered cranberry bogs that span for miles to the south behind them — but they end only a short distance ahead of them, at the foot of

66

some hills that are home to several massive windmills, a sight which looks entirely out of place to most people when they see them for the first time.

"I saw a girl that reminded me of my niece a few days ago," Rachel continues. "She even had the same snotty attitude."

"Was she sick?"

"No, she was healthy. She was with another couple in Grayland."

Sarah looks back at Curtis, wondering if he's heard any of this. "Do you remember their names?"

"His name was Larry, but I don't remember his sister's name — or the girl's.

"Beth and Amanda?" This time, when she glances back, she sees Curtis quickly catching up.

"Yes, Beth, that was the sister — but Amanda doesn't sound right."

"Wait!" Curtis says, stopping all of them just a few feet from the edge of the pasture, where the gravel farm road runs north-south along the hills. "How old was this girl?"

"I don't know, maybe fifteen or sixteen."

"Is she still alive?"

"I don't know, she was the last time I saw her. Why, do you know her?"

"Yeah, we know her."

CHAPTER 9
EAST OF COHASSETT: MARCH 29TH

Rachel can sense that the mood has changed dramatically in the group since hearing about their former companions, and although they seem sincere when they talk about her, Rachel's own impressions of the girl traveling with them was quite different. Curtis seems especially withdrawn, looking down at the road only a few feet ahead of him instead of at the picturesque forests and pastures that surround them — a landscape that would ordinarily look serene, if not for all of the deadly threats that could be lurking somewhere just beyond their sight.

Although she liked Sarah right away, she's still not sure what to think of Curtis. She completely understands the pressure that both of them are under, trying to protect their children from everything that's happening around them — but she can see cracks forming in his ability to control himself, and she wonders how long it will take before he allows those primitive temptations to take over. Everyone has their limit, that fine line that separates us from the animalistic behavior of our ancient ancestors. Curtis, for all of his good intentions, seems on the verge of reaching his.

The boys are quiet, but it's hard for her to determine whether or not they've always been that way. Ben had a look of absolute horror on his face at the mere mention of Amanda's name, and he hasn't spoken in the forty minutes since. Instead, he's spent nearly the entire time looking behind the group, toward the fading town of Grayland in the distance. When she glances back to check on him again, she sees him standing in the middle of the gravel road, facing away from them.

"Ben, are you okay?" Rachel asks. He doesn't respond, but she can hear the footsteps of the others stop.

"What's wrong, Ben?" Sarah asks, as she walks back and kneels beside him. "Do your feet still hurt?"

"There's someone back there — I saw them a minute ago..." he replies.

"What did they look like?"

Rachel looks back at the road they've just hiked, which has very few twists or turns, but doesn't see any sign of movement. It does, however, have trees and brush alongside much of it, providing plenty of spots for someone to hide.

"There was more than one of them," Ben says, pointing his finger straight ahead. "There they are!"

The others look again, and see several figures appearing out of a dip in the road, no more than a half-mile behind them. While not running, they are moving at a pace that will allow them to catch up rather quickly.

"Should we hide?" Rachel asks, looking around at the few trees that are sparsely scattered around them.

"No," Curtis says, looking north on the road ahead of them. "There's a bend coming up — we'll try to lose them on the other side of it."

"There's at least four of them," Sarah says.

Rachel can't pick out any distinguishing features on them from this distance, but they resemble many of the hunters from Grayland. They move and act almost normally, and wear clothing that covers their entire body — unlike the typical infected person that always seems to be only partially dressed, regardless of the weather or temperature.

Moving more quickly than before, Rachel and the Lockwoods head north again, seeing the curve just ahead of them as the road runs through the middle of a farm — complete with a small house, a couple of old sheds, and a massive barn that has a broken spine in the middle of the roof. Curtis looks back at the hunters and sees that they've gained some ground, but they're still probably at least ten minutes behind them. They go around the curve in the road, which takes them out of sight, and then cut across the yard in front of the farmhouse, seeing a wide open front door and trash littering the entryway.

"Should we risk going in there?" Sarah asks. "There could be someone inside."

"We don't really have a choice," Curtis says, as he hurries onto the front porch and briefly scans the living room from the doorway.

After everyone enters the house, Curtis, Sarah and Rachel quickly close not only the door, but also all of the curtains on the front facing windows — leaving the room relatively dark as they crowd together in one corner of the room, hidden from even the windows in the back of the home. Curtis leans over and peeks through a small slit beside the curtains and looks out at the road, and after a few minutes he sees four people approach the end of the driveway, and then stand at the end of it, staring in his direction.

"They're just standing there..." he whispers, still looking at the road as something crashes loudly in one of the back rooms.

"What was that?" Sarah asks.

"I think there's somebody in the house," Rachel replies.

"Curtis, give me the gun..." Sarah says, holding her hand out to him as he hands the pistol over. Rachel bends down and takes the kitchen knife out of her bag, then joins Sarah as she slowly makes her way back to the bedroom where the noise originated. Seeing another open door in front of them, Sarah leans over and whispers into Rachel's ear. "I'm gonna open the door, and if anything comes out of there, kill it."

Taking in a deep breath, she grabs onto the doorknob and pulls it open, aiming the gun around the room frantically before seeing two glowing eyes coming from underneath the bed. Feeling relieved, she shines the flashlight inside and sees two raccoons hiding under the box-springs. Joining her husband next to the window again, she leans forward and stares outside.

"Where are they?" she asks.

"They moved on. What was in the other room?"

"Raccoons."

He looks at his watch, which shows almost four o' clock in the afternoon. "We should stay here for the night, then take off at first light."

"Do you think they'll be back?"

"They'll be back." Rachel says. "These ones aren't stupid like the others."

Sarah hasn't seen as many houses as Curtis has, or Rachel for that matter — but she's seen enough to know that every one of them tells a different story. Some are still occupied by their infected owners, or contain the remains of what's left of them — others lie dormant as if they've been empty for decades, and others, like this one, show signs of a stubborn will to survive. The person who lived here before was meticulous and organized, keeping the garbage cleaned up and the canned foods kept in tidy alphabetized rows with expiration dates that are clearly marked on the label. Judging from the amount of empty jars and cans stacked up on the back porch, it seems they must have lived for some time after the outbreak. When Curtis told her that there was a body in the bedroom, one that had been there for some time, she immediately assumed that it was yet another suicide — but what she saw instead was just as troubling. Surrounding the body, looking almost like a shrine, is a mountain of cold and flu medications, along with thermometers, blood pressure cuffs, and bottles of hand sanitizers. Whoever they were, they certainly wanted to survive — and yet perished long after most of the world was already gone.

The house that they left behind, although somewhat drafty, is extraordinarily well-kept considering the circumstances. If not for the close proximity to the towns, Sarah would actually be tempted to stay for a while, if for no other reason than to allow Ben's feet to rest.

After covering all of the windows and barricading the doors to the best of their abilities, the group decides to sleep in shifts in one of the upstairs bedrooms for the night, while the others keep watch in another room across the hallway where they have a clear view of both the road out front, and the town to the southwest. Seeing the tired look in Curtis' eyes, Sarah informed him after dinner that she and Rachel would take the first watch, while he and Matt could take the second.

"Do you ever wonder why you never got sick?" Sarah asks Rachel, while each of them sit in front of separate windows and stare into the darkening landscape of dusk.

"I used to, but not anymore. I was certainly exposed to it enough when Travis got sick."

"I've wondered if we're all immune for some reason, like some rare gene that was passed on or something."

"I know that I should be grateful," Rachel says. "That I've been given this incredibly rare gift, but deep down I know that I should have died with him."

"Rachel..." Sarah says soothingly, turning toward her.

"Instead, I'm sitting here, hiding like some scared, defenseless animal that's being hunted."

"I know, but we'll find someplace quiet — I know we will."

"There's no life in Olympia, Sarah — there just isn't. The best case scenario is that we hide out there until the rest of mankind kills one another — and then what?"

"We start picking up the pieces." Sarah can't see the expression on her face, it's too dark — but she can hear her chuckle dismissively. "I know you think I'm being overly optimistic, but we've met some good people over the last few months, and the only reason that any of them are gone now is because we haven't been willing to make hard decisions."

"Travis made a hard decision, and now he's gone."

"But you aren't..." Sarah replies, watching Rachel stand up and look behind her, distracted by something out the window. "What's wrong?"

"Behind you... that's Grayland, isn't it?"

Turning around again, Sarah looks out across the pastures and forests and sees several bright orange spots on the horizon, each of them sending large plumes of black smoke and glowing embers into the night sky.

"It looks like half the town is on fire," Sarah says.

"That girl said that South Bend was on fire too."

"Which girl? Amanda?"

"That name still doesn't sound right — but yeah, she said it was all gone when they came by there."

"Amanda lived in Westport — that's where we found her."

"Well, then it wasn't her that I met."

Confused about what must have happened in those short couple of days after Larry and Beth left the cabin, Sarah continues watching out the window at the growing intensity in the distance, then notices some slight movements in the foreground, in the pasture across the street. "Rachel, do you see something in the field over there?"

"Yeah, I think so, but it's too dark to tell for sure."

A few moments later, they both realize that they're looking at people crossing over the field and into the woods on the other side — toward the town of Grayland. None of them are walking with any coordination or speed, and some of them are stumbling so badly that they're practically crawling across the tall grass.

"Did you hear that?" Rachel asks.

Before she has a chance to answer, Sarah hears a thump, like something is hitting the side of the house. "Yeah, I do. Stay here for a minute, I'm gonna check the other side of the house really quick."

"You might wanna wake Curtis while you're up."

Exiting the room, Sarah tiptoes past the bedroom where her family is sleeping, then walks down the hallway to another room that faces north. She's halfway across the floor, trying not to step on anything on the hardwood, when she finally looks up and sees somebody standing next to the window. Taking a couple of steps backward, she sees them turn around and face her, then stare back out the window again.

"Look at this..." Curtis says, motioning her closer.

She stands next to him, still feeling her heart pounding — then she feels him take her hand as she looks outside. Heading directly at them, moving south from the direction of Westport, is a line of people that extends into the darkness.

"How many are there?"

"I don't know, they just keep coming."

CHAPTER 10
ABERDEEN: MARCH 30TH

Dressed in warm, dry clothes, and armed with several guns, Larry walks into the waiting area and expects to see Christine still sleeping on the hospital bed in front of the windows. She moved it there from one of the other rooms the previous evening after the incident on the second floor, telling Larry and Mike that the view made her feel more comfortable somehow — like she wasn't trapped.

Instead, he sees her sitting in the bed and staring out the window, looking out at a massive plume of smoke that's billowing up from the south. It's still early, with the first trace of sunlight barely visible through the clouds and rain over the horizon, but he can clearly tell that the fire is spread out across a wide area, stretching from somewhere around Grayland and extending south for miles beyond. He approaches her, noticing that she's still sleeping in the same filthy, worn out clothes that she had on when they first met. Sitting down in a chair next to the bed, he watches with her as the strong wind coming off of the ocean carries the smoke and ash in their direction.

"I can already smell it," she says, sniffing the air.

"What, the smoke?"

"Yeah, it doesn't smell like woodsmoke — it smells like buildings, and garbage."

He breathes in deeply, taking the polluted air into his lungs. She's right, there is something peculiar about the smell, but he's not quite sure what to make of it. He can't imagine an accidental fire spreading like that, not with the rain soaking everything like it has over the past several months.

"Are you getting ready to take off?" she asks, finally turning around and facing him.

"I think so — I'm just waiting for Mike to get out of the bathroom. He's pretty nervous about it."

"He should be." She faces the window again, looking down at the streets below the hospital. "Those buildings still have people in them, Larry. I've seen them after the sun goes down."

"I know, I've seen them too. There aren't a lot of them though, not like we've seen in the past."

"Just make sure you watch your back — you can't trust him to do it. He hasn't seen what it's like out there."

"Is that the South Bend fire behind it?" he asks, pointing out the window at an even bigger wall of smoke and haze rising from the south and heading northeast by the wind current.

"Yeah, it must be. It looks huge, doesn't it?"

"Could you guys come here for a minute?" they hear Mike say from the hallway behind them. "There's something I wanted to talk to you about..."

Larry and Christine look at each other, both of them hearing the nervousness in his voice. When they reach the ICU desks, their surfaces bathed in bright white light from the fluorescent tubes above, they see Mike standing behind the counter, his forehead covered in sweat.

"What's wrong?" Larry asks, seeing Mike wearing his hospital scrubs again instead of the winter coat and jeans that he had on earlier.

"You know where we're going, right?"

"Sure, more or less. Why?"

"Are you going out in that outfit?" Christine asks. "You're gonna freeze to death."

76

Mike looks down at himself, then takes a few excited steps toward her, causing her to back up slightly in response. "I'll be fine, the cold doesn't really bother me all that much. I am a little concerned about you though, staying here all by yourself. You have a gun on you though, right?"

"Yeah — well, it's..." Christine reaches into her pocket, then remembers that she left it sitting on the bed.

Mike leaps forward in a flash, grabbing Christine from behind and placing her in a choke hold, then he positions her between Larry and himself. She struggles with him for just a moment, and then suddenly stops when he presses his pistol into her temple.

"Let her go!" Larry screams, aiming his own gun at Mike as he takes a few steps closer to them.

"If you come any closer, I'm gonna pull the trigger — I mean it!" Mike responds, tightening his grip on her neck. "Nobody has to get hurt — not if you do what I say."

After hearing the gun shaking in Mike's trembling hand, and the hammer on the gun pulled back and ready to fire, Larry stops moving forward and chooses to deescalate the situation instead. "I don't want to hurt anybody either, but if you keep that gun aimed at her head like that, something is going to happen — even if it's only an accident..."

"If you go now, I won't hurt her, I promise."

"Go where?"

"The supply center, just get me my medication and I'll let both of you go." He presses the gun into Christine's head even harder, making her wince from the pain. "I can't go out there, I'll get killed if I do."

The last thing Larry wants to do is leave Christine with him, especially after her experiences with Amanda and Jake, but he can also see both the determination and desperation in Mike's eyes, and he's almost certain that he'll at least try to kill both of them if he

77

doesn't leave.

Christine, whose face is reddened by her restricted airway, tries to say something to Larry, and Mike eases his arm up just enough for her to speak. "Larry, go... I'll be fine..."

"Listen to her, Larry, she'll be fine — you both will..." Mike tells him, his voice more frantic than ever.

Putting his gun away, Larry slowly backs up toward the staircase, stopping just in front of the door. "What if the supply center is burned down? What then?"

"You'll figure something out."

"Let her go as soon as I leave, understand?"

"You have my word."

He turns the handle on the door and starts to open it, then faces Mike again. "If you hurt her, I'll come back and burn this fucking place to the ground..."

The moment that Larry closes the door and begins walking down the stairs, he can feel his chest begin to tighten from the stress of what he's about to do, not to mention the horrible situation that he's left Christine in. When he gets about halfway down to the fifth floor, he can hear the door upstairs lock, and then everything goes quiet — until he reaches the second floor again. The door is still closed and locked, but the window in the top of it is shattered, and the broken shards of glass are covered in blood from the man that Larry shot the day before. Somewhere inside, down the corridor or in one of the rooms off of it, he can hear someone laughing — a slow, maniacal shriek that he mistook for pain when he first heard it. He only glances through the opening when he passes by it, seeing nothing but darkness on the other side.

His plan, when he thought that Mike was coming with him, was to take a shortcut straight down the hill from the hospital, instead of taking the street that runs alongside of it. He figured that the chances of coming across someone was less likely in the overgrown pathway that winds through the wooded area just above downtown. When he exits the hospital and stands out in the parking lot, the cold wind pounding his face with rain drops and debris from the trees across the road, he looks up at the main tower above and realizes that Mike is probably watching him. To dispel any suspicions, he decides that taking the more visible route might be safer for Christine, even if it places him in more danger from the lingering residents of the city. Already feeling the dampness making its way through his coat at the shoulders, he trudges through the mud puddles that cover the paved lot, then down the street that leads to downtown, trying to stay clear of the massive maple trees that grow next to the roadway and hang overhead, their trunks and limbs jerking violently in the high winds as he passes under them.

"*Larry, are you there?*"

Hearing Christine's voice on the radio, he fumbles around for it in his pocket, then looks up at the waiting area windows above him — but he can't see anything due to the rain and the glare off of the glass. "I'm here — are you okay?"

"*I'm fine, but we can see some people on the street ahead of you. They're moving slow, but they're coming toward you.*"

"How many?"

"*It's hard to say for sure, at least three or four though. I have to go, Larry.*"

"Okay, thanks. I'll see you soon."

Shielding his eyes with his hand and peering into the distance, he can see several dark objects lying around on the sidewalks and road surface, but none of them appear to moving, and he assumes that they're either the scorched remains of someone, or rubble that's fallen down from one of the nearby damaged buildings. It's only when he approaches the first cross street that he can hear the sound of something being dragged over the pavement, even over the howling wind that's blowing leaves and trash through the neighborhood. When he reaches the intersection, he crouches down behind a pickup and looks to the east, spotting a group of a people walking mindlessly down the sidewalk. One of them is dragging a children's bicycle behind him, which under different circumstances might look somewhat comical, but they're also creating a noise that can probably be heard blocks away from here. Larry considers simply walking right past them, figuring they're probably the same type of infected people they've seen in most of the places they've been to, almost incapable of causing harm out in the open because of how slowly they react to anything — but as they get closer, he sees a few differences that make him reconsider.

These people, five of them in all, are fully clothed — just like the people that they witnessed in Grayland. Worse than that, he can see one them talking to the others, and the others nodding in response. Their movements are stiff and painful looking, dragging their feet on the sidewalk as they stare straight ahead in the direction of Hoquiam. Larry crawls underneath the pickup that he's hiding behind and waits as they pass by, hoping to stay hidden from their view and avoid a confrontation — but when he looks up and sees their faces, with the skin badly scarred and their eyes swollen and hazy, he realizes that every one of them has been horrifically burned in the fires, and have most likely been blinded as a result.

When he climbs out again and continues down the street, he feels a sense of relief when he's no longer in sight of the hospital and under Mike's watchful eye. On both sides of the road, regardless of the building construction or age, the damage from the blaze has been devastating. Piles of crumbling debris from the buildings above are lying everywhere, blocking wide portions of pavement and forcing Larry to find a way around them. Ash and soot cover virtually every surface of the city, but here in the heart of the inferno it looks almost like a thick layer of fresh snow on the roadway and sidewalks. It takes him nearly a half hour to reach the block where the supply center is located, and when he finds the exact address his heart instantly sinks. He sees the supply center, or what's left of it anyway — but the only part of it that remains is the sign out front, and even that's been damaged in the flames.

He pulls the radio out again, wondering how he should break this to him. "Mike, this is Larry, come in..."

"*This is Mike. Are you there yet?*"

"I'm almost there, not quite though. As long as I'm down here, is there anyplace else I should check?"

"*There's a small pharmacy to the west of there, but I doubt they'd have much. Just clean out the supply center for now.*"

"Yeah, got it."

He looks to the north as he crosses the street and heads further west, making sure that Mike can't see his location and where he's going. The rain is coming down heavier now, and on the flat ground only a few blocks from the harbor, the unassisted drains are now spreading raw sewage and blackened trash into the blocked gutters and low spots in the parking lots, adding yet one more thing for Larry to avoid.

The pharmacy that Mike was talking about turns out to be three blocks away, and is fairly isolated from the surrounding buildings by a large parking lot that's still filled with cars — some of which are charred and indistinguishable from each other in their current state. As he passes by each one of them on his way to the store, he glances through the windows and open doors and sees nothing but bones and melted plastic inside. The walls of the store look undamaged for the most part, showing only minor signs of heat damage on the awning over the front entrance. Noticing that the glass door is already partially open, Larry takes out his gun and looks through the windows that line the front of the store, seeing shelves tipped over and items scattered across the floor and ripped open. Pushing the door open with his foot, he steps halfway in and listens closely for a sound of any kind, but the only thing he can hear is the wind outside, and the rough waves from the harbor only a short distance down the road. Only a few steps in, however, he can hear and feel the floor giving way, cracking and moaning under the pressure of his weight. Scanning the area around him with his flashlight, he can see that the surface of the flooring has been blackened from the fire in spots, turning the old boards into crumbling pieces of charcoal.

"Is anyone in here?" he yells, walking carefully down the main aisle toward the pharmacy counter in the back. The disarray lessens as he makes his way through the store, but when he reaches the pharmacy and jumps over the counter, he discovers that the medication shelves have been largely destroyed as well — the pills and powdered contents now spread out over the tile floor in front of him. In the corner of the room sits three countertop refrigeration units, which are also open, and the contents of which are also spilling onto both the counter and the floor. He glances at his watch, which shows 10:42AM, then begins sorting through the syringes and bottles, until he finally comes to an empty one labeled 'Insulin Suspension'. Searching through the other nearby bottles, he finds more than a dozen more, all of which are empty — but with their seals simply broken and their lids replaced, he wonders if they've actually been dumped out on purpose. Looking around at the rest of the room for a minute, and wondering whether or not Mike might be easy to bluff, he grabs ten dry, clean bottles and takes them to the front where he sets them down in a nice, perfect row. Next, he grabs a jug of saline from the floor and opens it, emptying the clear fluid into the insulin bottles and then closing them up and packing them into his bag. He knows they won't do Mike any good, but they probably won't harm him either — although at this point it doesn't really matter to him one way or the other. Getting Christine back in one piece is the only thing that matters to him.

He hops up onto the countertop again, then starts to swing his legs over the side, but he stops as soon as he hears the door up front closing. Only a moment later, as he jumps down from the counter and positions himself behind an overturned shelf, he stops and listens again as the sound of security gates come crashing down. A single set of footsteps can be heard, walking from one side of the entrance to the other as they close even more gates.

Larry stands up and shines his flashlight across the aisles, seeing a man with his back turned away from him next to the entrance. "Stand still, I have a gun!" The man stops momentarily, then continues down the row of steel gates as Larry inches his way toward him. He can see burns on his skin, especially his forearms, but unlike the severe injuries that he saw earlier in the day, this guy's face looks untouched. "Did you hear me?" Larry screams. Then he hears a loud rattling cough, followed by a raspy breath and more footsteps — all of them coming from just a few feet behind him. He spins around quickly and aims his gun at the dark figure that's now standing in front of him — but before he gets an opportunity to use it, they grab his arm instead and wrestle him to the ground.

With the wind temporarily knocked out of him, Larry struggles to catch his breath and fight for the gun at the same time, his attacker still relentlessly clawing at his hands as he tries to aim it in their direction. He manages to free himself from their grasp, but then he hears the other man in the room running up behind them, giving him just enough time to fire a single shot into the man's face. As he crumples down on top of the other infected man, Larry can hear something underneath all of them give way, and a moment later he feels the sensation of falling as everything around him fades to black.

CHAPTER 11
ABERDEEN: MARCH 30TH

With much of the city covered in a thick blanket of misty rain, fog, and smoke that's rolling in from across the harbor, Aberdeen appears perfectly normal from the waiting room of the ICU — aside from a few blackened buildings that are still rising up through the murkiness of the weather outside. Hidden are the burned and collapsed structures that are spread widely across the area, and the streets littered with the corpses of the former residents, many of which were probably dead long before the fire started. Aberdeen's chronically foul weather is well-known throughout the northwest, as it is for most of the Washington coastline, but as Christine tries to peer through the thick layer below her and catch a glimpse of Larry somewhere on the other side, it occurs to her that in this one instance, the rotten weather is an improvement over the death and decay that they could see from this view only yesterday.

Trying not to make eye-contact, she glances over at Mike and sees that he's still pacing back and forth on the other side of the room, his mood becoming more nervous the longer that Larry is away. Although he promised to let her go as soon as Larry left the hospital, he immediately broke that word when he tied her arms and legs to a chair in the waiting area, leaving her strapped to it for nearly two hours already. The restraints that he used are padded and lightweight, obviously intended to secure patients without hurting them, but so far she hasn't been able to loosen them in the slightest, and she's finding it difficult not to have a full-blown panic attack.

After saying almost nothing to her all morning, Mike suddenly approaches and sits down beside her, staring out at the vast nothingness of clouds over the harbor. "Where did you say you were going again?"

"East," Christine replies simply, not remembering just how much they had shared of their actual plans.

"Olympia, right?" he asks nervously.

"I think so."

"Listen, I know you probably think I'm some horrible person for doing this, but I'm really not. Having that insulin is life or death for me..."

"I know," she replies back, afraid of saying something that might set him off. "But there's no reason to keep me tied up like this — I'm not gonna try anything."

"I've taken in three people since the outbreak, before you two showed up... The first two came together and stayed for a couple of weeks, then moved on, stealing a bunch of shit before they left — but that was fine, there's plenty of stuff around here to go around. The third guy I found downstairs, close to death after being attacked by a bunch of those infected pricks."

Christine can see the agitation growing as his physical expressions become more animated — and there's no doubt in her mind that he's talking about Jake.

"I wasn't even sure he was alive when I found him," he continues. "When he woke up, he immediately wanted to leave, I finally had to sedate him in order to keep him from leaving."

"What happened to him?"

"It turned out that he was sick, but I never checked him out for bruising." He rolls up his sleeves and points to his forearms just below the elbow. "Right here, and on the face, that's where they show up... He had them all over his arms, but I never bothered to look until it was too late. He ended up tying me up in one of the rooms downstairs, sliced me open with a scalpel, then took off with every trace of amphetamines we had. He said he'd been on them for months."

"So he's the one that trashed the pharmacy downstairs?"

"Probably, who knows... It could've been any of them." He stands up again and faces her, then leans in close. "The reason I'm telling you this, is to let you know that I won't be taking any more chances. It's a dog-eat-dog world these days, and we're all capable of some pretty evil shit — me included."

"You said yourself that he was infected..."

"Right — but he wasn't the one that killed that guy downstairs when he had his back turned to you..." He steps back and looks outside again, where the rain is coming down even harder than before. "For your sake, I hope your friend doesn't decide to take off."

She watches him walk away, heading back down the corridor, then she turns her attention back to the water streaked glass pane in front of her. After a few minutes, she can hear what sounds like footsteps far off in the distance. It's only when she hears someone sitting in one of the chairs behind her that she realizes they weren't so distant after all. Very slowly, trying to act as calm and unsuspecting as possible, she casually turns her head to the side, and can see someone seated in the next row — someone who isn't Mike.

"Shh..." comes a voice in Christine's ear. "We wouldn't want him hearing us..." they whisper in a small voice.

Christine recognizes the voice, and her entire body tenses up as she tries to decide whether she should scream for help or not.

"Where did the fat guy go?"

"Larry? He went to get something for Mike."

"Mike won't be alive long enough to need it."

"Amanda, he's really not that bad..."

The girl laughs quietly behind her. "The guy who put a gun to your head and tied you up isn't that bad?"

"I... I mean, he isn't..." she mutters, hearing another set of footsteps behind her, this time louder than before — and when she turns her head and sees Mike walking into the room again, Amanda is nowhere to be seen. Without saying a word to her, Mike picks up the radio from the window sill and then heads back down the corridor to the main desk area. She listens closely, expecting at any moment to hear screams coming from down the hallway, but aside from the raindrops hitting the window, the hospital is eerily quiet.

Mike sits down at his desk and sits back in the chair, feeling his heartbeat throughout his entire body as he tries to calm himself down. He was certain that Larry cared too much for the girl than to just leave her behind, but after hearing nothing for the last two hours he's beginning to wonder if that's exactly what happened — which leaves him with two possibilities, neither of which he's looking forward to. The first is to either hurt her over the radio, or at the very least coerce her into acting hurt, in the hope that Larry will hear it and change his mind. That hinges on whether or not Larry is even listening to any messages, which he probably isn't if he's actually decided to run. The other possibility is taking Christine with him to find his medication, using her as a lure to draw attention away from himself. Eliminating her afterward would be unfortunate, but it would also be necessary to protect himself from retribution in the future.

Looking at his watch for the third time in the last ten minutes, and seeing that it's only a few minutes past eleven, he switches the computer monitor on and loads another game of solitaire — a more or less mindless game that's served as a useful distraction for months now. After losing a hand, he reshuffles the deck just as the lights go out, including the computer. Overhead he can hear the ventilation system slowing down to a halt, and the emergency battery lights on the smoke and CO2 detectors have come on, which can only happen for two reasons — the generator has finally run out of fuel, or somebody has shut it down. He fumbles around on the desk for his flashlight, then checks his pocket for his gun before standing up and shining the light around the room. As he pans it toward the corridor that leads to the waiting room, he sees a sudden flash of movement as someone runs from the other side of the desk and into the hall. Aiming his gun ahead of him, with sweat now dripping from his forehead, he slowly and cautiously steps forward, well aware of the fact that Christine has more experience on the outside than he does. He already went through the trouble of locking her guns inside one of the lockers, which only he knows the combination to — but there are still plenty of things lying around the rooms that could be used as an effective weapon.

He passes by each one of the patients rooms carefully, making sure that every door is closed before moving on, but when he finally reaches the waiting area, almost fully lit from the subdued sunlight outside, he sees Christine sitting in the same chair as before — with her back turned to him.

"What the hell do you think you're doing?" he demands, aiming his gun at her as he approaches her from the side. When she turns her head toward him, and he sees the surgical tape that's now covering her mouth, and the restraints still wrapped around her arms and legs, he takes a few steps back and begins looking around the rest of the room. "Larry... if you don't show yourself right now I'm gonna shoot her... I mean it!" He looks down and sees Christine crying and shaking her head at him, then he hears someone laughing from back down the hallway. He walks up to Christine and rips the tape off of her lips, tearing some of the skin off in the process. "What the hell happened?"

"It isn't Larry..." she says softly, trying hard not to scream in pain.

"Who the hell is it? One of those people from downstairs?"

Christine looks up at him, bleeding from both of her lips and onto her shirt. "She's gonna kill us."

He slaps the tape back onto her mouth, causing her to scream out in pain, then backs up until he can see down the hall with the flashlight. There's only one other way between the two areas, and that's through the offices on the far side of the waiting area. Grabbing one of the loose chairs along the back wall, he wedges the back of it underneath the doorknob to the office area, then tries unsuccessfully to force the door open. Certain that nobody can get through behind him, he takes another quick look around the room and then stands at the entrance to the hallway, facing the dozen rooms in front of him, all of which have open doors again. Hearing something move directly behind him, he turns around in a hurry and fires his gun twice, shattering one of the windows and sending a gust of cold, wet wind into the waiting area. He turns around again, shaking with fear, and begins walking toward the first set of rooms, which are right across the hall from each other. Listening first for any hint of movement, which is difficult with the noise of air rushing in behind him, he stands back and shines the light into the room on the right, seeing only an empty examination bed and cabinets.

From the moment he shot the window, he could instantly feel the draft of cold air against his body, moving easily through the thin layer of clothing he has on — but as he starts to turn around, he suddenly feels a warmth running down his lower back and down his legs, like a stream of hot water from a shower. He stands still for a moment, then begins to feel a dull pain in his back, radiating around to his sides and the back of his knees. He grabs onto the frame of the doorway and nearly catches himself before falling onto the floor, dropping his flashlight and gun in the process.

Christine listens intently to the sounds of struggle behind her, trembling with fear as tears fall down her face and onto the fresh wounds covering her lips — the saltwater burning as it soaks up the blood and drips onto her shirt and lap. She can hear whispering, and cries of agony as someone begs for their life — and then after an extended period of silence, she hears a single gunshot echo throughout the floor. For a moment she listens to the wind howling to her left through the broken window, and watches as the gusts of wind move the trees that surround the hospital violently back and forth.

She nearly screams out in terror when she finally sees the silhouette of someone standing next to her, and the image of a young girl, covered in fresh blood, as she leans down and stares Christine in the face.

"Don't worry, Christine," Amanda says soothingly. "It's only me..."

CHAPTER 12
EAST OF COHASSETT: MARCH 30TH

By daybreak, after a sleepless night of watching the caravan of people travel from Westport to Grayland, Curtis looks out across the flat farmlands to the south of the house, and sees absolutely no sign of anyone — only the massive billows of smoke rising into the sky from the fires that remain.

He's tempted to stay another night, leery of moving through an area so filled with infected people with only a few bullets for protection. With supplies running low, however, and with so few houses in the vicinity to gather food from, all three adults decide that moving on is probably in their best interest. South Aberdeen is only a few hours away, perhaps a little longer with Ben's sore feet, and the houses there are both plentiful and void of people compared to the coastal communities.

"Are we going back to the highway?" Rachel asks Curtis, as all five of them sit down for a meal of dry cereal and a single can of cold tomato soup.

"No, we'll stick to this road until we get to the bridge — it's probably safer."

"I was thinking that the highway has plenty of places to hide..."

"Yeah, and plenty of places for them to hide too."

"Were they from Westport?" Matt asks.

"I think so, they must have been following the fires."

"Or they were from Cosmopolis," Rachel adds. "If that's the case, there could be more where we're headed."

"You came through there, didn't you?" Sarah asks her.

"We went there, figuring it might be a good place to stay for a while."

"I take it you were wrong about that?"

"It was overrun with those things. None of us got any sleep there, with all the screaming and people trying to break into the house all night."

"So, if those people last night were coming from Cosmopolis, we'll be walking right into them — is there any way around?"

"No," Curtis answers. "Just miles of swampland."

"What about Westport, just for a while?" Rachel asks.

"Westport is out of the question."

"It could be practically empty now..."

"We're not going to Westport," Curtis says adamantly. "We've been there twice already, and it almost killed us both times."

There's a few tense moments of silence as the group eats their breakfast and contemplates the direction they'll be going, all of them well aware of the potentially deadly consequences if they make the wrong decision.

Sarah stands up and places her bowl onto the counter, which seems like an odd act of civility given the circumstances, but anything else would seem strangely rude somehow. "We can't be certain where those people were from, so I'm for sticking to the original plan and heading toward Olympia."

The others all look at Rachel, since she seems to be the only one arguing otherwise. She looks back at each of them, seeing the determination in their eyes, then she continues to eat. "I just don't want to get caught in the middle of them, that's all," she says.

"We won't, we'll be careful." Curtis tells her.

Just north of the farmhouse, the landscape along the road quickly turns from the man-made pastures and cranberry bogs of eastern Grayland, to the edge of the saltwater marshlands of the Elk River estuary — a pristine natural wetland that stretches for miles to the east, and empties into the harbor at the nearby crossing of Laidlow and Bay City.

Wearing raincoats and plastic garbage bags from the farmhouse they were staying at, the group walks in the tall grass alongside the dirt road, which is little more than a muddy drainage ditch when it's pouring down rain. They can see footprints everywhere in the mud, many of them barefoot, and some that were either crawling or falling down based on the multiple sets of hand prints as well. At times, when the wind shifts direction and starts blowing directly north, the smoke becomes so thick that it's difficult to breathe or see very far ahead of them — and even after it passes it leaves a lingering stinging in their eyes and throats.

Sarah, who's holding Ben's hand as he suffers through each painful step forward, slows down just enough to walk beside Rachel. "You know, we really don't know all that much about each other..."

"Like what?"

"I don't know — jobs, hobbies, whatever."

Rachel smiles slightly, for the first time in quite a while. "I was an accountant, which is a rather useless skill set it turns out. What about you?"

"I was taking a break from work when the virus hit, trying to focus on raising the boys."

"It seems like you did a pretty good job, they both seem like good kids," Rachel replies, smiling at Ben, who politely smiles back.

"Did you pay much attention to the virus? I mean in the early days..."

"Not really — I think Bill did though. He was glued to the television, listening to all those news anchors repeat themselves over and over again. I started paying closer attention when the school district sent a letter home with Travis, telling us that classes had been canceled until further notice. That's when I knew it was serious, that the virus was already here."

"I can't believe how quickly it spread when it got here," Sarah says, before noticing that Curtis and Matt have stopped walking, and are now staring straight ahead. As they join them, Curtis points up the road where something is sticking up out of the mud, and two more objects are next to it in the swamp. "What is it?"

"I don't know, but they're moving," Curtis replies.

They start walking again, but more slowly, watching all around them just in case it's a trap of some kind. Sarah lets out a gasp when they get close enough to discover that they're stragglers from the night before, hopelessly stuck in deep mud and now freezing to death in the rain and wind. The one in the middle of the road is an old woman, who's covered in dark purple bruises and is nothing but skin and bones. The other two, who are off to the side, appear to be dead already.

"What should we do with her?" Sarah asks.

"We don't do anything, it looks like the mud is handling everything," Curtis responds.

Sarah looks into the woman's eyes, which are bloodshot and staring back at her. She backs up as the woman reaches for her with her one free arm and grasps at the air, her blue-tinged lips trying to say something as she struggles to move in the thick mud.

"She looks close to dead already," Rachel says coldly. "We certainly can't save her, and if we shoot her we'll attract too much attention. Let's just keep moving."

Rachel walks away, with the two boys following closely behind her.

Curtis grabs Sarah's hand and holds it gently, then begins to pull her down the road with him — but she rips her hand away from him and looks back at the woman, breaking down in tears.

"Hon, we have to keep moving — it's not safe out here, especially in this weather," Curtis pleads with her.

She looks at him briefly, wondering where his compassion has gone, or whether he ever had any to begin with — then she marches past him and walks several paces behind Rachel and the boys.

"If things were different," Curtis starts to say, before Sarah raises her hand up and cuts him off.

"Things are definitely different, I get that Curtis — but I'm not discussing it with you, so save it." Her tone is blunt and bordering on rude, which is exactly the way that she meant it. She's more angry with the situation than Curtis or Rachel, but she's also disappointed in their reaction to it. Sick or not, the woman that they're leaving behind is suffering, and in a perfect or even halfway decent world, they would at least try to figure out how to help her, or ease her pain. Instead, the attitudes of her husband and children are to do nothing, and leave her to rot in a pit of mud in the pouring down rain. The children she can forgive, since their minds are clearly capable of adapting more quickly than adults, but she feels that Curtis should know better, and should be setting an example for how the boys should act in the future — if there is one.

For the next hour, they walk in complete silence, every one of them exhausted and sore from the constant walking — not to mention the stress and anxiety. By the time they cross the flooded marshes of the river delta, passing by even more trapped people along the way, Ben's feet are slowing their speed down to almost a crawl.

Sarah, noticing that he's both slowing down and beginning to walk strangely, stops him and takes off his shoes again. "Curtis, look at his

96

feet — he can't go any further. Not like this..."

Curtis kneels down and pats Ben on the knee, then looks down and cringes, seeing blisters and bruises covering both feet, and blood on the socks that he just put on this morning. "I'll carry him on my shoulders," he says to Sarah, then faces Ben. "Is that okay with you, buddy?" he asks, seeing Ben nod in return.

"You're as tired as the rest of us, how far will you get?" Sarah asks him.

"Laidlow is just up the highway, we'll find a wheelbarrow or something to use. The road is paved the rest of the way to Olympia."

"Hey guys, look at this..." Rachel says, pointing down to the ground beside of the highway.

The others don't even need to get closer to see what she's talking about. A path has clearly been worn down beside the highway, leaving the same crowded footprints in the mud that they've been seeing for miles now — all of them leading back to Westport, and not the direction that they're headed in.

"Come on, let's get going before there's more of them," Curtis says, as he bends down and picks Ben up, placing him on his shoulders. "We should be able to make it to Aberdeen by dark."

They reach the small community of Laidlow in only a few short minutes — a cluster of a dozen or so houses, half of them on the harbor side, and the other half along the river. The only one that's close to the highway sits by itself next to the bridge, and they can see an open door and broken out windows as soon as they approach it.

"Did you search this when you and Larry came by here?" Sarah asks Curtis, watching him set Ben down onto the front lawn and look around at the outbuildings for anything useful.

"No, we didn't really search a lot of houses."

"I was inside," Ben says softly.

"You were inside this house, sweety?" Sarah asks him.

"I was hungry, so we stopped for a few minutes. Amanda doesn't really eat much."

"Was there any food inside?"

"Just a couple of old candy bars, but I ate those."

Curtis looks closer at the place, half expecting Amanda herself to come bursting through the door with a knife in her hand. Even seeing a place that she's been to sends chills up his spine. "Come on, let's go inside for a few minutes while I look around for a cart or something. We can at least dry ourselves off."

The inside of the house smells like all of the others they've been to — damp, moldy, and full of decay. Sarah finds a more or less clean set of towels in the master bathroom, and some dry clothes that more or less fit everyone but Curtis in the closet. While Curtis looks around outside, Rachel searches the kitchen for any food that was left behind — but Ben was right, the cupboards and pantry have been cleaned out of anything non-perishable. Even the boxes of dry pasta, which normally have a long shelf life, have been lost to rodents and who knows what else, all of them having full access through the open front door. From the window in the living room you're only a stone's throw away from the dark, cold waters of the harbor, which is mostly obscured by fog.

"Is it wrong that even a dump like this seems appealing?" Rachel asks Sarah, who's standing at the window that looks over the harbor.

"No, I was kind of thinking the same thing."

"It's so quiet here, it's almost eerie."

Sarah suddenly feels Rachel's hand on her forearm, then she points down the road toward Westport, where a man and woman are walking in their direction. "I have to find Curtis, he's still outside somewhere," Sarah says in a panic — then she turns around and sees him standing behind them.

"I'm right here," he whispers. "I heard them coming down the road."

"Are they sick?" Sarah asks, as all three of them crouch down and watch from the window. "They're walking normal."

"I don't know, it's hard to say. They were talking to each other, but I couldn't really hear well enough to tell if it was gibberish."

With the boys sitting in the back of the room, completely out of sight from what's happening on the road, the adults can see the couple approach the driveway and stop for a moment, looking over the house carefully before moving on again. They stop for a few minutes across the street, pointing at a drifting boat that's run aground about fifty feet or so from the shore. Privately, they all wonder why one of the infected would even find something like that interesting, since it's barely worth noting even to them — but after they turn around and head back to the road, the man reaches down and takes the woman's hand to help her through the tall grass and weeds in the ditch, and they know without a doubt that both of them are probably healthy. Eventually they pass out of sight entirely, headed for either Aberdeen or Cosmopolis — one of them a burned out ruin, and the other crawling with the infected.

"Do you think we should have said something to them?" Rachel asks. "They probably have no idea where they're going."

"No, but we still can't trust them," Curtis replies. "Sometimes it's hard to tell the difference between the healthy and the sick."

"Well, they're holding hands for one thing..."

"Have you ever come across..." Curtis stops and turns toward the boys. "Matt, what did Jake call those people that act differently?"

"Daywalkers," Matt answers.

"Right, daywalkers." Curtis turns back and faces Rachel. "Have you ever run into someone that seemed perfectly normal at first, and then tries to kill you?"

"No, I haven't," she says, finding the question somewhat unnerving.

"You're lucky — we've met two of them. They can act and talk perfectly normal when they want to, but they're completely unhinged."

"Three," Matt says, correcting him. "Mom and I met another one at a beach house — an old woman."

"Right, I forgot about her. We can't trust anybody, not until everything settles down."

"So do we stay here for the night?" Sarah asks, seeing the sun dropping into the west.

"No," Curtis responds. "We'll give them some space, then we'll follow. We don't have much food left, and we need to find someplace we can stay at for a while so Ben can rest up."

"Did you find anything outside?"

"Yeah, there's one of those big plastic garden carts around on the side."

"It looks like the rain is letting up some." Rachel says, as a few rays of sunlight can be seen shining through the clouds over the water.

"Enjoy it while it lasts," Curtis says. "I think it rains on the harbor even more than the beach."

After waiting for almost an hour, the group begins walking down the road once again — this time with Curtis pushing the cart with both Ben and most of their supplies loaded into it. While it's not exactly beautiful weather, the rain seems to have stopped for the time being, making the walk less miserable and time-consuming.

"This stretch of road always seems to take forever, even in a car,"

Rachel complains.

"At least there's no mud," Sarah replies.

Although the highway along the south side of the harbor curves with the natural contour of the shoreline, this particular stretch of road is long and straight, with no view of the water or any sign of civilization. Only a fallen-down, obsolete power line and Douglas Fir trees can be seen, along with a few stranded cars that have already been picked through the last time they were here.

"How far are we walking today?" Matt asks.

"All the way to South Aberdeen, another three or four hours probably."

With Curtis in the lead, the group almost reaches the next bend in the road when they see an object in the middle of the road ahead of them.

"Dad, there's something..." Ben says, pointing straight ahead.

"I know, I see it too," Curtis replies, still moving forward at the same speed.

As they get closer, and they can see the bright red color, and the clear image of a woman lying face-down on the pavement, Curtis finally slows down as they approach the scene, recognizing her as the woman that passed by them earlier. Her partner isn't obvious at first, but by the time they reach her, they also spot his body sprawled out beside the road, his body presumably beaten with an ax handle that's still lying next to him.

"Curtis, I don't want to look at this," Sarah says, seeing him standing still and examining the bodies from a distance.

"I know," he says, looking around at the surrounding trees, and a private gravel driveway only a hundred yards behind them. "But whoever did this is still around here, and they're not alone..." He points to the ground next to the man, and two sets of footprints can be seen in the mud — one is wearing shoes, and the other isn't.

CHAPTER 13
ABERDEEN: MARCH 30TH

The sounds of gentle splashing water and moans of pain are the first things that Larry hears before opening his eyes to the dark basement around him. Eventually his sight adjusts to the dim light, and he finds himself lying on top of the old flooring and staring up at the large hole above him, his legs submerged in water from the knees down. Hearing the moaning once again, he looks to his left and sees one of the men that attacked him lying motionless in the water, his head still bleeding from the bullet hole. Next to him, however, is the second man, who's still alive and impaled on an old broken floorboard that's sticking straight into the air. He keeps clutching at everything around him, sending waves of the stinking, murky water across the room.

Larry pulls himself up onto the platform further, making sure that his legs are on a dry surface — then he begins looking around for an exit. From what he can see, the basement doesn't have any stairs, and only one door at the back of the building which he assumes leads to an exit. When he pulls his spare flashlight out of his pocket and looks around, he can see a faint movement of current in the water from that direction. The only clear pathway to the door leads right past the two men, and also requires walking through the flooded waters.

Very slowly, he lowers himself down into the water until it comes up to his chest, then limps along the cluttered pathway on a twisted ankle, stepping over objects that are scattered on the floor beneath him. He pushes the dead man out of the way as he passes by, and then tries to walk as far around the other man as possible, but just as he almost clears him, he feels a hand reach out and grab his coat.

"Let go!" he says sternly, but quietly, not wanting to attract any unwanted attention from outside.

"I'm sorry, I'm really sorry," the man says, letting go of him.

Larry rushes past him a few feet, clear out of his reach, then turns around. "You can speak?"

"I'm sorry, I didn't mean to hurt anybody..."

"What's your name?" Larry asks, suddenly feeling some sympathy for the man. When he shines the light toward him, not only does he see the massive wound in his abdomen where the piece of wood is piercing him, but he also sees that his eyes are dark red, with deep purple patches on his neck and jaw. Hearing no answer from him, he turns around and makes it to the far wall, listening to the continued splashing behind him as he jerks the door open and lets a rush of rainwater into the basement — which nearly knocks him off of his feet. As he pulls himself onto the concrete stairs on the other side, he glances back at the man and sees the water quickly rising in the room, already close to submerging his head underneath it.

He can feel just how tired his legs are as he climbs the stairs to the top and steps out into the parking lot behind the pharmacy — but he's shocked when he looks around and discovers how dark the skies are. Panicked, he pulls his sleeve up and looks at his watch, which reads a few minutes past seven. With his head still foggy, he has a hard time figuring out just how long he's been stuck down there, but he knows for certain that it's been several hours — long enough to completely run out of daylight anyway. He searches for the radio in his pocket, afraid that he might have lost it for a moment — but it's still in the same place as before, and the lights still work when he turns it on and presses the talk button.

"Christine, Mike, are you there?" Waiting for an answer, he

suddenly realizes that he can hear footsteps around him, mostly coming from the main street in front of the pharmacy. "Can anyone hear me? I ran into some trouble and got knocked out, but I'm on my way now — and I have the medication..." Still getting no response, he starts walking to the east, making it two blocks before he gets a clear view of the hospital above him. To his surprise, he doesn't see any lights on the sixth floor, or anywhere else for that matter. Fearing the worst, he begins jogging as quickly as his injured ankle will allow, heading north down the middle of the road where there's less debris and more visibility — but when he comes to the main intersection, where the highway joins the road, he sees another group of people coming toward him, splitting off into different directions as they come to the highway. As three of them approach him, he's forced to duck into a small building next to him, unsure of whether or not they noticed him.

He waits behind a large office desk for the people to pass by, seeing a large real estate poster on the wall in front of him, and a sign that says 'The Most Affordable Homes In Grays Harbor', with photographs of houses that are now almost certainly burned down and destroyed. This particular office though, as rundown as it is, appears to be mostly undamaged from the flames.

When the silence returns to the street outside, with no sign of activity in front of the office, Larry carefully peeks out at the neighborhood around him, and sees another intact building directly across from him — a bank from the looks of it. On the far corner of the intersection, between him and the hospital, he can still see several silhouettes standing beside a lamppost, as if waiting for a signal to cross the street. The more he looks around, the easier it is to spot movements throughout the city — movements that were impossible to see from the vantage point of the hospital. He's not sure if it's only here, or whether the same thing is happening everywhere, but the health of the infected seems to be getting worse overall. In Grayland he saw people that were talking and manipulating on a large scale, and on his way through Westport he saw more people active during the daylight hours — but all of them showed worsening signs of congestion and bruising.

All but Amanda, that is — she's the only one that they've come across that has actually improved over the course of the illness.

Taking in a deep breath first, Larry unlocks the door and reaches for the handle, then hears the familiar hiss coming from his radio.

"Larry, are you still there?"

Recognizing the voice as Christine, he immediately lets go of the handle and grabs the radio instead. "Christine? Yes, I'm here."

"Are you coming back soon? Mike is really anxious about those antibiotics..."

Larry presses the button on the radio to correct her, then pauses for a moment. "Yes, I have them. How are his symptoms?"

"His cough is getting worse."

He can hear the distress in her voice, which wouldn't be all that unusual considering the circumstances — but he can tell that something else is seriously wrong, Mike made it crystal clear to both of them that he needed insulin, not antibiotics. He personally saw dozens of large bottles of those on a shelf behind Mike's desk. "Okay, I'll be there as soon as I can. There's a lot of people walking around outside."

"Okay, just hurry, Mike said he needs you here as soon as possible."

"I'm heading out now, I'll see you soon."

Placing the radio back into his pocket, Larry opens the door and steps out onto the sidewalk, looking around carefully before quietly closing the door behind him. After only a few steps forward though, he hears the radio hissing again, the transmission filled with heavy static, and then a man's voice comes out of it. Larry quickly makes his way back to the office and closes the door behind him, but not before a woman from down the street notices him. Locking the door and watching her slowly come closer, he pulls the radio out again.

"*Larry? Larry Goss?*" says the static-filled voice.

"Yes, who is this?"

"*It's Curtis Lockwood.*"

CHAPTER 14

Crowded around Curtis and the radio, the rest of the Lockwood family and Rachel sit silently as they listen to Larry on the other end of the signal — all of them stunned to hear his voice again. They're sitting in a small living room, across the street from the harbor, and directly across the harbor from Aberdeen.

"*Curtis, are you serious? Where the hell are you?*"

"Across the harbor from Aberdeen — where are you?"

"*I'm in Aberdeen, a few blocks south of the highway, directly south of the hospital.*"

"Is Beth with you?"

"*No, I'm alone right now, but I'm on my way up to get a girl, Christine.*"

"Who is Mike?"

"*That's a long story, Curtis. One I'll have to tell you about in person.*"

"Right, I understand... We should meet up tomorrow."

"*Yeah, that'd be great. Listen, I have to go — it was really good to hear from you again though.*"

"Same here." Curtis says before putting down the radio and looking around at the others, still in disbelief.

"What happened to Beth?" Matt asks.

"I don't know, I'm sure he'll tell us tomorrow though." Hearing the radio again, Curtis picks it up and listens closely to the voice on the other end, and he can tell that it's the girl again, who's obviously further away from them judging from the amount of static on the line.

107

"*...to wait for them, he doesn't want to...*" the girl says, before cutting out.

"*Curtis, are you still there?*" Larry says.

"Yeah, I'm here. What's going on?" replies Curtis.

"*Mike wants me to wait for you, that way the two of us can pick Christine up. I'm sorry to hear you're alone, it'd be great to have more company.*"

"Yeah, I hear you. Where should we meet?"

"*Hang on a minute...*"

"Curtis, what's going on?" Sarah asks, her voice suddenly filled with worry.

"I don't know, but something certainly doesn't sound right."

"*You remember where you worked for an entire day after you finished school?*" Larry says over the radio.

"Yeah, I do."

"*Three blocks south of the highway. Everything is safe there.*"

"Got it. Be careful, Larry."

"*Same to you.*"

"What does that mean?" Rachel asks.

"He wants to meet at a bank," Sarah answers. "Curtis worked at one a long time ago, and got fired after one shift."

"It wasn't that long ago," Curtis replies. "I think he means for all of us to go there, that's why he said it's safe there."

"Do you think it's this 'Mike' guy that's the problem?"

"I don't know, we'll have to wait and see." He looks over at Matt and Ben, who are both sitting on the couch and looking sleepy. "Okay, everybody needs to get some sleep — it's gonna be a long day tomorrow. I'll take the first watch."

"I'll join you," Sarah says to him, as the two boys head into the bedroom behind them.

"I guess that means Matt and I for the next watch?" Rachel asks.

"Do you mind?"

"No, not at all. I'll see you in a few hours."

They watch as Rachel walks into the same bedroom, then shuts the door behind her. The room suddenly becomes completely quiet, except for the occasional wind gust that moves the wind chimes somewhere outside.

"Is it me, or is Ben quieter than usual tonight?" Sarah whispers to Curtis.

"No, it's not you."

"And he barely ate anything at dinner..."

"It's just this place, it has us both unnerved."

"Aberdeen?"

"No, Ben escaped from Amanda here — from this house."

Sarah looks at him incredulously, raising her voice slightly. "Then why are we here?"

"Because it's the only house in the neighborhood with an intact front door."

Feeling wide-awake herself, Sarah watches as Curtis nods off in a recliner and finally falls asleep. She knows that he'll hate himself when he wakes up, but she's also worried about how little sleep he's gotten over the last couple of weeks. Everything that he's doing, including the morally questionable acts, has been to protect the family, no matter what the cost — and as much as she disagrees with some of it, ultimately she knows that he's doing it for the right reasons, or at least she hopes so anyway.

Hardly a thought crosses her mind lately that doesn't include living in the serenity of Olympia, where they suspect the virus had a nearly complete mortality rate. It's something that would normally be considered catastrophic, a worst-case scenario for humanity — but compared to the reality they're now faced with, a lack of survivors sounds like paradise. Just having enough time to prepare for the inevitable — the days when the canned goods and dry pasta finally go bad, and they run out of bottled water, medications, and batteries for their flashlights and radios. At some point in the near future, the conveniences of the modern world will begin to disappear, leaving them alone with no real knowledge of how to survive in the stone ages.

The food situation alone is a constant concern. She used to grow a small garden every summer when they lived in Oregon, but she bought seeds at the local supermarket, and never had to worry about collecting more seeds to replace them — she knew that she could simply buy new ones the following year. Hunting is always a possibility, especially since Larry seems to know a thing or two about butchering the animal once they're killed, but storing the meat without refrigeration is another problem they haven't tackled yet. Meat used to be either canned or cured with salt to preserve it, but one small mistake could end up killing the entire group by poisoning them with a bacteria they're no longer capable of eliminating.

The stress of everything is beginning to take its mental toll on Sarah. No matter how many problems they eventually have to face, none of them will be solved as long as they're constantly running for their lives — which is what makes this trip so vitally important.

As she looks out the front window, she can barely make out the skyline of Aberdeen in the darkness. She lived here for a few months when she was a teenager, staying with an aunt for the summer while her parents moved back east for the company her father worked for. Compared to the long, warm, sunny days of summer that she was used to in Portland, the cold, gray skies of Aberdeen seemed like a winter that would never end. The harbor brought in a constant flow of moisture into the streets, bringing fog and rain showers to the area on a regular basis, even as the weather forecasters on the radio bragged about the hot, dry weather in Tacoma, only eighty miles to the east.

As horrid as the climate was, there was still something about living on the harbor that appealed to her. It seemed to have a life of its own, entirely different from the rivers of Portland or the ocean at Cohassett Beach. She thinks back to those few months of her childhood fondly, choosing to remember Aberdeen as a coastal city with lots of character and atmosphere, and not just the past reputation of prostitutes and serial killers that some like to associate it with.

Tonight, however, as she watches the moon cast a pale, white light over the city, it lies in ruin, decimated by the descendants of those who built it.

"Sarah, are you awake?" Rachel whispers from behind Sarah.

"Yeah, I'm awake — I'm just letting Curtis get some rest. What's wrong?"

Rachel sits down next to her, looking around at the neighborhood suspiciously. "Have you seen anybody out there?"

"No, not a soul."

Rachel points further down the road. "I'm just freaking out a little I guess — Bill was almost killed right down there. We'd crossed the bridge from Aberdeen, then we decided to check out some of the houses in Cosmopolis."

"Cosmopolis was pretty bad, huh?"

"It was like Grayland, only there were a lot more of them — it was like they..."

She stops in mid-sentence, as both of them notice the same orange glow coming from across the harbor. Another fire has started, this one coming from the eastern side of the city that was spared from the previous blaze. Within only moments, the fire spreads from a small, single location, to several larger ones — all of them on the other side of the Wishkah, along the highway to Olympia, which is where they planned to go tomorrow after joining Larry and Christine.

"That area was empty when we came through there before." Rachel says. "Or at least we thought it was."

"Is that the only way through?"

"No, there's another bridge north of there." Rachel stands up and takes another look around, still seeing no activity of any kind. "Okay, I'm headed to bed — for real this time. You're sure that you're okay out here by yourself?"

"Yeah, I'll be fine."

Hearing Curtis snoring from the other side of the room, Sarah gets up and walks through the house, scanning the perimeter of the property from the different windows. Everything appears to be quiet, and then she enters the second bedroom and peers into the east, where she can barely see the main bridge that heads into the city. Small bits of movement are visible through the fog, which she can only imagine are people heading toward the new fires.

"Which direction are they going?" she hears Curtis say from behind, startling her.

"Into the city. I thought you were still asleep..."

"You saw the fires?"

"Yeah, they're spreading fast."

"Their behavior is changing, have you noticed that? It's like they never move alone anymore."

Sarah can still see the movement down the street, and some flashes of light scattered throughout the crowd.

"Maybe you guys should stay here..." Curtis says.

"No, we'll come with you — we're not splitting up again."

"It might be safer on this side of the harbor..."

"There's no such thing as safe — not anymore."

CHAPTER 15
ABERDEEN: MARCH 30TH

Christine is shaking as she looks up at Amanda, not knowing what the young girl will do with her next. She's still tied to the chair, and she can feel a tingling sensation developing in her fingertips from being restrained in the same position for too many hours — but it's her bladder that's hurting the worst. Without a bathroom break since this morning, she's having a hard time concentrating on anything except how much she has to urinate, and Amanda's constant coaching as she holds the radio up to her face hasn't been helping. More than once she's thought about just going, figuring that sitting in wet clothes is probably preferable to having her bladder burst, but she's still holding out hope that she might be released from her shackles now that Amanda's message has been sent — if she doesn't simply kill her instead.

"Amanda, I really have to go to the bathroom... It hurts really bad," Christine says, watching the girl walk away from her, then pitch the radio out of the broken window and onto the rooftop below. "I know that Larry and Beth had you tied up for a while — so you know how it feels..."

"They had me tied up for a good reason," Amanda replies, picking up Mike's gun from a nearby table.

"I'm not gonna hurt you, I've never hurt anybody before..."

"No, but you left me to die in that barn."

"I'm sorry, I really am — I was just scared. I didn't know what to do."

Amanda looks the gun over, then pops the clip out, throwing both of them out of the same broken window. Christine tries not to look as she grabs her knife again, and then stands directly in front of her, holding the blade against her throat with the tip barely piercing the skin — the same way it did in the hayloft in Grayland.

"If I let you go, you have to do exactly what I say..." Amanda orders.

"I will, I promise," Christine answers, with tears running down her face.

"Trust me, you don't want to see me angry."

"I promise..."

Showing no compassion whatsoever, Amanda takes the knife and crudely cuts Christine loose, the blade lightly slicing into her arms and legs several times before she's finally released. Then Amanda backs up slowly and sits down in the corner, where she's almost entirely obscured in the darkness.

"Can I go to the bathroom now?"

"The water doesn't work anymore, so the toilet won't flush."

"I don't really care at this point," Christine says, feeling her legs nearly give out when she stands up and tries to take a couple of steps. She takes it a little slower, then turns around and faces the dark hallway in the back of the room — but when she checks her pocket for her flashlight, she discovers that it's missing. "Have you seen my flashlight?"

"It was on the floor — I tossed it out the window."

"How am I gonna find the bathroom?"

"I'm sure you'll figure it out. It's hard to escape when you can't see anything."

By the time Christine reaches the beginning of the hallway, she can hardly see anything in front of her. The movement of walking is only making her bladder situation worse, and as she hurries down the corridor, her feet suddenly slip on something wet and slippery, sending her tumbling to the floor. As soon as she places her hands on the smooth tile, feeling a gooey substance all over her skin, she realizes that it must be Mike's blood — and when she gets up and starts walking again, her suspicions are confirmed when she feels his body with her feet. Composing herself, and hearing Amanda in the next room giggling, she continues walking slowly until she finally makes it to the open door at the end of hall — then closes the door behind her.

As badly as she has to go, the first thing she does upon entering is feel around on the floor next to the toilet, searching for a flashlight that Larry left there the night before — just in case the power went out while he was sitting down. Not feeling it, she finally can't take it anymore, so she sits down and starts to go — then immediately hears footsteps in the hallway.

"Are you finished yet?" Amanda says through the door.

"Not yet — I really had to go..."

"Why is the door locked?" she asks, trying to jiggle the handle.

"I just wanted some privacy, that's all."

"It's pitch black in there, who's gonna see you?"

Christine can see a light coming from underneath the door, and Amanda's feet pacing back and forth anxiously. When she's done, feeling physically more relieved than she's ever felt in her life, she reaches around on the wall for the toilet paper and accidentally kicks something across the floor with her foot.

"What was that?" Amanda asks, her voice sound impatient and annoyed.

"I'm not sure what it was..." Knowing exactly what it was, she feels around on the floor and quietly picks up the small flashlight and hides it in her pants pocket, then finds the toilet paper just as Amanda begins banging on the door. When she opens the door and sees the floor lit up on the other side, she notices for the first time that

Amanda's skin appears clearer and more flushed with color than it used to be. At first she tells herself that it's probably the spectrum of the light that's causing that effect, but then she realizes that her once congested breathing and cough are gone as well, along with the faint clicking sound she made every time she inhaled.

"We have some things to do before they get here," Amanda tells her, pointing toward the staircase door.

"Downstairs?"

"On the second floor — there's something down there that we have to move."

"The second floor is filled with people — they're infected..."

"I know, that's what we're moving."

Walking down the dark staircase, with Amanda only a few steps behind her holding a flashlight to guide them with, Christine feels the rush of cold air moving up the shaft from below — which makes her wonder if the main entrance is wide-open and letting outside air in, but she's too afraid to ask. When they reach the second floor platform, Amanda stands up on her toes and peers through the window, seeing nothing but darkness in the corridor beyond a few feet.

"Step back," Amanda orders her, as she aims the flashlight through the window and concentrates on whatever is on the other side. The girl twists the handle, but it doesn't budge. Then she takes a large set of keys and inserts each of them into the lock one by one, watching the window after every attempt to make sure the noise hasn't attracted any unwanted attention. Finally, after at least a dozen tries, she manages to find one that works, and pushes the heavy steel door into the corridor with a loud screeching sound that echoes throughout that portion of the hospital. As Christine follows her inside and looks down the long hallway in front of them, she catches just a glimpse of someone in the flashlight beam, standing about halfway down with their back turned away from them.

"Amanda, I think there's someone down there," she whispers quietly, realizing too late that her voice, as low as it is, still carries a long way with hard surfaces and complete silence.

Shining the light at the person for only a moment, Amanda turns around and locks the door again, then hands Christine the flashlight. "Here, after I slip into one of those rooms, make as much noise as possible to get their attention."

"Why not just leave them down here?" Christine asks, aiming the light toward the person. She can see that they have long hair, but they're still dressed in a filthy, soiled hospital gown, and she can't tell for sure whether or not it's a man or a woman. Then she feels something press into her side, and she quickly backs up against the wall behind her when she discovers that Amanda's knife is cutting through her clothing and piercing into her abdomen.

"I didn't cut you loose so that could ask stupid questions..." Amanda says in a menacing tone, as she continues to hold the blade firmly against her.

"I'm sorry, I won't ask any other questions."

Feeling the pressure from the knife subside, she watches as Amanda turns around and sneaks across the tiled floor, her footsteps never making a sound as she silently slips into one of the open rooms along the side. For a moment, Christine just stays there, feeling the wound in her side begin to ache and bleed down onto her hip — then she slowly aims the light back up, seeing the beam dance around as her hand shakes uncontrollably. "Hey!" she yells out, hoping that more of them don't come crawling out of the other rooms — and well aware of the fact that Amanda has both of them trapped down here.

Still seeing no reaction from them, she bends down and picks up a small juice container that's lying on the floor beside her, then flings it through the air and nearly hits them in the head. Again, she leans over to pick something else up, but this time she hears something ahead of her, a slow dragging sound followed by a loud single footstep. When she points the light down the hall this time, she sees a young woman that's not much older than she is, using her left leg to walk as her right foot drags along uselessly beside it. Backing up against the staircase door, she watches nervously as the woman gets closer with every excruciating step she takes, and becomes even more scared when she passes by Amanda's room with no sign of the girl doing anything to help. With the woman only ten feet away — close enough for her stench to fill the entire hallway — Christine reaches behind and tries desperately to open the door handle, fearful that she's been tricked by Amanda to be taken out in the most horrible way possible.

"Amanda!" she screams, seeing the red, bloodshot eyes staring her down, and horrible, blackened teeth as she opens her mouth and tries to say something — but the only thing that comes out sounds like a low-pitched groan. Now just a few feet away, Christine takes a step sideways as a glint of metal suddenly shows up in front of the young woman's throat, then slices across it rapidly as she falls to the floor and begins to flail around. Amanda, who must have been standing behind her, kneels down and grabs the woman by her hair, then holds the knife to her head as Christine closes her eyes to drown out the gory imagery.

"Help me drag her upstairs," Amanda orders her, wiping her blade against the woman's hospital gown as Christine opens her eyes again. "First we need to take her clothes off, then we have to lay her just inside the door up there."

Curious as to why she would want to do something so gruesome and pointless, Christine tries to run a dozen scenarios through her head, hoping that one of them will make the slightest bit of sense — but she still doesn't dare ask her any questions about it. "What do you want me to do?"

Amanda unlocks the door and swings it open, then takes one of the woman's wrists and holds onto it tightly. "Grab her other arm, we'll just pull her up there."

"She's kinda heavy, isn't she? Maybe we can find another way to do it..."

"I've done it before by myself — just grab her, she won't bite."

Wishing she had gloves on, Christine wraps her fingers around the woman's forearm, then helps to pull it through the doorway and onto the first step of the stairs. They have to yank on her with every step they take, and each one gets harder than the last. When they finally reach the last one, Christine almost mentions to Amanda that the door downstairs is still unlocked — but then she notices the metal keychain that's dangling loosely from her coat pocket. Taking in a deep breath, she picks the woman up by the shoulders, using every ounce of strength she has, and then begins carrying her inside as Amanda backs up through the doorway and guides her into reception area of the sixth floor. When she gets close to her, Christine pushes the limp body onto Amanda and pins her onto the floor. Knowing that she just sealed her fate, she hesitates for a moment and tries to decide whether she should attempt to kill Amanda, or simply try to get away from her and warn Larry and Curtis of her plans. Seeing the keys lying on the floor, she leans over carefully and picks them up, then starts to reach over for the knife that's still held firmly in the girl's small, delicate-looking hand — but when she sees the woman's body being pushed off to the side, she backs up quickly toward the stairs and starts running, not sure of whether to head outside or hide somewhere else in the hospital. Hearing the sound of rapid footsteps behind her though, she makes the quick decision to duck into the fifth floor, shutting the door behind her just in time to hear the blade scraping against the steel shell.

"Christine, open the door!" Amanda screams at the top of her lungs.

Holding the door closed with only the weight of her body, Christine fumbles through the keys and tries a few of them before finding the correct one. Hearing Amanda beat against the window in the top of the door, she turns around and shines her light quickly around the hallway, then runs toward the end of it, carefully stepping around a dried puddle of blood. She hears the pounding behind her stop as she comes to an intersection, where she turns to the right and runs down another corridor with a waiting room at the end of it. Glancing at each room, she finally chooses one that has an open solid-wood door with no window — and a lock. Hearing something faintly, she listens closely for a few seconds — then recognizes the sound the running footsteps, coming from somewhere close. She pushes the door open and jumps inside, not bothering to even make sure the room was empty first. Next, she quietly locks the door, takes a quick look around the office, then turns her flashlight off as she backs up toward a desk that's only a few feet away.

She can still hear the footsteps, sounding further away the longer she listens to them. Then another noise appears — a deep, raspy cough that's followed by a scuffling sound.

It was obvious from the cough that they're close, possibly even in the next room — but when the shuffling becomes louder, and she can feel something brush against her foot, she knows they're much closer than that. They're on the other side of the desk.

CHAPTER 16

Pressing a clean washcloth against her side, Amanda sits down in the waiting room of the sixth floor and looks out at the gloomy landscape of the city. She didn't even realize that she'd been cut until the pain suddenly appeared while running down the stairs after Christine. The only time it could have happened was when she was pushed to the ground, which meant she was likely injured by her own blade — although it's impossible to tell for sure considering how much blood was already on it. Still, she was lucky that the wound was so superficial, and by the time she was able to treat it with antiseptic wipes the bleeding had all but ended. Unfortunately, her arm is a different story. When she fell backward, the woman that Christine threw on top of her landed directly onto her elbow, and ever since then, that arm has felt weak and tingly. Even holding onto her knife has proven to be difficult.

She remembers sitting here in this very spot a few years prior, waiting to hear news about Diane's sick mother. She cared little about the welfare of her stepmother, Diane, and even less about the prognosis of her mother's stroke — but she remembers being fascinated by the view from this room. Her father told her that on a clear day you could practically see their house on the other side of the harbor, which was probably rubbish, but she believed him at the time. Tonight, with no electricity and the air filled with smoke, you can hardly even see that Westport exists at all, or even the nearby city of Hoquiam for that matter. Her entire world seems to be disintegrating around her — the people that loved her, the few of them that she loved back, and now even the stores and city parks that were so much a part of her childhood. All of them are disappearing — as if she were an old woman looking back at the days of her youth.

The longer she sits and looks over the water at Westport, the more she misses her former life, and even the people in it. Aaron is likely dead by now, trapped in a basement with no food or water, which doesn't necessarily bother her all that much considering the way he talked to her last. She misses the way they used to get along though — the board games and trips to the state park, where they would search the wooded dunes for lost items that would blow in from the beach from the countless tourists. She remembers the feeling of the cold sand underneath the pine trees, where the sun hadn't touched the ground in decades, and the constant roar of the ocean that would block out any of their secretive chatter from the outside world.

All that she has left today, is Ben — and the only evidence that he's still alive is her own gut feeling, which still tells her that he's out there somewhere, maybe even in this city. Hearing Curtis' voice was a shock, and knowing that he's on his way gives her hope that Ben is probably nearby, since there's no way he would ever allow them to be separated again.

At one time her plan was to kill all of them, including Ben — but now she feels differently, she feels alone. The others will all have to die, otherwise Ben would never stay with her — but there's no possible way she can imagine herself harming him.

She takes the cloth from her side and looks at it, noting the lack of new blood that's been deposited since the last time she checked. Standing up, she wraps a blanket around her shoulders, shielding her skin from the cold air that's blowing in through the broken window, then she walks down the hallway and unlocks the door to the staircase. Mike has several sets of keys in his desk, so it wasn't a problem finding another one — but it annoys her that Christine has one too. She's already prepared for Curtis and Larry's visit, with only one extra thing to take care of, but she's beginning to wonder if it might be best to take care of Christine before they arrive. She seems harmless enough, but she also has a weird friendship with Larry, which might complicate things down the road.

With her flashlight in her hand, she moves down the steps quickly and silently, stopping only momentarily at the fifth floor to listen for any signs of activity from Christine. Hearing none, she continues all the way down to the second level, where she can already hear the sounds of scratching and pounding, as at least two people try to claw their way through the busted small window in the door.

"Get back!" she yells at one of them, as she takes her knife and jabs into the back of their hand. That arm disappears from sight, but it takes her several more blows before they all retreat back into the dark cavern that used to be a hospital. She unlocks the door and then stands back, waiting for one of them to get curious enough to come back to the opening. The hunters in Grayland were still smart somehow, sensing when they were about to walk into a trap — but the infected of Aberdeen were just like all of the others, too dimwitted and gullible to understand even the most basic strategy.

In only a few minutes, one of them finally appears in the doorway — a tall, older woman whose coordination is so shaky that Amanda isn't even certain she can make it up the flights of stairs. Right behind her is a woman that isn't much younger, but she's far more steady on her feet. Seeing no one else come through the doorway, she begins to back up the stairs slowly, waiting every few steps for the women to catch up. She really wanted three of them, and at first she was disappointed when only the two came out — but as she reaches the third floor landing, she hears yet another set of footsteps coming up the staircase. It takes the man only seconds to reach the other two, and as he pushes both of them to the side and hurries up the steps, Amanda grips her knife tightly and steadies her feet on the rough surface beneath them. The man doesn't hesitate at all before attacking her, but he makes the same fatal mistake that almost all of them do. As he grabs for her shoulders, intending to tackle her to the ground, she quickly ducks underneath his reach and spins around behind — pushing the knife into his back several times before he has a chance to react. By the time he turns around and faces her, his knees are already beginning to buckle — and as she calmly approaches him, ripping the large blade across his throat, she feels her hand begin to shake.

Hearing the women getting closer, she places the knife in her other hand and makes a few quick stabbing motions with it to test her agility, hoping that she doesn't have to resort to using her less coordinated hand for protection. Instead, and much to her delight, the pair of them simply step over the man and continue following her — all the way to the sixth floor.

CHAPTER 17

Christine slowly picks her foot up and moves it forward a few inches, breaking free of whatever is under the desk and holding onto it — then she spins around quickly when she hears them grasping for something else. She fully expected to see a hand when she turned on the flashlight, but she never expected it to be so thin and frail looking. Hearing fast-moving footsteps in the hallway again, she turns the flashlight off again for a moment and stays perfectly still until they pass by, and then carefully leans over the desk and catches just a glimpse of the person behind it — but then she quickly turns her head away and covers her mouth, trying not to get sick.

Wearing a black sweat suit that's now several sizes too large, she can hear the person wheezing and struggling for every breath, and the upper portion of their face is buried beneath a stack of papers. It's impossible to tell for certain whether it's a man or a woman, but at this point it doesn't really matter — they'll be dead soon anyway. None of these people have been completely without food and water since the outbreak first began, far too much time has passed for that to be true — but this person is obviously starving to death, and their pathetic, labored breathing is almost more than Christine can handle. Her mother ultimately died of cancer, but she looked and sounded nearly identical to whoever this is. At first she prayed for a miracle, that her mother would spontaneously improve despite the lack of drugs to fight the cancer — but in those last couple of weeks, as her condition became worse and the drugs to comfort her began to

125

dwindle, Christine started to hope for something she never thought possible. Since that horrible day, when her final wish was granted, and her mother drew her last breath, Christine has felt an overwhelming guilt that she somehow let her down.

Being in the same room as this person, as they make the same sounds and give off the same smell of death, is bringing all of that heartache and anguish back. Covering her mouth to block the smell, she leans over the desk, hoping that by seeing the person, it will somehow convince her mind that it's not really her mother lying there. After convincing herself that they're incapable of putting up any kind of a fight, Christine takes her foot and carefully pushes the papers away from their face, revealing the emaciated face of a woman underneath, who's looking up at her with dark, sunken, bloodshot eyes. Christine just stands there and stares at the woman, wishing that she could help end her suffering somehow — but when she hears the tapping of shoes somewhere outside the room, the woman lets out a high-pitched scream and begins to frantically claw at the floor again.

As soon as they start beating on the door from the outside, Christine knows that it's pointless to turn off her light and pretend that she isn't here — the fact that the woman on the floor continues to scream is more than enough reason to continue their assault. She glances around the room quickly, looking for something that might serve as a better weapon than her flashlight, and ends up grabbing a pair of scissors that are lying on the floor next to the woman's feet. The hinges that hold the door look strong, and are barely moving through the repeated hits that they're taking — but the door jam on the lock side isn't holding as well, and she can hear the splintering of wood as the sounds of slamming hands turns into kicks instead. She stands back, gripping the scissors tightly in her hand as the door finally begins to give way, and she sees a half naked man burst into the room and look around with a frenzied look in his eyes, first at

126

Christine, and then at the other woman, who's still yelling at the top of her lungs. The man tries to climb over the desk at first, reaching desperately for the woman who's only slightly out of his grasp — then he drops to the floor and shoves his arms underneath, giving Christine an opportunity to either make a run for it, or to take him out with only a pair of scissors. Looking at the broken door, and hearing the agonizing cries coming from the woman as she fights for her life, Christine kneels down beside the man and shoves the blades of the scissors straight into the back of his head. She hears a loud moan as soon as they go in, and she sees him grabbing at his neck where the steel is still deeply buried.

She waits for a few more seconds, thinking at any moment that the man in front of her will simply lie down and die — but when that doesn't happen, she lets go of the scissors and jumps back, listening to the woman continue to scream and draw attention to the room.

Still backing away, Christine stands next to the open doorway and carefully looks down both directions of the hallway with the light, expecting to see Amanda standing there waiting for her. Seeing nothing though, she steps into the corridor again and turns to the right, where there's a waiting room and a small kitchenette off to the side. The sounds of screaming is still echoing down the hallway behind her as she turns off the flashlight and hides behind a small couch in the corner of the room — and then she hears something else, a small squeak, repeating itself every few seconds or so on the far side of the room where the kitchen area is. Exhausted, she leans back against the wall behind her and closes her eyes, finding herself drifting off despite the commotion throughout the rest of the floor.

Existing halfway inside of a dreamworld, she remembers another night similar to this shortly after they left their home in Adna — a night in which all three of them, her father, David, and herself, nearly died at the hands of a psychopath. In their first real experience with that type of infected, they were followed for hours down the highway and across winding pathways through the thick forests of the Boistfort Hills, until they finally came across a farm that sat miles from anything else, tucked back into a small valley and overshadowed by the hills on either side of it. It was there, hiding in an old, deteriorating farmhouse with no supplies and little protection, that they were relentlessly tormented through the night. It wasn't until the early morning hours, when the glow of the approaching sun illuminated the land around the house, that David was able to fire several gunshots through a window as the man ran past it — killing him instantly.

The man that was following them was clearly different from the others, although Christine has since seen several others just like him. The man and woman in the office down the hall frighten her, especially when she's more or less defenseless against their infrequent attacks — but they're also easily outwitted, and are oftentimes confused, but harmless. Amanda and Jake, however, and the others like them, are anything but harmless, and are never confused about anything surrounding them. Even now, with the area around her filled with screaming and loud footsteps in the distance, she can still hear something being dragged across the floor above her. She knows exactly what, and who, it is — the murderous young girl only has a few hours of darkness to prepare everything for the arrival of Larry and Curtis, and her singular focus will be aimed at killing both of them before they have a chance to escape her torment.

Hearing a few drops of rain against the building, Christine opens her eyes again and sees a floor-to-ceiling window only a couple of feet ahead of her. Still hidden behind the couch, she scoots herself across the carpeting, her tired legs protesting against every movement, and finds that the window is looking east toward the cascade mountains in the distance — their silhouette barely visible from the rising sun

128

behind them. The city itself is still mostly shrouded in darkness, although she can see what looks like fires burning on the east end of town, near the pharmacy where Larry and her found one another again. That part of town seemed deserted at the time, and they talked about it being a possible place to settle down and rest for a while — but she doesn't find herself discouraged or disappointed from the fact that it's obviously overrun, her mind has become far too calloused and desensitized for that to happen. One building at a time, the world that she once knew is being destroyed, and replaced with nothing but crumbling ruins that serve no purpose whatsoever.

Watching the flickering lights of the fires a few miles away, she lets her mind briefly escape from the situation that she finds herself in — but then something suddenly draws her attention again, not a noise inside of the building, but a lack of one. The woman down the hallway has been screaming and crying almost non-stop — until now. Christine turns her head away from the window and listens closely to the sounds emanating from inside the hospital, but she only hears the slight squeaking coming from the kitchen, the faint footsteps from far away, and now the sound of someone struggling to crawl down the hallway, grunting painfully with each movement. As the noise becomes louder, and Christine realizes for certain that they're getting closer, she peeks her head around the edge of the couch and stares at the beginning of the hallway, which is just barely visible in the darkness of the room. In only a few moments she can tell that they've entered the waiting area, and are now crawling across the floor as she feels the couch being pushed toward her from the other side. They're moving at a regular pace, pulling themselves along as their legs drag across the floor behind them — but then they suddenly stop, and the only sound they make are the grunts and moans of somebody desperately struggling. She waits for what seems like forever, listening as they continue to grasp at anything within reach, and then she quietly climbs out from behind the couch and shines her flashlight onto the floor.

There's a thick streak of blood across the carpet, leading back to the man that's scrambling around in front of the couch, and she can see the office scissors still sticking out of his neck where she shoved them in only a short while ago. Both of his legs look like they're paralyzed, and one foot is wedged underneath a table, which prevents him from going any further. As she approaches him, he turns his head slightly and then reaches one of his hands in her direction in a pathetic attempt to grab her. Stepping down on his elbow, she bends over and grabs onto the scissors, wishing more than anything for the strength to put the man out of his misery — but instead, she just pulls them out and then steps back, watching the blood pour out of his neck and onto the flooring in giant spurts. In a few minutes his body finally goes limp, and she wipes the scissors onto the couch cushion beside her and then shines the light back down the hallway.

Relieved to see nobody else around, she turns the light off and feels her way to another chair — then hears the squeaking behind her stop as well, leaving the entire hospital suddenly quiet. Her body tenses up as footsteps make their way across the floor, then back again, followed by the squeaking noise starting up once again. With her fingers fumbling nervously for the power switch on the flashlight, she turns it on and slowly moves its beam toward the kitchen, where she sees the back of a woman standing at a small sink, attempting again and again to pour water into an empty glass. Each time she lifts the faucet handle, it makes a slight squeak before she pushes it back down and then tries again.

The woman then stops, still facing away from Christine. As she reaches to her side for another glass, Christine gets up from her chair and starts to slowly back away to the corridor, keeping her light on the woman the entire time. Instead of reaching for the faucet again, which Christine was hoping she would do, the woman spins around quickly and throws the glass in her direction, nearly hitting her head as it smashes against the wall behind her. Christine stumbles backward, trying to regain her footing after ducking out of the way — but when she aims the light back in the woman's direction, she doesn't see her anywhere. Shining the light around the room frantically, she finally spots her back in the kitchen, where she was apparently bent over and hidden by the cabinets. This time though, her frail, gaunt frame that looks dangerously close to death, has a small revolver aimed directly at Christine.

"I don't want to hurt anybody," Christine says softly, hoping not to arouse anymore attention than necessary. "I'll leave you alone, okay?"

She starts walking backward again, noticing the usual purple blotches of skin all over the woman's face and arms. Then the woman takes a couple of steps forward and pulls the trigger just once, but nothing happens. With a completely blank expression, she then holds the gun up to her own head and pulls the trigger repeatedly, and on the fifth shot the gun fires a bullet into her head, dropping her body to the floor.

At first Christine just stands there in shock, and she actually begins to back up further into the hallway before her mind begins to clear once again. From somewhere down the long corridor behind her, she can hear multiple sets of footsteps quickly approaching, along with incoherent yelling and someone beating against the walls as they make their way toward the gunshot. Christine looks around for someplace to hide, seeing another room on the other side of the waiting area that's marked 'Staff Only'. As she passes by the suicidal woman, she reaches down and grabs the gun off of the floor and then slips into the other room, not even bothering to look around inside first. The room, which appears to be another small office, is empty aside from a desk and a few metal file cabinets — but it also has a large window next to the door, which has a view of the entire waiting area as soon as she shuts the flashlight off. She locks the flimsy door, then hides behind the desk and watches through the window as the first people come barging into the waiting room. In only a few minutes, five of them are standing over the bodies of the man and woman, all of them looking confused as they begin searching around the rest of the area — including the window of the small office that Christine is hiding in.

CHAPTER 18
ABERDEEN: MARCH 31ST

Seeing the first rays of sunlight hitting the building across the street, Larry tries to rub the sleepiness from his eyes as he looks out at the clear morning sky — a rarity in this area, especially during this time of the year. He barely slept last night, with his mind racing in circles over what might be going on inside the hospital. He could tell Christine was scared, but he can't think of a single reason why Mike would want to delay getting his medication — especially to wait for someone he's never even met. Every scenario that ran through his head last night came back around to the same conclusion — one that he prays isn't true.

They saw Amanda Williams in front of the pharmacy not long before they left, and they both assumed that she'd followed them through the city, watching their movements for any signs of letting their guard down. For whatever reason though, neither one of them took the threat of her seriously after confining themselves in the locked sixth floor of the hospital, which is a mistake he's just now beginning to realize. He knows that the odds of finding Christine alive this morning are low, regardless or whether it's Mike or Amanda that they'll be facing — but he also keeps reminding himself that she kept Christine alive in Grayland, and never harmed her despite her threats to do so. Just like Ben, she seems to have a soft spot for the teenager, which might have something to do with their ages.

At first light, he contacted Curtis and found out that he was leaving right after sunrise — Larry assumes with the rest of his family, but he can't even be certain that all of them are still alive. After discovering how violent and cruel the virus had made Jake, he wasn't holding out much hope that any of them survived his rampage. After that he tried radioing Christine to give her an update status, but the only thing he heard back was empty static.

Grabbing his gear and pushing the desks and chairs away from the entrance of the real estate office, he steps out into the brisk morning air and shivers as the wind blows between the buildings from the harbor to the south. Even on a dry, sunny day like this, the air along Grays Harbor always carries a chilled feeling to it, a dampness that cuts right through to the bone.

The streets look empty once again, which gives him at least some confidence that the infected here are different than they are in Grayland and Westport. Here, at least as far as he can tell, daywalkers seem to be quite rare. He crosses the road and pushes the door to the bank open, both surprised and relieved that it did so without any resistance — then he looks around at the mess of ripped up papers and turned over chairs and desks that have been thrown around the place. Besides the trash though, the only sign of violence that he can see is a rather fresh trail of blood that leads from somewhere behind the counter to the doorway where he's standing, then down the sidewalk and around the corner. Following the other end of it, he traces it through the back of the bank and to a partially open vault, where he can see scratches on the carpeting in front of the massive door, and more bloodstains on the handle. He pulls the door further open with his foot, and releases a horrible scent of death and decay that's obviously coming from a pile of human innards lying just inside the opening.

Pushing the door closed again, he turns around and sees an office sitting by itself in the opposite corner of the lobby. As soon as he approaches it, he can tell there's something different about the glass window that overlooks the rest of the lobby — it's far thicker than any normal window, and when he hits the glass, it sounds strange and feels heavy somehow. He looks around the rest of the lobby, making sure that he's actually alone, then locks the entrance and grabs a metal chair from the waiting area. After dragging the chair to the office window, he picks it up and swings it directly at the large pane, feeling the impact in his shoulder and elbow, but the hit does absolutely nothing to the glass. He swings it again, this time letting go of it right at the end in order to protect himself, but after three straight hits to the same place, it barely shows even a scratch — although the chair itself is bent beyond usability.

He drops the chair, then uses his flashlight to look around the inside of the office, finding some fancy ink pens, some paper, and a variety of dollar bills in the top desk drawer — along with a single key that works on the sealed, reinforced door in front of him. This room was apparently once used as a safe room for the bank manager or owner, but it offered little help to the unfortunate soul that died in the vault — a vault they obviously didn't know was impossible to lock from the inside.

Curtis looks east toward Cosmopolis as they pass by the intersection before the bridge, seeing wisps of smoke rising from the fires that are still burning on the south side of the river. He hopes that the thick smoke that he can see down the highway might deter some of the infected from coming this way, but he can tell from the look of mayhem on the bridge that they've been making this a regular route in recent days. Newly deceased corpses are lying next to old bones scattered across the pavement, and he can see where people have been clawing at the doors and windows of abandoned cars, leaving deep gouges in the thick layer of ash piled on each vehicle.

"It stinks here..." Ben says, holding his arm over his mouth and nose to cover the scent.

"I know, buddy, we'll be past here before you know it," Curtis says, looking down at him in the garden cart, and knowing that he's probably lying to him. "That's the hospital up on the hill — Larry and Beth said that the light on top used to come on at night."

"After the outbreak?" Rachel asks.

"Yeah, that's where Beth and Jake became separated."

"Mom, look at those..." Matt starts to say, looking at Sarah while pointing down at the Chehalis River below, right as it dumps into Grays Harbor.

"I know, honey," she says calmly and quietly, as she gently pushes his arm down. "There's no reason to make a big deal out of it — is there?" She nods toward Ben, and watches as Matt turns his attention back to the river.

Debris is being washed downstream, everything from sheets of plastic to building materials and even a few cars that have been lodged against the side of the riverbank. None of those, however, compare to the clusters of dead bodies floating on the surface, dozens of them passing under the bridge in only the few minutes they've been walking over it — and they just keep coming. Sarah looks out toward the harbor itself, which is barely visible from here, and sees the same dark spots on the top of the water stretching as far as her eyes can penetrate.

"They're all dead, aren't they?" Matt whispers.

""Yes, but at least this way they can't hurt anyone."

"Have you ever been to Olympia, Matt?" Rachel asks, trying to distract him from the river.

"That's the place with the capital building, right?"

"Right, it's the state capital — or at least it used to be. It's also warmer and drier than the beach."

"I don't really mind the rain that much, or the cold. I kinda like it here."

"Sure, what's not to like..." Rachel says, smiling a little at Sarah as she looks around at the scarred city covered in ashes and bones.

The smell does improve a great deal as they distance themselves from the river, but there's still a lingering scent of smoke and rot that's permeating the air around them — and the clouds of smoke and ash that's still blowing in from Grayland certainly doesn't help.

As they walk down the smaller side streets and wind their way through the city in an attempt to stay hidden, Curtis notices footprints and drag marks in the layer of ash on the road — a clear indication to him that Aberdeen wasn't quite as dead as they'd hoped it would be. Throughout much of the city, however, he can see the remains of people, their bodies burned and decayed, and picked apart by animals and the weather. Even now, there's an unusually high number of seagulls, crows, and ravens in the area, taking advantage of the abundance of food that's suddenly become available to them. One thing that they haven't seen though, something that's been plentiful in the other towns they've been to, is domestic animals. Since crossing the bridge, they haven't come across a single dog, cat, rabbit, or livestock animal anywhere — and while it would be more than a bit unusual to find a horse or cow in the middle of a city, Curtis finds it strange that so many people have obviously survived the fire, but none of their pets did.

"How much further is it?" Sarah asks Curtis, looking at her water bottle that's almost empty.

"It should be on the next block or so."

"Why don't you radio Larry and let him know that we're here..."

"Yeah, that's probably a good idea," Curtis says, as he stops and takes the radio out of his pocket. "Larry are you there?"

137

"Yeah, I'm here," Larry says after a moment. *"You must be a lot closer, you're coming in clearer."*

"I think we're in the general vicinity."

"Do you know where the Sullivan Hotel is?"

"I can see it."

"Well, I'm kitty-corner from it, on the opposite side of the street."

Curtis looks up the street, where a brown, crumbling three-story building sits nestled between two modern structures — and across the street he sees Larry standing in front of a bank, waving his arms to catch his attention. "There he is..."

"Where is the Sullivan Hotel?" Sarah asks.

"That's the ugly building across from him. It used to be a whorehouse in the old days, but it's been shut down and abandoned for decades."

"What's a whorehouse?" Ben asks.

"It's a place where whores live," Curtis says without hesitating.

"What's a whore?"

"It's a job that used to exist, but doesn't anymore."

"Like yours?"

"Exactly, just like mine."

Sarah runs up and hugs Larry as soon as they get close, but he nervously motions them inside before Curtis has a chance to shake his hand. Once they all enter the bank, he locks the door and then quickly retreats back into the manager's office, where the others follow him.

"Okay, we don't have much time, and I don't want anyone else knowing that you're all here," Larry says, who suddenly notices Rachel for the first time. "I know you..."

"Hi Larry, my name is Rachel — remember?"

"Yeah, Rachel, of course. It's good to see you again."

"Why is it important that nobody knows we're here?" Sarah asks, interrupting them.

"Because Christine is in trouble, and I don't think it's Mike that's holding her."

"And you think that it's someone considerably younger..." Sarah says, nodding to Ben.

"Right..." Larry opens the office door and steps out, then turns to Rachel. "Do you mind if I have a quick word with Curtis and Sarah alone? It'll only take a minute..."

Without waiting for an answer, only a look of confusion on her face, Curtis and Sarah join Larry in the lobby, closing the door behind them.

"You think it's Amanda, right?" Curtis asks, as soon as the door shuts.

"I honestly have no idea — but I know she's in the city."

"You've seen her?"

"A few days ago, east of here — she followed one of us here. Look, I really need to get moving, and I don't mind going alone."

"No, I'm going with you," Curtis answers quickly, drawing a look of surprise from Sarah.

"Do you have a gun?"

"Yeah, but it only has a few bullets."

"You can take one of mine," he offers, handing him a loaded semi-automatic.

Sarah sees Curtis lean in to give her a kiss, but she pulls back and pushes him away before he gets a chance. "Wait, aren't we going to talk about this?"

"We'll be back before you know it," Curtis says, placing the gun inside of his coat. "Besides, I'm sick of looking over my shoulder every time I turn around. If she's up there, I need to find her."

Sarah doesn't say anything else — she's tired of arguing, especially when she knows that it won't do any good anyway. She simply watches as Curtis heads back to the office to talk to the boys, and then sees Larry handing her a key. "Here, this is to the office — I don't think anyone can get inside."

"Thanks," she says, taking the key from him. "Larry, what happened to Beth?"

"Jake killed her, back in Grayland."

"Oh my god... I'm so sorry, Larry," she responds, her voice choking up. "Is he still alive?"

"No, I shot him."

Hearing the office door open again, Sarah looks inside and sees both boys crying as Curtis says goodbye to them and leaves the room. "Don't do anything stupid," she tells him, as he hugs her briefly and then joins Larry by the front entrance.

"I won't, I promise."

"Oh, and Sarah," Larry says. "Don't open the bank vault."

Leaving the bank, Curtis looks ahead at the long climb up the hill that leads to the hospital, and at the massive amount of footprints visible on the street in front of them. "Was it quiet here last night?"

"No, not really. None of them got in though."

"Does this Christine girl know how to handle herself?"

"As far as defending herself? Not at all — but she's been through a lot, and I'm hoping she's a lot stronger than I think she is. She made it from Grayland to here on her own though, so I guess that says something about her."

"And Mike... what about him?"

"Mike is desperate, so I guess he's dangerous in that regard — but he's also a coward. If he's still alive when we get in there, I'm gonna kill him before we leave."

"And if it's Amanda up there?"

"I think she's had more than her fair share of second chances too."

About halfway up the hill, Curtis looks up at the hospital and realizes that it's virtually impossible to sneak up on anybody with that vantage point, especially when they know you're coming — but this morning all of the rooms appear dark, even on the top floor where Christine is supposedly being held captive. As they reach the top of the hill where they can see the main entrance ahead of them, Larry tries contacting Christine on his radio again, but he hears nothing in response.

"Was the entrance closed when you left yesterday?" Curtis asks, pointing at the shattered glass front door.

"It was closed, but it wasn't locked. I didn't have a key."

"So why did they bust it up?"

"I don't know, but I think there's still someone moving around in there," Larry says, seeing a shadow pacing against the back wall near the staircase entrance. As out of shape as he is, Larry has been the one pushing them across the city and up the hill this morning, but even he begins to slow down as soon as they step through the missing glass pane and enter the lobby of the hospital, hearing someone thrashing around on the far side of it and screaming obscenities at a closed staircase door. Curtis stops as soon as he catches a glimpse of the man, who's covered in blood from head to toe, and carries an equally bloody ax that he's using to cut his way through to the emergency stairs.

"Larry, hold up..." Curtis whispers, trying to get Larry's attention before the man spots him. Instead of stopping though, Larry walks calmly up to the information desk and knocks on it. At first the man doesn't do anything, but after knocking yet again, he turns around and looks Larry in the eyes, then lifts his ax up and screams again to intimidate him. Curtis takes a couple of steps forward just as the man

141

swings his ax in Larry's direction — which misses by a mile, but he still continues to get closer. Then Larry takes his pistol from its side holster, aims it carefully at the guy, and fires a single shot into the man's face.

"Well, I guess everyone knows we're here," Curtis yells, his ears still ringing from the gunshot.

"I'm sure they already knew," he replies, stepping over the still-twitching body as he tries opening the staircase door.

"Is it locked?"

"No," Larry responds, still pushing with all of his strength. "The latch works, but there's something on the other side that's blocking it."

Careful not to step on anything, Curtis tries shining his flashlight into the space beyond, and sees a stack of gas cylinders, chairs, and other objects filling up the area between the door and the steps behind it. "You're not gonna open it, we're gonna have to find another way up there."

Holstering his gun again, Larry turns on his flashlight and shines it on an emergency exit map next to the door. "We're being led down a maze like fucking mice."

"Is there another set of stairs?"

"Yeah, on the other side, but they only go up to the third floor — we'll have to find this set again when we get up there," Larry answers, ripping the map of the first floor from the wall.

Walking to the other end of the lobby, they can hear light footsteps on the level above them, and the occasional loud thump as something heavy hits the floor. Behind the information desk, Larry pushes the door marked 'Staff Only', which opens into a long, dark corridor that stretches farther than his flashlight will shine with any clarity. It does illuminate enough, however, to see something moving slowly across the floor, low to the ground.

"Any idea what that is?" Larry asks.

"No, but we have to assume that Amanda is probably waiting for us somewhere down here."

They move carefully down the hallway, Larry's light fixed on whatever is in front of them, and Curtis' light moving around elsewhere just in case this is merely a diversion. When they make it about thirty feet from the door, they hear a loud crash behind them, followed by a click of metal from the door as it locks — but it doesn't slow Larry down. His eyes are focused on the object, hearing a painful whimper coming from it as he finally realizes what it is.

"I think that's a woman ahead of us — but her back is all twisted up or something."

Curtis glances inside some of the rooms as they pass by them, seeing stacks of body bags covering the floors of many of them. He only sees a living person in one, but they have their back turned to the door, staring straight ahead at an empty wall. "Does that map of yours show another way out of here?"

"There's an exit if you go all the way down this hallway, then turn to the right," Larry says, as he stops and taps Curtis on the shoulder. "Look at this..."

Curtis looks ahead and sees the woman lying on the floor, her back obviously horribly broken. She has her face turned away from them, with her arms pinned underneath her body in a completely helpless position — and he can hear her muted cries for help as she tries to lift her head up.

"Can you speak?" Larry asks her, walking around to get a look at her face.

"Yes..." she whispers weakly.

The moment Curtis sees her face, he knows from the coloring around her eyes that she's infected — but that doesn't seem to stop Larry from bending down and opening the small bag that he's carrying. "What're you doing? You can't do anything for her..."

He fumbles through the bag, then grabs a syringe with a small needle and jabs it into her arm. In only a few moments the woman's eyes start drooping, then go completely blank as the light disappears from them.

"What the hell is that?" Curtis asks him.

"Something I picked up at the pharmacy. I grabbed a few of them, just in case I got into trouble." Closing the bag again, he grabs the sign and walks down the hallway another twenty feet, then stops at an open door with a staircase inside. "Whoever is in here with us, they must have another way of getting around — or there's more than one of them. Somebody had to close that door behind us."

"You feel that cold air coming down the shaft?" Curtis asks.

"Yeah, there's a door open somewhere up there."

They start climbing up the steps, with Larry still leading the way, and almost immediately they hear a rumbling noise coming from above them. As soon as they reach the second level landing, Larry sets the map to the first floor down and draws his gun out. Curtis can tell that the sound is coming from this floor, and the noise becomes even louder as they stand in front of the open door and look inside, seeing two office chairs roll across the floor, landing only a few feet away from them.

"Stay here and guard the door, I'm gonna check it out," Larry tells him.

He steps into a small waiting area with only a half-dozen chairs in it, and then hears some commotion from the other side of the room. Footsteps can also be heard, both fast and slow, from down a corridor to his right, and also from the third floor above him. He aims his light straight ahead, and sees an open door behind an enclosed desk area, with both small and large objects being tossed out into the waiting room. The closer he gets, the more angry they sound — and as their labored breathing becomes louder, he aims his pistol at the doorway and waits for them to come out from behind it. Just as their arm becomes visible as they exit the room, Larry feels someone pull hard on his shoulder, and before he realizes what's happening, he sees a grotesque looking set of teeth staring back at him as he falls backward onto the carpeting. The dark figure above him grabs at his gun, and then he hears two loud gunshots, followed by a third that splatters blood down onto his face.

"Are you okay?" Curtis asks, holding out his hand to help pull him up.

"Yeah, I'm fine — just a little shaken, that's all."

Bending down to pick his flashlight back up, he aims it down at the man, recognizing severe burns all over his naked body. "This guy isn't from inside here — he's from the streets."

"Well, he's dead now, so it doesn't really matter," Curtis says, standing on the stair landing once again.

"I can still hear someone on this level..."

"It's not Christine, it sounds like another man — so we need to keep moving."

"I have to be sure, Curtis."

"Larry, listen closely..." The footsteps coming from somewhere down the hallway are slow, dragging both of their feet as they hobble across the floor — and even from this distance, where the sounds are barely audible, you can still make out the deep, raspy cough as they gasp for breath. "If that's her, there's nothing we can do for her."

CHAPTER 19
ABERDEEN: MARCH 31ST

Sarah watched out the window as Curtis and Larry left the bank and headed out into the streets of Aberdeen, until they eventually disappeared from sight about a block away. Sitting in the dark, watching their sons huddle up together against the cold, damp air, she has no idea whether or not she'll ever see her husband again. Both of them are breaking their pledge to always stay together no matter what — him by leaving, and her by letting him go without trying to stop him. As angry as she is right now though, she can't imagine living with herself if they allow an innocent, healthy person like Christine to die needlessly, especially considering how few of them exist today.

All of them need a breather, a time where they can heal their wounds and start making long-term plans for how to deal with future struggles, like growing food and dealing with illnesses that were once easily managed by a primary physician. They also have to create their own set of laws to live by, which will likely include how they deal with infected people from now on. When Curtis tried to kill Amanda at the cabin, it seemed overly violent at the time, even to her — but after looking at everything with more perspective, it was an incredibly foolish thing to ever question his motive, as barbaric as it was.

For now though, all they can do is sit and wait for the others to contact her — and for their eventual return.

"How are you holding up?" Rachel asks, sitting down next to Sarah in front of one of the windows that face the street.

"They've only been gone about fifteen minutes."

146

"I'm sure we'll hear from them soon," Rachel says, not knowing what else to say. For a few moments they sit quietly, looking out the windows at the ash-covered pavement and empty streets of Aberdeen. "It's quieter here than I thought it would be."

"It seems like that now, but it won't be when the sun goes down. The streets must have been crawling with infected last night from the looks of the footprints," Sarah says, as she reaches inside of her coat and feels the cold, hard steel of a loaded pistol that Larry gave her — which despite its weight and cumbersome feel against her side, still gives her a sense of comfort just knowing that it's there. Her change of attitude toward guns has been dramatic to say the least, since less than a year ago she despised everything about them, telling Curtis that they weren't even allowed to be in the same house with their sons unless they were locked securely in a safe.

Rachel points down the street, where a man is stumbling around a corner and headed toward the harbor, his feet stumbling over the ground as he barely manages to stay upright.

"Considering everything that's happened, who would've thought that finding some peace and quiet would be so difficult..."

"It'll settle down after they're all dead."

"You know, it's kind of sexist when you think about it," Rachel says.

"What is?"

"The two men, running off to save a helpless girl — while us poor, defenseless women stay behind to take care of the kids."

Sarah glances out at the burned ruins of the city, and at the smoke seen rising from the east — then looks back at Rachel. "Well, it's hardly a fucking fairytale is it?"

"No, I just thought it was odd."

"There's a reason that they left both of us here."

"Why is that?"

"Because there's a decent chance that Amanda is waiting out there somewhere, maybe even across the street," Sarah says quietly, pointing her finger at the real estate office on the other side of the road.

Rachel, feeling even more paranoid than before, looks more closely at the surrounding buildings, hoping that she doesn't spot any signs of movement inside. "Matt talks about her like she's supernatural or something — like she's a ghost."

"Did he tell you that she killed her entire family?"

"He mentioned it, yeah."

"Did he happen to mention that it was before she got sick?"

"No, he didn't. How do you know that?"

"She told us, when we had her tied up at the cabin. She'd been planning to do it for months, at least her step-mother anyway, and she saw the evacuation as a perfect time to get away with it. I don't even think the kids know about it — although the bitch probably told Ben every grisly detail."

"Have you asked him about it?"

"He won't discuss any of it with us, not even after he's had a nightmare." Her attention suddenly turns to the corner of the lobby, where Matt and Ben were both sitting together only moments before and are now staring out another window that looks out toward the harbor in the south. Both of them are now standing with their faces pressed against the glass, speaking excitedly about whatever is on the other side. "What's going on over there?" Sarah asks them.

"Come look before it disappears, mom!" Matt yells out.

Sarah and Rachel both hurry over to the other side of the room and stand next to the boys, who are pointing between two buildings where you can barely see a sliver of the harbor "You two need to keep your voices down, we just saw somebody down the street."

"Look though, out on the water..."

She sees a glimpse of something dark as it disappears behind one of the buildings, but in a minute it shows up again on the other side, floating upstream against the current of the river. "What is it?"

"It's a boat — it has to be."

Rachel runs into the office, then comes back out carrying a pair of binoculars. She glances out the window quickly as she walks by, then unlocks the front door and steps out onto the sidewalk.

"Rachel, what you doing?" Sarah says incredulously, following her to the door, but staying mostly inside.

"It's only for a minute..." Rachel answers back, focusing the binoculars onto the cabin cruiser that shows up more clearly out in the open. "Do you think we should signal them or something?"

"No, I think we should get back inside before somebody sees us..."

"There's someone standing on the back of it — I think they're looking this way." Still watching them, Rachel waves her free arm in the air, which prompts Sarah to step out onto the sidewalk behind her. "If you listen closely you can hear the engine."

"Rachel, get inside, now..." Sarah warns her.

"Just a second, they're doing something... I think they're turning the boat."

Sarah walks up behind her and rips the binoculars out of her hands, then grabs her by the arm and pulls her back inside.

"What the hell are you doing?" Rachel yells.

"You can risk your life all you want, but you're not risking the lives of my family!" Sarah yells back. "We have no idea who the fuck those people are, or even if they're healthy..." She tosses the binoculars onto a chair, then turns to Matt and Ben. "Go grab your stuff, quick..."

"Are we moving?" Ben asks.

"Yes, but just down the block."

"What about dad, how will he find us?"

"We'll keep an eye out for him. Go do what I said — now!"

Rachel, who's standing there speechless, picks the binoculars up and looks out toward the harbor again — but wherever the boat went, it's now out of sight. "Sarah, is this really necessary? Those people are operating a boat for God's sake..."

"For all we know, that's one of those assholes from Grayland, or some other psycho that's looking for someone to kill," Sarah says, her voice frantic with fear and anger. "I'm not taking any chances, not anymore — especially after dealing with Jake."

Since their bags were already more or less packed, it only takes a few minutes for them to get ready — although Ben is being forced to walk on his own now that Curtis isn't there to wheel him around. With Sarah leading the way, they exit the bank and turn left toward the hospital, seeing a small cluster of businesses about two blocks up the road that look largely undamaged from the fire. When they come to an intersection, she looks north and sees a large pack of wild dogs running down the street away from them, chasing two deer through the center of the abandoned city.

"Which place are we hiding in?" Matt asks her, looking at the businesses ahead of them.

Sarah looks the shopping center over, seeing five businesses scattered around the shared parking lot. There's a gas station and grocery store on the corner, a laundromat, fast food restaurant, an insurance agent, and a credit union. Only the insurance agency looks like it's suffered damage, which is located by itself on the far end of the complex. "Let's check out the laundromat — if we're lucky it'll already be open."

"The store might have some food," Matt says.

"Yeah, but it also attracts people. The laundromat doesn't have anything." Every so often, Sarah glances down the hill to make sure they haven't been seen by any of the people from the boat, but as they reach the parking lot and head for the entrance of the credit union, they all hear the loud barking and howling coming from the woods behind the shopping center. "Ben, can you run?" Sarah asks, listening to the dogs quickly closing in on them.

Without answering, Ben starts running through the empty parking lot, all of them trying to keep up with Matt as he runs up to the door and pushes against it.

"It's locked," Matt says frantically.

Looking around at the other businesses, Sarah grabs onto Ben and pushes him behind her as she hears a dog growling ahead of them. She hands one of her bags to Rachel, then aims her gun as all of them begin backing up in the direction of the credit union. "Matt, check the next door," she says calmly, keeping her eyes on the mutt that's now approaching with its hackles up. When it gets to within about ten feet, she grips the handle of the gun more tightly, then begins squeezing the trigger — but right before she fires, she sees more movement out of the corner of her eye, and several more dogs start spreading throughout the parking lot, all of them staring directly at her.

"It's open!" Matt says, holding the door open for Ben and Rachel to enter. "Mom, come on..."

Afraid to even move, Sarah stays still as the dog in front of her waits for the others to join in — and it's not until they all hear a gunshot somewhere in the distance that the dogs are momentarily distracted enough for Sarah to back through the doorway and into the credit union. Once she moves, the dog focuses on her once again and lunges at the door, smashing its face against the tempered security glass. Within a couple of minutes they can see more than a dozen other dogs of mixed breeds move in and jump at the door and windows.

"Everybody get back, they might leave if they can't see us," Sarah says, as the group moves behind the teller counter and sits down on the floor, still hearing the barking and fighting going on outside the entrance.

"Did you hear that gunshot?" Matt asks.

"Yeah, it sounded like it came from down by the water." Sarah answers back, looking over at Rachel, who's staring straight ahead with a blank look in her eyes. "Rachel, are you still with us?"

Snapping out of whatever mental trap she was in, tears begin to run down her cheeks as she hands the binoculars to Matt. "I'm sorry Sarah, I didn't mean for any of this..."

"Listen to me — we can't afford to lose it right now, we have to stay focused on getting through this, okay?" Seeing her nod in agreement, Sarah starts examining the layout of the credit union while still remaining on the floor. The layout isn't all that different from the bank they were in before, except that there's no heavily secured corner office here. It's just a lobby, several teller counters, a few cubicles on one side, and a massive safe that's wide-open just a few feet from where they're hiding. The dogs, who were scratching at the door and barking just a few seconds before, are now almost completely silent. "Matt, take a peek around the corner and see if they're still there."

He leans his head out from behind the counter and watches for several seconds, then turns to the group. "They're still out there, but they're watching something down the hill."

As Matt leans over again, they all hear another series of gunshots, this time sounding as if it's from a fully automatic rifle. Glass can be heard crashing down behind them as bullets come flying through the air above, and a few of the dogs start whimpering in pain as the gunfire continues. After several seconds the firing finally stops, and the sounds of humans screaming and dogs barking can be heard instead. Then, as suddenly as it all started, the air becomes quiet once again. They all lie there motionless for a minute, waiting for some sort of confirmation that it's all over — but when the sound of crunching glass echoes throughout the small lobby, and the strong scent of cigarettes fill the air, they know that it's only a matter of time before somebody discovers where they're hiding.

CHAPTER 20
ABERDEEN: MARCH 31ST

On the last several steps of the staircase, between the fifth and sixth levels of the hospital, Curtis and Larry are forced to walk on the far right side of the walkway, hoping to avoid stepping in the pools of blood that are covering most of the floor surface. Considering the massive amount that's spilled across the landings and running down the steps, there's absolutely no doubt in Larry's mind that whoever it once belonged to is now dead — it's just not possible for someone to survive that much loss. It appears to have originated at one of the lower floors, where a bloody trail winds its way up the staircase and ends on the sixth floor landing, where it disappears beneath the locked steel door.

"What now?" Curtis whispers, watching Larry quietly and unsuccessfully trying to turn the handle on the door.

"I don't know — I wish someone would answer the radio." Larry tries to peek through the window in the door, but someone has fastened something to the inside of the glass, preventing him from seeing anything but darkness through the thin cracks in the surface of the material. "Maybe I'll try it again, in the off-chance that Mike is still alive."

They switch places, with Curtis standing next to the door as Larry steps behind him and tries the radio one last time. Curtis hears a faint noise, barely audible, coming from somewhere around the door — like a scratching sound against the steel panel of the entry.

"Mike, or Christine, come in... We have the insulin, and we're right outside the door," Larry says into the radio, suddenly noticing the noise himself.

Seeing that the covering over the window is loose on the bottom, Curtis peers through it and sees a speck of light from somewhere on the other side, but otherwise only darkness in the room beyond. When he focuses once again on the glow of light, trying to see what it could possibly be coming from, he sees a quick flash of movement in front of it, and then what looks like someone's face staring back at him. He steps back slightly and shines the flashlight at the window, thinking that he might catch a glimpse of Amanda's evil grin in the small opening — but instead of seeing something, he hears a metallic click coming from the door, and then the handle slowly turns as the doorway opens up a couple of inches.

"Larry, turn the radio down," Curtis says, referring to the low hiss coming from the handset. With his flashlight in one hand and his gun in the other, Curtis uses his foot to open the door the rest of the way, as Larry stands behind him and aims his gun through the opening.

"Careful," Larry whispers. "I can see something moving in there."

Curtis leans forward some, moving the flashlight beam around the room full of scattered papers and jumbled furniture, all of it smeared with streaks and hand prints of blood. As the thick, metallic smell of blood enters his nose, he stops moving for a moment and just listens for any sound at all that might be coming from the area. He hears and feels the sharp howling of wind coming from the hallway that's straight ahead of him, and a low thump coming from some direction that's indiscernible — but it's a miserable sounding whimper that actually attracts his attention, also coming from down the hallway. Looking ahead, he can see the daylight shining in through the windows of the waiting room, and a chair that's sitting in the middle of the corridor with someone in it, facing them. He still can't tell what they look like, but he can see the struggling movements of their body

155

as they try to get up, and the desperate sounds that they're making, as though they've been gagged.

Forcing himself to move, he takes a few steps forward into the room, not aware that Larry isn't following from behind — and as soon as he passes completely through the entryway, he feels someone push him off balance as he falls onto the floor, and the door to the staircase slams shuts. Scanning around the room frantically with the light, he just barely sees a blood-soaked black coat before the flashlight is knocked out of his hands, landing somewhere on the other side of the room with a loud crash, and immersing the entire room into darkness. He aims his gun in the direction of every noise, no matter how minuscule or insignificant, but he's afraid of wasting the few rounds of ammunition he has on him — so he decides instead to scramble to his feet and back up against the wall, hearing at least two sets of footsteps ahead of him and to his right. Larry's voice, dampened by the steel security door, can be heard on his right, yelling at him to open the door — but he's afraid if he moves toward it that it might give away his location to whoever else is in the room.

Knowing that Christine is likely the one tied up in the chair, he listens for a moment, waiting until he hears someone walking into a desk just a little to his left. He fires his gun, hearing them cry out and screaming in pain — and then he hears a gleeful laugh from another direction, coming from a voice that he instantly recognizes. As more footsteps are heard, this time coming toward him from the right, he fires another single gunshot, and again hears a body hitting the floor in agony. He tries to listen closely through the screaming and thrashing around coming from both sides of the room, but he hears absolutely nothing else — until a whisper appears in his right ear, so close that he can feel their breath on his skin.

"Did you think that was me?" Amanda asks coldly, holding a blade to his side.

As soon as the door shuts, trapping him outside on the stairwell landing, Larry immediately grabs the handle and tries to open it again — unsure of whether it closed by accident or on purpose. What distracted him was a voice from somewhere down the staircase — a voice that sounded an awful lot like Christine's.

"Curtis, can you hear me?" he yells, still trying to twist the handle. "Curtis, open the door!"

He stops and listens, hearing nothing but a slight wind coming from down the stairwell shaft — and then he hears the the girl's voice again, this time screaming.

"Curtis, open the damn door!"

With no answer coming, and the screaming continuing downstairs, Larry runs back down the stairs until he reaches the open door of the fifth floor, his mind conflicted on whether he should stay with Curtis or possibly fall for a trap chasing after Christine's voice. As he enters the main corridor and begins walking past the various patient rooms and offices, he can hear Christine yelling at someone to stop, and then call for help in a desperate, sobbing plea. When he reaches an intersection and starts to turn right, still following her pitiful cries, he suddenly hears a loud gunshot coming from upstairs, and then another one only moments later. He starts to turn back, shining his flashlight beam back toward the stairwell again — but as the beam illuminates the doorway at the end of the hall, he sees several dark shadows pass by it, all of them heading up to the top floor. Knowing that there's nothing he can do with a stairwell full of infected, he turns back around and walks carefully toward a large room at the end of the hallway, where the screams are becoming closer. He can see a body lying on the carpet just ahead of him, and several people standing around a heavily damaged door on the far side of the room.

"Christine?" he calls out, aiming his gun from one person to another, before finally keeping his sights set on a woman that's slamming her fists against the glass window next to the door. As soon as the words leave his mouth, all five of them turn around and face him, then quickly return their attention to the office in front of them. "Christine, can you hear me?" he yells out again, looking behind him to make sure someone doesn't sneak up on him.

"Larry, I'm in here!" she yells out, appearing in the window right behind the woman.

"Okay, listen... I need you to duck down on the floor, okay?" After watching her disappear from sight, he waits for a moment to allow her enough time to find cover, then breathes in deeply to clear his head before firing his first shot. The first one strikes the woman in the head, passing clear through her and into the window — shattering the glass onto the floor in both rooms. The next three men each take a couple of shots to take down, none of them even bothering to turn around and stop their assault as the others drop to the floor and writhe around in agony. The fifth person, with one hand on the doorknob, stands still for a moment — their long, gray hair that runs down to the small of their back disguising anything else about the physique of the person. They slowly turn their body toward Larry — and the withered up face of an older woman stares back at him as he sends a barrage of bullets into her torso and shoulder. None of them, however, have any effect on the woman — and after firing several more shots he starts to back up as she takes a few steps toward him, her wounds making a trail of dripping blood behind her as she passes by the counter of the kitchenette.

Hearing footsteps behind him, he turns around and quickly glances at the hallway again, seeing shadows running back and forth on the main corridor — but thankfully, none of them are moving in his direction. Focusing once again on the approaching woman, he reaches into his pocket and grabs another loaded clip and slaps it into place, letting the empty one fall to the floor. Her movements are slow and deliberate, but obviously hostile, slamming her hands onto the countertop repeatedly and screaming incoherent words at him. After waiting patiently for her to get close enough, he carefully aims the pistol at her forehead and pulls the trigger, sending her momentarily to her knees before she finally collapses to the tile.

Noticing his flashlight getting dimmer, and confident that all five of them are dead, he works his way through the waiting room, trying to stay clear of any splattered blood or corpses as he gazes through the window of the office. "Christine, are you okay?" Larry asks, keeping his voice low.

"Are they gone?"

""They're gone, it's safe to come out," he says back, in a voice only slightly louder than a whisper.

Climbing out from underneath the desk, Christine unlocks the door and tries to open it, but it takes both of them to break it free from the jam after being bent out of shape and wedged tightly in the opening. "Amanda is in here somewhere — she's in the hospital..." Christine says, hugging Larry as soon as the door is opened.

"I know, I had a feeling something was wrong when we talked last night."

She starts walking toward the hallway, but Larry grabs her arm and holds her back. "Larry, we need to get out of here before she finds us..."

"I know, but Curtis came with me — and he's still upstairs."

"Shit, I think..." Before finishing her sentence, they both hear a scream coming from somewhere far away, in a voice that definitely sounds like a man in pain. "Was that her or Curtis?"

"Curtis. Do you know if there's another way out of here besides the stairwell?"

"Amanda is getting around in here somehow, but I don't know how she's doing it."

Another scream echoes throughout the hospital, and then more footsteps can be heard coming from their floor, and they're getting closer. Reaching into his pocket, he pulls out another gun and hands it to her. "If you see anyone but a man about my age, kill them."

"I already have a gun, and it still has a few bullets in it — just not enough to take care of all of these people."

"Take it anyway, you're gonna need a lot more than a few bullets."

CHAPTER 21
ABERDEEN: MARCH 31ST

From the other side of the bank counter, Sarah can still hear the crunching of glass as someone walks slowly around the lobby, their footsteps out of rhythm as they limp around the room. Every five or six steps they pause for a few seconds, then continue on again, each time getting closer to where Rachel and the boys are hiding silently next to her — and then she looks up when she hears their breathing above her, each one sounding labored and excruciating. Looking over at Rachel, who's staring back at her with a frightened look on her face, Sarah grips the gun in her hand and holds it straight up into the air, expecting at any moment to see a face appear over the edge. Instead, there's a loud thumping sound, and they feel the floor shake as something falls right behind them.

"Jim, can you hear me?" a deep, gravelly voice says. "Jim — I'm in a credit union at the bottom of the hill, and I think I'm hurt pretty bad." They hear him start to groan as he repositions himself against the counter, and a congested cough after taking a long drag from a cigarette. "Foreign-made piece of shit..."

Sarah starts to get to her feet, then feels Matt try to pull her back down again — but she motions for him to stay put and stands up anyway, cautiously glancing around the lobby first before making her way around to the front of the counter. The man is older, most likely in his 70s, and is leaned up against the front of the teller counter, a cigarette hanging loosely from his mouth, and a radio and pistol lying on the floor next to him. He looks up at her and waves his hand

161

slightly, then looks down at his leg where there's a large red bloodstain on his torn jeans.

"Don't even think about reaching for the gun," she tells him sternly, pointing the gun at his head as she keeps several feet of distance between them.

"Don't worry, I won't touch it," he says in a weakened voice. "Go ahead and kick it away if it makes you feel better, it's out of ammo anyway."

"You're hurt?"

"Yeah, those fucking mutts got me."

"Are you with somebody?"

"I was with another guy, but he didn't make it — neither did the dogs though."

The gun is lying only inches away from his hand, which makes her leery about getting any closer to him — especially when he believes she's alone. "Matt, come on out," she says, backing up a few steps to meet him, then handing the gun to him. "I'm gonna grab his gun — if he moves at all, shoot him in the head."

"Okay, I will," Matt says, trying to make his voice sound older and more mature.

"Have you ever shot someone before, boy?" the man asks, watching Sarah circle around to the other side.

"I wouldn't have handed him the gun if he hadn't..." Sarah answers, kicking both the gun and radio away from him and then picking them both up.

"I need that radio..."

After checking the gun, and seeing that it's out of ammunition just like he said that it was, she looks down and sees the pool of blood that's running across the floor from beneath him. "Judging from the amount of blood you've lost, I don't think the radio will do you much good anyway."

"Is she always this heartless?" the man asks Matt.

"Hey, don't speak to him, speak to me..." She steps back away from him and takes the gun back from Matt, then grabs a nearby chair and places it a good distance away from him. "You came in on that boat?"

"My brother's boat, who'll be looking for me if I don't radio him back — and trust me, you don't wanna meet him."

"Where are you from?"

"Lady, I'm not answering any more of your pointless questions — just give me my damn radio back..."

"And you'll do what, call your brother for help? I'm sorry, but I can't let you do that."

"He'll come looking, I can promise you that."

"Well, it's a damn big city, I'm sure he'll do his best."

"Sarah, just give him the radio," Rachel says, standing behind her in plain view. "We can find somewhere else to hide."

"You can't let me die like this — it's not right," the man says.

"Answer my question — where are you from?" Sarah asks again.

"Coos Bay, Oregon. We left as soon as the weather started clearing up."

"Are you gonna give him the radio now?" Rachel asks.

"Nobody can know we were here..." Sarah starts to say to her.

"I won't tell anybody, I promise," the man says.

"...and he's dead already, whether help arrives or not," she finishes saying, seeing the look of disappointment on Rachel's face.

"Should we at least try to stop the bleeding?" Rachel asks incredulously.

"No, nobody goes near him — he has a knife hidden under his coat, I saw it when he turned toward me." While still keeping an eye on the old man, Sarah walks to the front of the lobby and looks through the broken glass door at the parking lot and street, seeing one human body lying on the sidewalk, and several dead dogs scattered all

163

around it. There's also a trail of blood running across the lot and into the credit union — but there's no sign of anybody else, not even down the street where the bank is located. "You saw us, didn't you? You came here looking for us..."

"We saw the binoculars — we thought you might be healthy." With some effort, he takes a large knife from underneath his coat and throws it onto the floor in front of Rachel. "There, now I'm completely unarmed."

Sarah watches as Rachel kicks the knife across the room, and notices that it has a fair amount of blood on it — then she looks back through the door and sees some movement down another street just a few blocks away, where two more men are walking quickly in their direction. "Matt, check the back door, make sure we can get out."

"Why, what's wrong?"

"Just do as I say, and don't go outside." She steps back, making sure that she's out of sight, then picks the knife up from the floor and kneels down beside the man. "I'm truly sorry, I really am," she says tearfully. Without any further hesitation, she drives the knife deep into his chest, holding his arms down for just a moment to prevent him from fighting.

"What the hell did you do that for?" Rachel yells out.

"Shh, be quiet — there's two men coming this way from the north. We need to get out of here before they find him."

"Why did you kill him though? You didn't have to do that..."

"I didn't kill him, the dogs killed him," she responds, placing the knife back under his coat near the stab wound. "If they find him alive, they'll hunt us down and kill us — or worse. He was as good as dead when he came through that door anyway."

"Where are we going?" Rachel asks, staring at the man's body as Sarah stands up and wipes her hands on her jeans, then fishes something out of one of their bags.

164

"We'll go up to the hospital and find someplace to hide, then wait for them to come out," Sarah answers, standing over the man again. She can tell that Rachel's nerves are still rattled — in truth, they have been since they first met her. "Rachel, don't look at him — just go help Matt and Ben move our things out back. I'll be out in a minute..."

Although Sarah is looking at the man's corpse, she can feel Rachel staring at her for a moment — then she sees her walk around the counter and grab a few of their bags before heading out through the back with Matt and Ben, leaving Sarah alone in the lobby with a dead body, two approaching men, and a set of smaller footprints that have left marks of blood across the carpet and toward the rear exit. She didn't even think about it when she asked for Matt to come out, but when she forces herself to see the room with fresh eyes — like the two men will — it isn't hard to figure out that other people have been here. She walks to the window and glances down the road again, seeing the men about a block and a half away now — then she takes a bottle of lighter fluid from out of her bag, and begins squirting it over the man's body and the surrounding carpet, focusing especially on the areas where Matt's footprints are visible. After nearly emptying the bottle, she takes a wadded up piece of paper and ignites it with a lighter, then drops it onto the floor where the heaviest concentration of fluid was placed. The first flames start out slow, spreading leisurely across the paper — and then after almost going out, the fire reaches the fumes from the lighter fluid, and the flooring is soon covered in fast moving flames that quickly engulf both the stained carpet and the body.

Sarah looks closely at the floor leading to the back door, and is relieved when she doesn't spot any other trace of blood from Matt's shoes. By the time she picks up the remaining bags and heads to the door herself, the room is beginning to fill with foul-smelling smoke, which pours out of the doorway as she exits the building and sees the others waiting for her.

"Did you set the building on fire?" Matt asks.

"I'll explain later — we have to find someplace to hide before they spot us."

"What about up there?" Ben says, pointing at a small shed that's only about a hundred feet away, sitting along a pathway that winds uphill through some woods at the foot of the hospital.

Without saying anything herself, and hearing some commotion in the bank behind them, Sarah motions for the others to keep quiet, then starts up the hill in the direction of the shed, looking back occasionally to see if they're being followed. When they finally reach the shed, which thankfully is unlocked, the smell of filth and rot instantly hits them as they open the door and enter — and when Sarah's eyes finally begin to adjust to the darkness, she sees exactly why it smells so horrible. Besides the two mostly-rotten corpses that are leaned up against the back wall, there's also buckets of human waste and open bottles of urine lying around on the floor. Moving over to a small, mildew-covered window that looks down at the back of the credit union, she can hear the sound of breaking glass beneath her feet as she walks across old syringes and other garbage that's been left over from whoever lived here before.

"Nobody move, and don't touch anything," Sarah whispers, peering through the nearly opaque window at the back of the strip mall below.

"Can I turn the flashlight on, just for a second?" Ben asks.

"No, leave it off — just until these guys go away."

She can see smoke rolling over the roof from the front of the bank, and the noxious black fumes streaming past the rundown shack that they're hiding in, partially obscuring the dreadful smell that surrounds them. In only a few minutes the smoke appears at the back door of the credit union as well, and then the neighboring stores as the inferno quickly spreads throughout the complex. For a moment

166

she worries what Curtis might think if he happens to look down the hill right now, seeing a fire only a few blocks from where he left all of them — but she's afraid to use the radio to contact him, knowing that there's a good chance that he has it turned off anyway, to stay hidden from anybody still lurking inside the hospital walls. That particular anxiety and worry, however, disappears from her mind when she sees the two men run around the corner of the strip mall, and head straight to the closed back door of the bank.

One of the men, who has long, gray hair and a thick beard, is obviously the brother of the man she just killed — although he appears from this distance to be the younger of the siblings. The other is much younger, a young man probably in his late teens or early twenties. The younger of the two is carrying a rifle in his hand, and has two very visible pistols strapped to his hips — while the older one is holding a single handgun in his hand as he opens the door to a wall of smoke and flames. Falling back onto the ground, the brother screams something that Sarah can't quite understand, then picks up a rock and throws it against the building as he continues yelling at the top of his lungs. He stares at the ground for a few minutes, clearly upset from the way his right hand keeps tugging obsessively at his beard, as if he's trying to rip it out — then he stands up and yanks the rifle out of the other guy's hand. At first he simply looks around at the surrounding area, focusing mostly on the pathway through the woods — then he brings the gun up to his chin and looks through the scope, aiming it toward the pathway, and then directly at the shack.

"Does that door have a lock?" Sarah asks quietly, backing away from the window for a moment.

"No, I don't think so — I can't feel one," Rachel answers back, having trouble seeing anything in the darkened space. "What's going on?"

"I think they're coming this way..."

She peeks out of the window again, just long enough to see the two men running up the pathway toward the hospital — and the shack. With her flashlight aimed low, she looks around at the interior, which has little in the way of furniture besides a small twin bed and a couple of old wooden chairs in the corner — and she finally comes to the determination that it's futile to try to hide here. She takes out her gun instead, motioning for the others to stand clear as she steps into the far corner and aims the pistol at the door.

"Check that building, I'm gonna check up the hill..." they hear a voice say from right outside the door, along with a set of footsteps that slowly disappear.

Sarah's hands are shaking horribly as the doorknob slowly turns, and when the door opens and floods most of the shack with light, she notices that the others are still hidden in the shadows, and it's obvious that he doesn't see any of them as he shines his light around the middle of the room. When the light finally reaches her, he calmly points his gun at her head and closes the door behind him — glancing briefly at the others before returning his attention to Sarah.

"If you shoot me, Sam will hear the gunshot, and I can guarantee that you don't want that to happen..." the young man says quietly. He slowly lowers his gun, placing it into one of the holsters on his hip, then he aims the flashlight back at Rachel and the boys. "Listen, we don't have much time, we have to get back to the dock before the others take off without us — but you need to stay quiet until we're gone, otherwise Sam could get all kinds of fucked up ideas in his head."

"We didn't kill him, the dogs killed him..." Sarah says, her voice shaking with fear.

"Frankly, I couldn't give a rat's ass whether you killed him or not, he was an asshole who took up too much room on the boat — but he was also Sam's brother." He opens the door just a crack and looks outside, then turns around again and faces Sarah. "Like I said, stay quiet..." With a quick jerk of the handle, he vanishes through the doorway and slams the door behind him. "Find anything? Yeah, me neither."

The others stay motionless, hearing two sets of footprints on the gravel pathway as they disappear into the distance once again — this time down the hill instead. When the sound is completely gone, Sarah carefully moves over a couple of steps and peeks out of the window again, seeing the two of them rounding the corner of the complex below and out of sight.

"I think they're gone," she whispers. "We should stay here for a while though, just in case they come back again."

"What if he was lying? What if they're planning on coming back?" Rachel asks.

"He wasn't lying, they clearly had us outgunned."

"Where are we gonna go?" Matt asks.

"We'll head up the hill through the woods — I think there's some houses across the street from the hospital."

"Will we be able to see Dad when he comes out?"

"Of course we will, sweetheart," she answers back, hoping that her words sounded more convincing than they felt.

CHAPTER 22
ABERDEEN: MARCH 31ST

The hallway ahead of Larry is getting darker — partly because of his dimming flashlight, but mostly because the sun outside is already beginning to sink lower into the sky, shading the already limited amount of light coming through the windows. With Christine walking silently behind him, he can hear footsteps and voices coming from somewhere ahead of them, all of them moving in the same general direction — the main staircase that connects all six floors of the hospital.

"We're going upstairs?" Christine whispers.

"I can't leave him behind," Larry answers, stopping suddenly when he sees a flash of movement in the next corridor. Muttering a few word of encouragement to himself, he starts walking again, more swiftly than before. When they reach an intersection in the hall, Christine points to the left when Larry stands there for a moment, confused and turned around by the multiple similar hallways surrounding him — but when he begins walking down that path, seeing the stairs and elevator signs just up ahead of them, he also sees a man standing in front of the stairwell door and staring straight ahead toward them.

"Larry..." Christine says quietly, pulling firmly at his coat. "I think he sees us..."

"Yeah, I know he does."

They slow their approach to the man, both of them aiming their guns at him as they creep ahead steadily. Larry is trying to avoid most of the wet blood spilled over the floor, and the obvious drag marks that are leading to the end of the corridor, but he's also trying to keep a close eye on the man in front of them, who still isn't moving aside from the exaggerated chest heaves from his congested breathing.

"Cover your ears," Larry says to Christine, stopping momentarily to aim carefully at the man's head. Standing only about twenty feet away from him, he nearly fires a shot at the man before seeing something in his gaze that Larry finds unsettling. Although he's facing two people, each with a gun pointed right at his head, the man doesn't look the least bit nervous or afraid. In fact, his eyes aren't even looking at either of them — they're focused on something behind them. He turns his head quickly and glances back down the corridor, seeing the outline of someone sneaking up from behind, then he hears Christine screaming as the man in front of the door starts running at the two of them, tackling Larry to the ground just as two quick gunshots go off right next to him. At first he isn't even certain whether it was his own gun that fired the deadly shot, which sends the man to the floor right next to Larry — but when three more shots ring out, he looks up to see Christine firing her gun at the vague outline that's now closing in on them.

Feeling the blood pour down his face from the wound in the man's head, Larry pushes his lifeless corpse away from him and struggles back to his feet, then fires his own gun just once at the approaching figure — slowing him down only slightly as Christine continues to fire rounds into his chest. Finally, after at least seven bullets enter his body, he drops to his knees and starts crawling instead.

"Come on, they're not going anywhere," Larry tells her, as he reaches his hand out and lowers her gun back down to her side, feeling her arms quivering from the fear and adrenaline. "You did good, but we have to save our ammo, okay?"

Seeing her simply nod her head in agreement, Larry turns around

171

and hobbles to the end of the hallway, stopping at the entrance to the stairs where he takes a moment to look through the bloodstained glass at the stairwell beyond it. At first he doesn't see anything but the wall on the other side, but then something streaks past him as he hears loud footsteps coming from the other side of the door. Just a few seconds later, something else passes by, this time slowing down just long enough for Larry to recognize the dark figure as human.

"What're you waiting for?" Christine asks from behind him.

"There's people on the stairs — a lot of them I think."

"How many bullets do we still have?"

"You should have six or seven in the clip," he answers, ejecting the clip from his own gun as he sees yet another person walk by. "I have four more in this one, and then another thirteen in my pocket."

"That's not a lot, is it?"

"Not when it takes seven to take a single man down — no." He shines the light back down the hallway, and sees the man still crawling slowly toward them. "One of us is gonna have to keep an eye on the people coming up the stairs, and the other has to take care of the people ahead of us."

"I guess I'm watching the people behind us?"

"Yeah, it's the least dangerous — are you ready?"

With Christine nodding again, Larry opens the door just a crack and shines his light through the doorway, seeing nobody in either direction, but hearing a lot of commotion from up above. Feeling the cold breeze of fresh air rushing up the steps from below again, Larry steps through the door and starts climbing the first few stairs — then hears the door behind them slam shut, and then a click as the lock traps them on the other side. After another few steps, he sees the bare feet of someone lying down, their body twitching slightly as the people ahead of them trip over the nearly lifeless body in their haste to climb the stairs. By the time Larry realizes how many are packed

172

onto the steps ahead of them, blocking any possible way forward, the closest man turns around and notices him, then reaches out with his right arm and takes a swipe at Larry's head — but misses him by a wide margin. Seeing the man trying to steady himself against the railing, Larry backs up and motions for Christine to do the same, until both of them are standing in front of the fifth floor entrance once again.

He hears keys jingling, and looks down to see Christine fumbling through a large set of them. "Forget it, there's no time," he whispers. "We need to get as far down the stairs as we can."

"Why don't you just shoot him?" she asks, seeing the man rounding the corner and stumbling with nearly every step.

"The whole fucking staircase up there is full of them. If we fire a gun in here we'll have the entire building chasing us..."

With only a few steps separating them from the guy, Larry motions for Christine to keep going down, trying the fourth and third floors and finding them locked as well — until they finally reach the second floor landing. As soon as he grabs hold of the handle and turns it, feeling the mechanism open up and release the door from the jam, Larry breathes in a deep sigh of relief as the door swings open and reveals another dark hallway in front of him. The feeling of relief, however, turns out to be short lived — and as sound of a metal object is heard falling from somewhere ahead of him, and then the intense heat and deafening roar of an explosion quickly fills the corridor around him, sending his body through the air and back into the staircase behind him.

For a moment, the only thing he can sense is a quick flashing of lights in front of his face, and the sickening smell of human flesh burning — a scent that he's become all too accustomed to smelling.

"Larry — please wake up..."

Feeling a light slap on his face, Larry opens his eyes to the worst headache of his life, and sees a bright beam of light aimed directly at his face — something that doesn't necessarily help the pain.

"Come on, we have to get some of this stuff out of the way..." Christine says, shining the light at a mess of various objects surrounding them.

When he sees the chairs and oxygen bottles stacked up in front of the door next to them, Larry immediately recognizes the doorway as the exit to the main lobby of the hospital — the one that he and Curtis couldn't get through when they first arrived. As Christine starts pitching chairs onto the steps behind them, he grabs onto the bottom step and tries to lift himself to his feet, feeling every muscle in his body screaming in pain as he struggles to a sitting position. Compared to the floor, the air even a few feet up is filled with strange-smelling fumes that cause him to cough, which only exacerbates the pain in his chest, and sends a series of loud sounds up the otherwise silent staircase.

"Try not to breath too deeply — I think the air is pretty toxic," Christine says quietly. She's still trying to clear the landing in front of the door, doing her best to throw the objects as far up the steps as possible.

"Where's the guy?"

"He's dead — the flames caught him on fire."

"How did I get down here?"

"I dragged you down. Can you walk?"

"I think so — I'm kind of light-headed."

He looks up and sees her jerking on the door, opening it a foot or so, and then chucking oxygen bottles through the doorway to make more room around them.

"You might wanna be careful with those bottles, or we'll end up with another explosion," Larry says, as he manages to get to his feet and step clumsily through the remaining debris, until he's standing behind Christine next to the door. She pushes against it with all of her weight, and the mess of junk behind it slowly gives way to the effort — allowing the two of them to squeeze through it and into the crisp, clean air of the ground-floor hospital lobby. Christine holds onto his arm and tries her best to help him along toward the exit doors, but as soon as they reach the first set of chairs, Larry pulls away from her and collapses into one of them.

"Larry, we have to get out of here," Christine says in an almost panicked tone.

"Curtis is still in here somewhere, I'm not leaving without him."

"The hospital is on fire, Larry — and Curtis is dead, we both heard those screams."

"That doesn't prove that he's dead..."

"Maybe not — but this entire building is going up in flames, and we're both gonna end up dead if we stay here."

He closes his eyes for a moment, attempting to control the throbbing pains in his head every time his heart pounds in his chest. Besides his own pulse, and the heavy breathing of Christine next to him, he begins hearing other sounds as well, coming from elsewhere in the hospital. There's a low rumble, and sounds of distressed steel and wood as the building creaks and moans above them. In his mind, he retraces the steps that he and Curtis took to get to the top floor, weaving through the dark hallways and twisting stairwells — and his heart sinks as he comes to the realization that it's impossible to make it through before the fire fully engulfs at least one of the floors, making their safe return completely impossible. He opens his eyes again and sees Christine standing over him, pleading with him to stand up.

175

"Do you need help? I can get a wheelchair if you need one," she says, pointing to a row of them beside the exit.

"No, I'm fine." Feeling his hips and back giving out as he gets to his feet, he manages to slowly make his way to the open doors, with Christine walking next to him and helping to hold him upright. The air outside feels good against his skin, but it also causes him to cough deeply, which drops him to his knees when they reach the sidewalk next to the parking lot. Christine kneels down and looks him in the eyes, placing her hand on his shoulder in an attempt to calm him down. Then she rises up again, pulling her gun out of her pocket and aiming it across the parking lot as his breathing normalizes again. He turns his head and sees someone running in their direction, and he grabs onto Christine's pants and tugs on them gently as soon as he realizes who the person is. "Wait, don't shoot..."

"Who is that?" she responds, still aiming the gun.

"It's Sarah, Curtis' wife..."

CHAPTER 23
ABERDEEN: MARCH 31ST

Feeling the sharp tip of Amanda's blade against his side, Curtis freezes for a moment as the young girl slowly applies more pressure, expecting at any moment for her to thrust it deep into his kidney — but then he hears something hit the wall next to him, thrown by someone on the other side of the room. He feels the blade ease up just a bit as Amanda ducks away from the flying object, and Curtis uses the distraction as an opportunity to knock her hand away and then jump back, firing his gun twice in her direction. He still can't see anything unless it's right in front of him, but right after he fires the pistol, he hears a swishing sound as her knife cuts through the air, the steel coming so close to his face that he can feel the rush of wind. On the very last swing, which he partially blocks with his forearm, she finally makes contact with his right cheek, slicing it open as he falls backward onto the floor with the hallway and waiting room directly behind him. Not knowing where she is, and now sitting on the cold floor with only a gun and no flashlight, he crawls backward into the hallway where he can see a small amount of light coming through the windows, then climbs back to his feet and stares into the darkness.

With the hall ahead of him faintly illuminated, he takes another step back, then lightly touches his face where the blood is beginning to run down to his chin. He doesn't see any sign of Amanda in the room ahead of him, but he does see someone else struggling to crawl across the floor toward him, the older woman's face and arms barely visible in the darkness — but then she stops suddenly and gasps for

177

air, looking up at Curtis with a desperate look in her eyes. In only a few seconds the expression on her face goes completely blank, and Curtis sees the life disappear from her completely as her body is slowly dragged back into the darkness.

He hears a sickening noise from that direction, and he can only assume that it's Amanda plunging her knife repeatedly into the woman's lifeless body — but when he aims his gun at the sound and starts to squeeze the trigger, he stops himself at the last second, figuring that any blind shot is only a waste of ammunition. Instead, he keeps walking backward toward the outside light of the waiting room, forgetting about the person tied to a chair in the middle of the corridor until he trips over them and sends them both crashing to the floor. He immediately scrambles to get up, then realizes when he gets to his knees that the gun was thrown from his hand. Looking at the floor around him, he glances quickly at the person who's tied up — an extremely old-looking man that's very near death, virus or otherwise. Then he spots the gun, which is lying underneath a chair about ten feet away. He starts to quickly crawl in that direction, over a rain-soaked carpet that has pieces of glass covering it, then he hears a noise from behind him just as he reaches for the pistol — but as soon as his skin makes contact with the rubber grip, he feels a sharp pain in his hand as Amanda's blade pierces through the top of his wrist and into the tendons and ligaments, causing Curtis to scream out in agony. He rips his arm away and grabs for the knife with his other hand, but she pulls it out too quickly and slices it against the side of his head just above the ear. After yelling out in pain again, he curls over onto his back in a defensive position, then watches as Amanda backs off for a moment, taking the time instead to bend down and pick the gun up — aiming it at him for just a moment before lowering it back down to her side.

"You tried to kill me, Curtis," the girl says, taking the clip out of the gun and looking at the bullets that are still left. "You tried to strangle me with your bare hands, when you could've simply shot me and ended it right there. Why did you do that?" Slapping the clip back into the gun, she tosses the entire thing out of the broken window, then drives her knife across the back of a chair, tearing a large hole in the upholstery. "Why didn't you put me out of my misery quickly instead of trying to choke me to death?"

"Amanda, I'm sorry, I shouldn't have done that..." He sits up, then starts to stand up, but she takes a quick step forward and backs him onto the floor again. "We can both go our own way, there's no reason to kill each other."

"Where are the others?" she asks, her tone suddenly more threatening. "Where is Ben?"

"Ben is dead — they're all dead..." he answers back, suddenly conscious of the fact that his family's lives will be decided in the next few moments.

"I know they aren't dead, Curtis — they're probably somewhere close."

He slowly starts to stand up again, knowing that her reaction will be to attack him again — and when she does, he swings his arm at the knife, unfazed by the pain caused when his forearm hits the tip of it. The blow knocks the girl down, and sends the knife flying across the room where it lands next to the wall of windows that look out over the city. As Curtis glances at his newest wound, Amanda struggles back to her feet and rushes toward the knife — but just as she extends her arm and begins to bend down, he runs up behind and picks up her small, lightweight frame and throws her through the window opening and onto the roof below, then falls back onto the floor in exhaustion.

He lies there for a minute, wondering if his sudden weakness is a sign that he's bleeding more severely than he realized, and whether he has enough energy to get out of the hospital by himself. Hearing raindrops against the windows, and feeling the spray of mist coming through the jagged opening above him, he grabs onto a nearby chair and pulls himself to his feet, then staggers into the closest exam room along the hallway. With his head finally beginning to clear, he feels his way through the cabinets and manages to find some bandages and tape, then he walks back to the waiting room and sits down in front of one of the intact windows, intending to use the fading sunlight to help him cover the wounds that are still actively bleeding — but after trying to soak up enough blood to see the lacerations more clearly, he ends up just wrapping the areas with gauze and taping them tightly to his body.

Standing up again, he starts to walk over to the window that Amanda was pushed through, to convince himself that she's actually gone, and that this nightmare is finally over — but after only a couple of steps he hears a knocking from somewhere down the hallway, a knock that sounds friendlier than the aggressive pounding that they normally hear from the infected. He limps down the hallway, flinching every time his swollen ankle makes contact with the floor, and wishing that he still had a radio to find out whether this mystery person is Larry. When he reaches the end of the corridor and enters the reception desk where the stairwell door is located, the knocking suddenly stops, and the only sound that can be heard is a light scratching from somewhere on the other side of the room.

"Larry?" he calls out, standing still for a moment. "Larry, is that you?" Hearing nothing else, he takes a few steps forward again and kicks something with his right foot, sending whatever it is tumbling ahead of him in the darkness. He feels around on the floor with his foot, too afraid of what he might find to use his hands — and eventually finds the object again. The moment he touches it, he recognizes it as the flashlight he'd dropped earlier — and much to his surprise, it still works when he pushes the button and illuminates the room around him.

Besides the dead woman on the floor beside him, he also sees a man lying face-first on the other side of the room, a man that he's quite certain he unknowingly shot — and next to him is yet another woman, her body still moving slightly as she hopelessly grabs for the desk in front of her. As he shines the light back at the door, he hears the knocking continue again, this time somewhat more forceful than before.

"Christine, are you there?" he yells out, grabbing onto the handle and feeling no sign of movement from the other side. Seeing the light growing dimmer by the minute, he braces himself against the floor and then slowly turns the handle, opening the door just a couple of inches. "Larry, Christine, is that you?" he yells at the gap — but instead of hearing a response, he sees an arm thrust through the doorway and hold onto the jamb, then feels someone pushing hard as they try to force the door the rest of the way open. Whoever is on the other side is either inhumanly strong, or there's more than one person — and as his feet begin to slide backward, he sees another arm reach through beside the first one, this one badly scarred from a fire sometime in the past. He looks around the room frantically, searching for something within reach that he can use to push the people back through — and then he suddenly feels himself flying through the air, as a rush of hot gasses and flames enter the room and ignite some of the furniture and papers lying around on the desks.

Against the wall next to the hallway, with his body pressed up against a file cabinet, Curtis squints as he looks through the smoke and haze that have filled the room, and he sees several people coming through the open doorway from the stairs — all of them entirely engulfed in flames. After quickly checking himself over, he stands up again and starts backing away from the room. The fire is still burning in the stairwell, but it's beginning to die down — but the same can't be said about the reception area. Seeing no other way out, Curtis turns around and hobbles quickly down the corridor until he's standing in front of the broken window, feeling the crisp, cold outside air against his face. He was hoping to find some sort of escape route fastened to the side of the building, but he sees a strange mixture of both good and bad news instead. While there is no platform outside, the drop is only about fifteen or twenty feet to the next rooftop below — and while that's good news for his escape, it also means that Amanda didn't fall nearly as far as he hoped that she would, and he doesn't see any sign of her body that would prove her demise. He does see a few others that have obviously been there for a while though, each of them riddled with gunshot wounds.

Since the edges of the window frame are still lined with broken pieces of sharp glass, Curtis breaks away as much of the debris as possible, then takes a cushion from one of the couches on the side of the waiting area and places it onto the bottom of the frame. The heat from the raging fire behind him is becoming uncomfortable, and by the time he steadies himself into a seated position on top of the cushion, the flames have already begun to spread across the floor along the hallway, and he can see smoke billowing from the air vents in the ceiling — something that he's quite certain is from another part of the building. With the flashlight in his hand, he takes a few deep breaths and then slides off of the window frame, landing much more softly on the tar-covered roof than he anticipated.

As soon as he gets back to his feet, which are becoming increasingly sore, Curtis looks around the nearly flat rooftop for any signs of Amanda, but the only thing he can find besides the other corpses is a small trail of blood that leads over to the western edge of the building — and a small black shoe that's lying only a few feet from his own landing position. He can see smoke rising from the window that he just jumped out of, and even more smoke from a building just down the hill from the hospital — but when he looks to the east, past the blackened ruins of downtown Aberdeen, he can see a massive amount of smoke and ash rising into the sky from far away. It's hard to judge exactly what distance it is, but it doesn't appear to be close to the city, or possibly even the county. The area of the sky that it takes up is immense though, stretched both north and south for miles.

Not seeing his gun anywhere in sight, he turns toward the west and follows the blood to the edge of the roof, then climbs down a ladder that leads to a fire escape, seeing drops of blood on the steel steps all the way down to the pavement below. Once his feet are on solid ground, he loses any trace of blood from his victim, which has been diluted in the wet asphalt and deep potholes of the pavement. What he can see though, is a trail of muddy footprints on the other side of a flower bed, which he follows down to the entrance road of the hospital — where he can also see, still several blocks in front of him, a small figure limping along a sidewalk at the bottom of the hill.

Feeling aches and pains throughout his entire body, he walks down the hill as fast as his legs and feet will allow, never losing sight of the girl until she turns to the left and heads east toward Olympia. When he reaches the same intersection, with the rain now pouring down on his already-soaked coat and bleeding scalp, he looks to the east where Amanda was headed, and catches just a glimpse of her as she disappears behind a dip in the road. For a moment, he actually considers following her, since he knows that part him won't ever be able to fully rest until she's put down for good. Then he thinks about his family, who are still waiting for his return — and Larry, who he hopes got out of the hospital with Christine before the fire broke out.

He watches for another few minutes, seeing her reappear several blocks away, a tiny speck that's only barely visible to the naked eye — then he turns and starts walking south, toward the bank that's hopefully kept his family safe for the past several hours.

CHAPTER 24
ABERDEEN: MARCH 31ST

Although it's now completely obscured by a mass of black clouds rolling in from the west, Sarah can tell that the sun is beginning to fall quickly toward the Pacific — and that makes the chances of finding Curtis before nightfall that much more grim.

After a mostly sleepless night, she woke up this morning with a bad feeling in the pit of her stomach, like she somehow knew that her life at the end of this day would be unrecognizable from when it started. She tried to explain the apprehension to Curtis before the family left South Aberdeen, telling him that she wasn't at all in favor of the family splitting up if that's what Larry had in mind — but she also knew that it was highly unlikely that he would listen to a word of it, especially if he thought the belief was somehow tied to psychic powers on her part. Both of them are skeptics of the supernatural in general, but while she believes in such things as instinctual presentiment, where people have a certain level of intuition that's programmed into our DNA from birth — Curtis believes in absolutely none of it, instead choosing to believe that life is a random set of circumstances with no possible way to predict the future.

As she stands in front of a living room window, looking across the street at the smoke and flames spreading rapidly throughout the hospital, she can't help but feel anger toward Curtis for not listening to her, and for leaving her and the boys to fend for themselves in this godforsaken world. Part of her wants to believe that he's still alive, that he somehow escaped his encounter with Amanda — but the rest of her is already becoming numb, a parental instinct that somehow finds a way to move forward despite the unpleasant hardships of life. Thankfully, the boys didn't get to witness the hysteria that she unleashed on Larry when he and Christine emerged from the hospital — and even now, distracted by Rachel in one of the bedrooms, they still have no idea just how dire the situation is.

Even from here, separated by two large parking lots, she can hear the roar of the inferno as it fills the surrounding neighborhood with a thick layer of smoke and raining embers. The house they've chosen has a direct view of the hospital entrance, and is located in a housing community that looks virtually untouched. Food is still sitting in the cupboards and pantry, the beds are tidily made in each of the three bedrooms, and there's a dining room table that has a full setting arranged for a family of five — including one chair obviously meant for a baby or small toddler. Something else they found useful was a pair of shoes in one of the bedrooms, which are only a half size bigger than what Ben normally wears.

Pictures are also hanging on the walls, leaving nothing to the imagination as to who once lived here. They looked happy, and healthy, complete with unexceptional sports trophies hung proudly on the fireplace mantle for everyone to see — and yet their fate was the same as everyone else. When they first arrived, Rachel found all five members of the family lying flat out on their backs on the back lawn, every one of them badly decomposed and picked apart by birds and rodents. Glancing at a family portrait that's sitting next to her on the window sill, Sarah reaches over and places it face-down and out of her sight — thinking of it as a painful reminder that she had that same happiness only hours ago.

Behind her, she can hear Larry snoring on the couch as he sleeps through his possible concussion. Christine is sitting beside him, looking worried as she watches every movement that he makes, even going so far as to check his breathing whenever his snoring stops for more than a few seconds. In Sarah's eyes, it would make sense for her to be upset with Christine, considering that it was her that Curtis and Larry were trying to rescue when all of this happened — but for whatever reason, she can't help but like the girl. It might be the fact that she's alone, just like her daughter might be somewhere — or it might be that she seems perfectly normal despite the horrendous things that she's already experienced in her young life. Whichever it is, she seems to have formed a bond with Larry, and looking at them now, you'd swear that she was looking after her own father.

"I think he'll be okay now — why don't you get some sleep yourself..." Sarah whispers to Christine.

The teen stands up and stretches, then slumps down into a chair beside Sarah and looks out across the parking lot. "Do you mind if I sit here? I'm not really tired."

"No, I don't mind — but you look exhausted."

"Have you seen anybody out there?" Christine asks her, ignoring the comment.

"No, just a couple of cats." Out of the corner of her eye, Sarah looks over at Christine and notices the incredibly short and mangled hair on her head. She would never say anything, but it looks horrible, although it's probably no worse than her own — but she also wonders how long it's been since the girl has had a bath or a decent meal, and not something out of a cold soup can that she consumed without any utensils. "Have you been on the road since the beginning?"

"My dad and I stayed at home until my mom died," Christine replies.

"She died of the virus?"

"No, she had cancer."

"I'm sorry to hear that — that must have been difficult..." She sees her simply nod in agreement, as she continues to stare out the

186

window. "Did your family isolate itself from the virus early on?"

"Not really — I kept going to school until they closed it. We didn't really see any sign of it in our town until it was too late."

"Did anyone else live through it?"

"Yeah, some people lived through it, but they became like all of these others."

"Kind of like zombies, huh?"

"No, they're worse than that — zombies aren't real." Christine spots another pack of dogs on the far side of the parking lot, heading north and away from the burning hospital. This one looks smaller than the last, but all of them are large breeds — which is probably the only size of dog that's survived all of this. "What about you? Did you stay away from everybody?" Christine asks.

"No, we didn't — but somehow our entire family managed to stay healthy. That seems like more than just a coincidence, doesn't it?"

Christine can hear the dogs barking in the distance, and notices that Sarah heard them too. After hearing what they just went through, she can't blame her for being wary of the noise, especially when her husband is still out there somewhere. "With all of these dogs running around, it's a wonder that there's any infected left in the city."

"Were you there when Beth died?" Sarah asks her quietly, her voice barely audible.

"Both of us were."

"That must have been horrible for Larry..."

"Yeah, but it was bound to happen eventually," Christine says coldly, drawing a curious gaze from Sarah. "This world isn't right for everybody — and especially not for someone like her."

Sarah is taken aback by the comment, and her first instinct is to defend the person that she grew so close to over the past several months — but she also can't entirely disagree with her. Beth seemed strong-willed and even callous at times, seemingly unaffected by the cruel injustices around them — but she also knows that the tough exterior that she displayed to everyone around her was beginning to show some cracks shortly before she died, and her lapses in judgment were growing more frequent with every passing day. All of them have their breaking point, where the constant stress of surviving the plague, while at the same time being hunted by the infected, strips them of their sanity — and Beth, having already lost her husband, was already closer to the edge than the rest of them.

"We haven't really checked this house for supplies yet, have we?" Sarah asks her, more as a distraction than anything. As much as she appreciates the company, she's not really in the mood for it.

"Just briefly — was there something you were looking for?"

"Just set anything useful on the dining room table, and we'll figure out what we can take with us when we leave. Non-perishable food, weapons, matches, those small propane tanks like you use in a lantern, batteries — whatever you think we might use."

"Are we gonna stay here for a while?"

"Until we find Curtis, and Larry recovers well enough to move."

"I'm sure we'll find him," Christine says, as she stands up and starts to leave the room.

"Christine..." Sarah calls out, stopping her just as she heads into the hallway. "Larry said that you guys heard Curtis upstairs, but he didn't tell me what he was saying..."

"We couldn't understand it, we're not even sure it was him."

"Larry said he recognized his voice. Did he sound angry, or hurt?"

"Honestly, you couldn't really tell. I'm not sure what Larry told you, but he took a pretty good blow to the head when we came out of that place."

As she makes her way down the hallway, Christine wonders whether it was a good idea to lie to Sarah like that — but the relieved look on her face afterward was certainly a welcome sight, even if it only lasts for a short while. It's true that they couldn't understand what was being said upstairs, but that's only because the things they heard were screams of agony, and they were clearly coming from Curtis according to Larry — but she doesn't see the point in traumatizing the poor woman any more than necessary, especially over something that may or may not have happened in that hospital.

Figuring that any weapons would probably be in the master bedroom, she walks to the end of the short hallway and enters a good-sized room that looks as though it's never been touched by human hands — aside from the messed up blankets and sheets on the bed that is. Otherwise, the room is pristine, with knickknacks sitting on shelves throughout the space, and a perfectly aligned row of shoes placed neatly in front of a pair of mirrored closet doors in the corner. Clearly, one of the people that lived here was a neat freak — but one thing they weren't, was a gun fanatic. After going through all of the drawers and closet shelves, throwing everything haphazardly onto the bed with only a small amount of guilt for having ruined the perfect order — she finally gives up on finding anything that even resembles a weapon, and continues onto the next door along the hallway instead. Room after room, she searches through every box, drawer, and cupboard, finding absolutely nothing of use aside from the large amount of canned food still sitting in the cabinets and pantry.

Then a vision suddenly flashes into her mind, of the family spread out so peacefully onto the lawn — and one of them with a bullet hole that can still be seen, despite the horrible decomposition present. She glances at Sarah and Larry as she passes through the living room, and then at Rachel and the boys, who are all fast asleep in the back bedroom that sits by itself. Not wanting to disturb any of them, she quietly opens the sliding back door in the dining room and steps out onto the back patio. The family, or what's left of them, is resting about halfway across the yard, near a small vegetable garden that's now full of weeds and volunteer plants that have reseeded themselves back into the soil. Lying just a few feet away from the first body, she can see a handgun on the gravel pathway next to the garden beds, sitting fully exposed to the downpour of rain that's coming down. She tries not to look at the bodies as she approaches them and picks up the gun, plucking part of the barrel from the wet mud and noting how much rust is covering both it and the cylinder of the revolver. Then she tries to open it, curious as to how many bullets might be left — but seemingly every moving part on it is now frozen in place with rust and decay.

Disappointed, she looks out at the rest of the lawn and sees that the entire place is surrounded with a tall chain-link fence — and after studying the perimeter of it for a few minutes, she suddenly notices a young man standing on the other side of the barrier, watching her every move as his hands grip the heavy wire. All of the men these days, healthy or not, have facial hair that gets longer by the day, and hair on their scalps that's even longer — but the man staring at her from the other side of the fence clearly had long hair even before the outbreak. He starts beating on the wire, then pacing back and forth as his state of mind becomes agitated — which prompts Christine to back up toward the house again, still holding onto the rusty revolver. A few moments later, as she nearly trips while stepping back up onto the concrete patio, the man begins screaming at the top of his lungs, his fists still beating violently against the chain-link — and by the time she opens the sliding door again and closes the curtains behind her, she sees another figure joining the man.

"What were you doing out there?" Rachel asks her, standing in the doorway of the spare bedroom. "I've been looking for you

190

everywhere..."

"I thought there might be a gun out there," Christine answers, her voice shaking with fear. "Why were you looking for me?"

"Sarah is afraid that Curtis might be headed back to the bank, so I volunteered to go look for him." She looks down at the pitiful excuse for a gun that Christine is carrying, then takes it from her trembling hand and sets it on the table next to them. "I was wondering if you wanted to come with me..."

Christine looks over at Sarah sitting in the next room, and sees the desperation in her eyes — but she also sees the darkening skies outside the window as the sun sinks deeper into the west. "It's getting kind of late, isn't it?" she whispers.

"It's not very far away — just down the hill a bit." She sees Christine nod nervously, then walk past her and into the living room, where she picks up a gun and holster from the floor next to the couch. "Were you gonna tell me who's yelling out there?"

"A guy who saw me — but there's a fence in the way," Christine replies, her sleep-induced mind forgetting about the second man.

Rachel opens the curtains just a crack, and sees a single man standing quietly next to the fence. "You're okay to stay here alone?" she asks Sarah, walking back into the living room.

"I'm not alone, I have Matt and Ben — and Larry," Sarah says, still looking out at the hospital, which is beginning to cave in on itself as the fires spread throughout the entire group of buildings. "You guys should leave right away, it's gonna be dark soon."

"Are you ready?" Rachel asks Christine, who's standing next to her with bleary eyes.

"Yeah, I'm ready."

"Keep your radio handy, okay?" Rachel says to Sarah, as Christine opens the front door and starts walking down the pathway to the street. "Oh, and there's a guy out back, but he's on the other side of a big fence — so you shouldn't have any trouble."

"Just one guy?" Sarah asks.

"Yeah," she answers back, leaving the house. "Be sure to lock this behind us..."

"Okay, I will. And thanks, Rachel, I can't even begin to tell you how grateful I am..."

She watches the door close, and the two women as they cross the street and head out across the hospital parking lot. It only takes them a few minutes to disappear behind the brush at the top of the hill, and then the scene in front of her turns static again, with only the flames of the fire moving in the distance. She's aware that there's no longer a reason to keep an eye out for Curtis, since he obviously won't be coming out of its doors now that it's fully engulfed — but with Larry still snoring next to her on the couch, and the boys asleep in the other room, she figures that it doesn't hurt to watch their surroundings anyway.

Picking up her gun and radio, she walks over to the kitchen and grabs a bag of saltine crackers, then turns around to head back into the living room — but she hears a faint ticking sound coming from somewhere behind her, and she turns back around and faces the sliding door, listening for the sound to repeat itself. Hearing nothing, she walks to the door and slides the curtains open just enough to see through them, and she sees the man that Rachel was talking about, still standing motionless against the fence. She closes the curtain again, then heads back into the living and sits down in the chair, opening the package of stale crackers from the plastic wrapper as she looks back at the parking lot.

Then she hears the sound again, this time with a scratching sound along with it. Facing the back door again, with her hand gripping the pistol, she nearly screams when there's suddenly a knocking against the glass — hitting the door hard enough that Matt comes staggering out of the bedroom beside the dining area.

"What's going on?" he asks.

"Go get your brother," Sarah tells him. "And grab the other gun..."

CHAPTER 25
ABERDEEN: MARCH 31ST

Between the downpour of rain in the city and the splitting headache from the gash on his head, Curtis doesn't even notice the numerous dead dogs that are scattered on the street until he nearly walks into one. Once he does though, he stops and looks around carefully, counting at least nine of the animals in the vicinity of the intersection, and the body of one man whose throat has been ripped out — presumably by the same dogs. The scene by itself, as horrific as it is, doesn't necessarily bother him all that much, but the fact that it happened only a few blocks from where he left his wife and kids is worrisome to say the least. He also sees what's left of a burning strip mall on the other side of the street, but all that's left are a few brick walls and the parking lot out front.

After checking the man for weapons or a radio, and finding that his pockets are remarkably empty, he begins walking further into the downtown area where the bank is located, his legs burning from the abuse they've endured over the last few days. The sun is still barely visible in the sky to the west, but he can already see a couple of people walking down the street by the harbor — both of them clearly infected from the awkward way that they walk, like every joint in their body is inflamed and painful. He can see someone else as well, lying motionless and face-down on the sidewalk just past the bank.

Sensing that something isn't right, Curtis carefully makes his way down the sidewalk, keeping his body as close to the buildings as possible until he reaches the first window in the front of the bank. At first he only listens, hearing a fair amount of clatter from inside — but after a few minutes of hearing no voices or anything he recognizes, he looks through the window and sees a shopping cart parked in front of the open bank vault, but there are no people anywhere in sight. He watches for a few more minutes, then finally sees a gray-haired older man emerge from the vault with bags in each hand. After the man re-enters the safe, Curtis sneaks over to the entrance and slips inside, glancing over at the man lying on the sidewalk as he passes by, who looks deceased from the amount of blood running from his body and into the gutter.

As soon as Curtis enters the building, the old man comes out from the safe once again and places more items into the cart, completely unaware that the front door still hasn't closed entirely. Curtis hides behind a desk and looks around the rest of the bank, seeing no sign of Sarah, the kids, or Rachel — and certainly no sign of Larry or Christine. As far as he can tell, he's the only other person in the building besides this old guy — a man who at first appears perfectly normal, judging purely from his mannerisms and fluid movement. There's still something that doesn't seem normal about him though, besides the fact that he appears to be stealing piles of cash that now has as much value as a ream of typing paper. It's not until the man turns in Curtis' direction that he sees the fresh blood splattered across his face and the front of his clothing, and the two handguns resting in holsters on his hips. He stays there, crouched down impatiently on the opposite side of the lobby, and waits for the man to enter the vault one last time before moving quickly across the room. Hearing metal clanging from inside, he throws his weight against the thick, reinforced vault door and closes it, muting the screams from inside to little more than a whisper.

Paying no attention to the noises coming from inside the safe, Curtis wedges one of the desks between the door and the wall

195

alongside of it, trapping the man and his guns in what he hopes is a bulletproof cage — with only a small crack on one side exposing the innards of the safe. Behind him, filled to the brim with canvas bags and metal safe deposit boxes, is the shopping cart that the man was loading up. Although some of it is cash just like he thought, most of it appears to be personal items that were stored inside the boxes — like jewelry and gold coins, and even a few unloaded pistols. He has absolutely no interest in the jewelry and cash, but he does slip the pistols into one of the bags and sets it on the desk — then he searches the entire rest of the bank for any sign of his family, but finds nothing. The only hopeful thing about the situation is the fact that their bags are also missing — but without a single clue left behind as to where they've gone to, finding them in this city could prove to be both difficult and dangerous.

Feeling discouraged and frustrated, he walks outside onto the sidewalk again and looks around at the nearby buildings and streets, hoping to see either one of his family members, or a message of some sort that might lead him in the right direction. All he sees, however, is another small group of people, looking weak and moving slowly to the east. He heads back inside again and picks up the bag of guns from the desk, then spots an assault rifle leaned up in the corner of the lobby, complete with a scope. Placing the bag onto his shoulder, he picks the rifle up and pops the clip out, seeing what looks like a full magazine of ammunition inside. Ready to move on, he looks over at the bank vault and wonders if he should be feeling at all guilty about leaving the guy locked up with no food or water — but regardless of whether he should feel something, he also knows that the man inside poses a threat to him, and for that reason alone, there's really nothing he can do to help the guy out.

As Curtis starts to leave, the old man begins yelling something again, this time in a voice that sounds more calm and rational.

"You wanna repeat that?" Curtis says loudly, leaning in close to the door. "I didn't quite catch it."

"I said..., are you looking for two women and a couple of boys?"

Feeling as though his heart is about to beat out of chest, Curtis yells back, more loudly this time. "Yes, I am — have you seen them?"

An evil, hoarse laugh comes through the thin crack beside the door. "Yeah, in fact I have — they're in here with me right now. A little rough around the edges, but they'll be okay."

A million thoughts race through Curtis' mind as he tries to figure out how to get his family out safely, but every one of them involves opening the door. There's a possibility that the man is lying, either about them being in there at all, or the fact that they're still okay — but at this point, he really has no choice but to trust him.

"Listen, we're just passing through, we don't want to hurt anybody," Curtis says, checking to make sure there's a round in the chamber of the rifle. "I'll open the safe, and we'll be on our way — does that sound reasonable to you?"

"Sounds good to me — as long as you leave my shit alone."

Curtis drops the bag with the pistols back onto the desk, then readies the rifle as his foot pushes the desk off to the side. As soon as the door is clear, he steps back and aims the gun, feeling the stab wound on his wrist begin to throb as his hand grips the handle. "Go ahead and push it open!"

Little by little, the vault starts to open, and an older man that stands several inches taller than Curtis slowly emerges with his left hand raised in the air, and the right hand still hidden behind the door. "Drop my rifle, and your wife won't get shot — okay?" the man says.

"Drop yours and I won't put a bullet in your head," Curtis says, his voice shaking horribly.

"You're not gonna shoot me," the man replies, laughing again. "The safety is on..."

Curtis quickly squeezes the trigger, but nothing happens. As he glances down at the side of the rifle, the man picks up an office chair next to him and throws it toward Curtis, then rushes toward him and grabs the rifle — wrestling it out of Curtis' arms before finally striking him over the head with it. Curtis' legs give out from underneath him as he crumples to the floor, and the room starts spinning as the man stands over him with the rifle aimed at his head.

"By the way, I lied, your family isn't in there — but you're gonna help me find them..."

As Rachel and Christine make their way down the hill, taking a different path than earlier in the day, both of them are a bit dismayed when they see a bat flittering around in the sky above, an unwelcome sign that darkness is approaching quickly — although it is a sign that spring has finally come to the coast. By the time they reach the bottom of the hill, more dogs can be heard from somewhere behind them, no doubt the same group that Christine could see from the living room window. They don't sound as if they're getting any closer, but it's enough to keep Rachel glancing in that direction often.

"What kind of dogs do you think those are?" Christine asks.

"When they're wild like this it doesn't really matter — they're all dangerous." Rachel points at the road up ahead, where the remains of the last pack is now visible. "Don't get any ideas about saving any of them either — those ones tried to kill us the moment they laid eyes on us."

Christine looks the other way as they pass by the carcasses of the dogs in the road, finding it easier somehow to look at the dead man lying next to them instead. She's been an animal lover since she was little, although neither of her parents would allow any of them in the house. Her mother had a valid excuse, since she was allergic to seemingly every type of hairy creature imaginable, but her father was a different story — he simply didn't like them. More than once in the last several months, Christine has stayed awake at night wondering what happened to all of the pets that used to be under the care of people. Some were trapped in homes, livestock were locked in fields, exotic animals in zoos, poultry farms with countless birds all crammed into ventilated buildings — and all of them were more or less dependent on the human race for their food, water and shelter. Besides these dogs and a few cats in the city, they've seen relatively few domestic animals on their journey — mostly cows and horses wandering around in the countryside.

"Did you have any pets before all of this?" Christine asks quietly, seeing a few people further down the road, walking away from them.

"We had some goldfish in a pond, and my son had a tarantula that I hated."

"What happened to them?"

"The fish are still in the pond as far as I know — but we turned the spider loose before we left. Hopefully it's dead by now."

"I always wanted a cat, but my dad..." She stops in mid-sentence, feeling Rachel pull on her sleeve as she points down a cross street.

"There's a man down there, and I think he's watching us," Rachel whispers, keeping the same walking speed as before.

Confirming her suspicions — as soon as the two of them reach the middle of the intersection, with only another block to the bank, the man starts picking up rocks and pieces of loose brick from the sidewalk and throwing them in their direction, but missing wildly. Christine aims her gun at the guy as they hurry toward the next building for shelter, but Rachel motions for her to lower the weapon.

"He's not gonna hit us throwing like that — just ignore him," she

199

tells the girl. "Don't shoot anybody unless you absolutely have too, there's no telling how many people are within earshot of us."

Seeing no indication of the man following them, they cross the next intersection without a problem — but right after spotting the sign in front of the bank ahead of them, Christine spots something else lying on the sidewalk just past the front entrance.

"What is that?" she asks Rachel, pointing straight ahead of them. "It looks like a body — was that there earlier?"

Rachel holds out her hands and stops both of them, recognizing the clothing immediately. "No, that's the guy from the shed — the guy that saved us."

"Is he dead?"

"It looks that way." She looks around the area closely, knowing that there's a good chance that the old man could be nearby — but the only people she can see is the growing crowd of infected wandering around down by the harbor. "Stay here for a minute," she says, leaving Christine behind as she sneaks quietly down the sidewalk with her gun pulled out — stopping just short of the first bank window. She can hear talking inside, and when she peeks through the glass she sees Curtis tied to a chair on one side of the lobby, and another man slapping him across the face and yelling at him. She looks around at the rest of the bank and sees nobody around, then she slowly backs away and returns to where she left Christine.

"What'd you see?" Christine asks.

"That old bastard has Curtis tied up — we need to get him out fast."

"How do we do that?"

Rachel thinks for a moment, looking at a line of cars parked across the street from the bank, and then at the people down the road. Finally, she pulls her radio out and glances at it quickly, then holds it out and offers it to Christine. "One of us has to get his attention, and the other has to shoot him. Do you have much experience killing people?"

"Not really, no," Christine says, taking the radio from her. "What do I have to do?"

"Sneak up to that window and wait for my signal, which will be a thumbs up — then turn the radio to alarm and run like hell. You can hide around that last corner."

"Where will you be?"

"I'll be hiding behind that car across the street. As soon as he comes out, I'll shoot him."

"And what if I can't make it around the corner in time?"

"Just set the radio close enough to the corner to make it work — it doesn't have to be right in front of him." She waits for Christine to nod her lukewarm approval, then she points at the alarm switch on the radio. "Just flip that switch — but make sure you wait for my signal, okay?"

"Okay, I got it."

Keeping low to the ground, Rachel jogs down to the first car that's parked across the street from the bank, watching the windows of the building closely to make sure she isn't seen. A light is coming from inside the lobby that wasn't there before, and she can see a lantern burning on top of a desk just a few feet from where Curtis is tied up. The old man is standing over it, warming his hands as he continues talking to his captive. She glances to her left, where the infected are still several blocks away, and then back to Christine, who's kneeling down about thirty feet from the front entrance of the bank. Rachel closes her eyes and takes a deep breath, then opens them again and gives a thumbs up to Christine, who then sets the radio down onto the pavement and turns the alarm on, which blasts out a loud siren that echoes throughout the entire section of town.

The alarm is louder than Rachel anticipated, and her immediate fear as she watches Christine run for her life back up the hill, is that it might attract too much attention during a time when the infected are gathering in numbers. Seconds later, she sees the door to the bank fly open, and the old man exits with a rifle in his hands, taking only a short glimpse at the radio before he looks around at the rest of the surroundings — spotting Rachel easily as she stands up and aims her pistol at him, firing several shots before he has an opportunity to defend himself. Her first couple of shots miss him entirely, hitting the brick wall behind him instead — but the next one hits him in the left shoulder, followed by another one that strikes his abdomen just below his sternum. He fires off a quick shot of his own as he falls back against the brick, holding the rifle with only his right hand, but the bullet flies clear over her head. Seeing him drop the rifle and grab for his handgun instead, Rachel fires twice more, but misses both times, causing her to duck behind the car as he points his own pistol at her and unloads several rounds into the vehicle.

She can hear more gunshots coming from further away, which she can only assume are coming from Christine's weapon — but when she looks down the street she can't see any sign of her. Hearing some loud, painful moans coming from across the street, she waits a few moments after the last gunshot to peek around the car tire, and sees the man slumped down into a seated position with his hands at his side. His head is slumped too, but she can see his chest heaving as his lungs take in the cold, damp evening air.

After taking another look up the road to the north, where she still sees nothing, Rachel rises to her feet and slowly approaches the disabled man — then she carefully aims her gun at him again and sends another bullet into his chest, which elicits absolutely no reaction from him. Hearing footsteps to her right, she sees a disheveled Christine appear from around the corner, her jacket and face covered with blood as she walks in a trance-like movement down the sidewalk.

"Are you okay?" Rachel asks. "Are you hurt?"

The man suddenly moves his hand and raises his gun into the air, causing Rachel to jump back and pull the trigger once more before the magazine runs out of ammunition — but his arm continues to lift his pistol, until the muzzle of it is pressed firmly against the side of his head. An instant later, a shot is fired, and his body falls completely to the ground.

With shaking hands, Rachel loads another clip into her gun, then turns to a frightened looking Christine who walks carefully around the newly formed stream of blood on the sidewalk. "Christine, are you okay?"

"I'm fine — it's not my blood," she responds, staring past Rachel and toward the harbor instead. "We should get inside, they're coming this way."

Rachel spins around, and sees a small group of people walking up the hill toward them — but the larger crowd behind them is also looking their way. "Grab the rifle," Rachel tells her, as she reaches down and snatches the two pistols from the old man. "We might be here for a while."

CHAPTER 26
ABERDEEN: MARCH 31ST

Retreating into the living room with her sons, Sarah aims her pistol at the sliding glass door and waits for the knocking to continue, then cocks her gun when it finally does. What started out as a friendly rapping has now turned into a violent assault on the door, and she's afraid of what might happen if they actually manage to break the glass panes.

Matt is standing beside her with a gun himself, and Ben is sitting on the couch behind them, armed with an aluminum baseball bat that he found in the closet of the back bedroom.

"Why can't we shoot through the glass?" Matt asks, his voice shaky with fear.

"Because we'll be left with no protection at all. Besides, we need to make as little noise as possible, so we don't arouse any attention from the neighborhood."

"*Who's outside?*"

The voice startles Sarah, who quickly points her gun at the hallway and sees Larry standing there with a bottle of water in his hand. "Jesus, Larry, I almost shot you!" Sarah yells, turning her attention back to the door. "I didn't even see you get up..."

"Yeah, clearly — but who's at the door?"

"One of those things I'm guessing," she answers.

"I think it might have followed me," Matt says. "I went outside for just a minute to see if that family had a gun with them when they died."

"Well, they're gonna wake up the neighborhood if they keep this up." Larry motions for Ben to hand over the baseball bat, then he checks his sidearm for ammo and puts his coat back on.

"Where're you going?" Sarah asks him.

"To take care of it. Wait here, I'll be back in a minute."

"You must be feeling better..."

"Not really, I feel like shit," he says, still limping badly.

He leaves through the front door, and a minute later they hear the rusty hinges on the metal gate beside the house creaking as they're forced open. Then they hear Larry's voice behind the house, bringing an end to the constant banging on the glass — but the noise is soon replaced with a sharp thud, followed by another. Sarah rushes to the sliding glass door and looks out through the curtains, seeing Larry standing over a small-framed man who's lying on the ground with his arms raised into the air in a defensive stance — and when she closes the drapes again and turns around, she hears more hits as Larry continues the beating.

"Is Larry okay?" Ben asks.

"He's fine, he's just making sure the guy can't hurt us."

"What if they're healthy?"

"They aren't."

"Yeah, but they could be. Maybe they just need our help..."

"Ben, listen to me..." she says, in as soft and soothing of a tone as she can muster under the circumstances. "Nobody in his right mind would just beat on someone's door like that, especially not anymore — and he also has bruises all over his body."

In truth, she didn't see the man well enough to tell whether he had bruises or not, but she was hoping the innocent lie would be enough to ease Ben's conscience. After the sound of the assault stops, they hear the gate open once again, and then they see Larry dragging what's left of the frail man across the front yard and down the street.

"Where is he taking him?" Matt asks.

"He's probably afraid he'll attract too much attention," Sarah answers.

"From who?"

"From anything that wants to eat him."

They watch as he disappears from sight, walking further into the neighborhood that extends up the hill past the hospital. When he returns a few minutes later, he's busy wiping his face and hands with a sanitizing wipe, followed by the bat and his shoes — then he simply tosses the contaminated wipe onto the pavement and continues along the pathway to the house. At one time, not so long ago, littering like that would've enraged Sarah, especially something filled with so many toxic chemicals — but at this point it seems like an incredibly foolish thing to argue about. Even if he were to throw it in the garbage can next to the house, it's not as though there's anybody around to pick it up anymore.

He walks in and sets the bat down in the corner of the room beside the door, then takes his coat off and throws it onto the couch. "Any sign of Curtis?" he asks Sarah.

"No, Rachel and Christine went to the bank to look for him there," she answers back, a little concerned as to what his reaction might be.

Without saying anything, he walks in front of the window and stares down the hill, and then at the hospital that's still burning in places, with massive streams of smoke rising from the broken windows throughout the entire complex of buildings. "I heard gunshots a few minutes ago, coming from that direction," he finally says.

"Oh my god..."

"There were a few different guns going off — did they take a radio along with them?"

"Yes," she answers, handing him the other handheld radio. "Should one of us go check on them?"

"Rachel, Christine, are you there?" he says into the radio. When there's no immediate answer, he turns to Sarah again. "How long ago did they leave?"

"Not long, just before you got up."

"I'm gonna go outside — I might get a better signal out there."

"Are you mad?" she asks as he opens the door.

"I'm too tired to be mad, Sarah — I just want this to be over."

He steps outside and sits down onto the wet grass, oblivious to the feeling of the cold ground soaking into his pants. "Rachel, Christine, can you read me? This is Larry." He can see the clearing horizon to the west, where the setting sun is painting the remaining clouds a golden color against the blue sky, and sending the last few rays of sunshine into the city of Aberdeen below him. If not for the terrible circumstances, this would be the first pleasant evening of the year, with even the wind blowing across the harbor feeling somewhat warmer than usual — although still bitterly cold by most standards. He also sees numerous silhouettes in front of the hospital, moving through the thick smoke as it rolls out of the doors and windows and into the parking lot next to it.

He holds the radio up to his mouth again, feeling the dreaded sense of despair wash over him as he speaks into it. "Rachel, Christine, please come in — we're worried about you up here." Waiting another couple of minutes, he then stands up and starts to make his way back to the house, his mind grappling with whether to stay here with Sarah and the boys, or to find out what happened down the hill before it's too late to save anybody.

"*Larry, we're fine, we're with Curtis now. I'll get back to you in a few minutes,*" he hears from the radio, the voice obviously coming from Rachel.

Although the bank faces east, Rachel and Christine can see the bright glow of light from the sunset behind them, covering the charred buildings and blackened cars across the street in a brilliant orange hue, and then disappearing completely — leaving the city looking desolate and forsaken once again.

It's not only the ruined structures and emptiness that makes it feel that way — in fact, the downtown area doesn't feel the slightest bit empty. What roams the avenues and sidewalks throughout the city though, feeding on what little scraps are still left, are no longer the residents that once occupied the houses and apartments — those people are long gone. The infected that remain resemble them physically, but their memories and personalities died shortly after the virus became active, and the living shells that have been left behind are now destroying the last pieces of humanity that survive.

Rachel has been living in the present now for as long as she can remember, never looking past the next day or two when her head hits the pillow at night. As horrible as the present is, thinking about the past is even worse, each memory a painful reminder of just how much they've all lost. Family and friends, hobbies — and even the relatively unimportant things like television and music. All of them are gone, likely for good — and accepting that unpleasant truth is something that she simply doesn't have the strength to do.

The most depressing, however, is the future. In all, she's only heard of slightly over a dozen people that survived the virus completely, having never experienced a single symptom. Considering the fact that those same people came from areas as far reaching as the Olympic peninsula, Portland, and the Puget Sound, she has to figure that the odds of living through this were astonishingly low. Even if people were to someday recover, the chances of it happening in her lifetime are practically zilch in her estimation — and the chances of finding happiness again, are even lower yet. It's a discouraging situation to say the least, and one that she hasn't allowed herself much time to think about until quite recently   but as she looks out across the landscape in front of her, where dozens or more infected are scouring the surrounding buildings for food, she can't help but think that the virus' greatest crime was not being thorough enough.

"We should probably stay away from the windows," Christine says from behind her, sitting in the dark and away from the dim light coming through the windows. "In fact, you might wanna get some sleep while everything is quiet."

"When was the last time that you slept?"

"It's been a while. Every time I close my eyes, I see her staring back at me."

"Amanda?"

"No — Beth."

"I know that must have been horrible, but it was Jake that shot her — you don't have anything to feel guilty about."

"I didn't pull the trigger, but I wanted to."

"That's nothing to be ashamed about," Curtis says from behind them, rising from the uncomfortable couch in the corner of the room and into a sitting position. "If we run around feeling guilty about every disgusting thing we do, we'll end up dead just like all of the others."

"You don't feel the least bit guilty about anything?" Rachel asks him.

"I'm sure I will someday — but not today, and certainly not when it protects my family."

"How do you feel?" Christine asks him, as she sits down next to him and checks his various wounds with her flashlight, noticing for the first time the welts and bruises developing all over his face.

"I have a headache, and my hand hurts like hell."

"Do you wanna talk to Sarah again?"

"No, we'd better save the batteries on the radio," he says sleepily, as he struggles to his feet and limps over to a seat beside Rachel. "How many are out there?"

"They keep passing by," Rachel replies. "Hopefully they'll clear out by morning."

"We need to come up with a plan."

"For getting back to the house?"

"No, for after that. We can't stay in the city — not with this many people wandering around. As soon as Larry and I get stronger, we have to move on again — and it can't be east."

"You saw the smoke?"

"Yeah, from the hospital. I don't know if that's Olympia or not, but that was a shitload of smoke on the horizon," Curtis says, taking a sip of water from a bottle that the old man had on him.

"I had an uncle that used to live out on the coast somewhere north of here — we used to visit him a couple of times a year in the summer," Rachel says.

"Was it Ocean Shores?"

"No, it wasn't that touristy. It was really quiet, or at least it was back then."

"Copalis?"

"Yeah, that was it. Have you ever been out there?"

"Just passing through, we usually stayed on the south side of the harbor when we'd come out here. We had a cabin just south of Westport," Curtis answers.

"Copalis is a pretty sparsely populated area — it wouldn't take much to clear it out."

"Clear it out?" Christine asks, her voice sounding indignant. "You mean kill everyone?"

"They're already dead, Christine, or they might as well be anyway."

Curtis watches Christine shake her head as she heads back into the darkness, hearing the squeaking springs of the couch as she throws herself into it. He agrees completely with Rachel, and understands why she feels that way after hearing about the way her son died — but he also doesn't want to force Christine into changing her own perspective. Sooner or later, the circumstances of life will likely change her mind as well — but until then, he doesn't see the harm in feeling some level of compassion for the infected, just as long as that sympathy doesn't interfere with the safety of the group.

"I think she's just tired," Rachel whispers, hearing a slight snoring coming from the other side of the room after only a couple of minutes.

"You know, there's nothing wrong with feeling the way that she does."

"I know there isn't, but there's too much at stake to worry about things like that."

"The infected here are weaker and slower than they are in Grayland — have you noticed that?"

"They're weaker everywhere compared to Grayland."

"If they're the same way in Copalis, it shouldn't take much to take care of them.

"All of them?"

"Like you said, they're dead already."

CHAPTER 27
ABERDEEN: APRIL 5TH

Four nights have passed since the incident in the bank, and although Rachel and Christine managed to get Curtis back to the house safely, neither he or Larry have been physically capable of making the long trip west to Copalis — a destination that everyone agrees is probably their safest bet to avoid as many of the infected as possible. The only possible problem could be Hoquiam, a city that sits on the other side of the western bridges from Aberdeen, and is the only real way of reaching the beaches north of the harbor. From what both Curtis and Larry saw in the early days of the fire, it looked as though it originated in Hoquiam — and from the viewpoint of the waiting room at the hospital, the damage seemed to be even more severe than Aberdeen. Looks can be deceiving, however, and all of them are concerned that the infected could be in much greater numbers than what you can see from this side of the bridge — and worse yet, there's always the possibility that the people there might be similar to the vicious residents of Grayland.

The night before, both Curtis and Larry told the others that they would be ready to move out the following morning, and the timing couldn't be more perfect. With seven mouths to feed, their resources were quickly running low, and the variety of food that was found in the kitchen was proving to be less useful than they hoped it would be — with ancient, spoiled jars of meat and seafood sprinkled throughout the homemade stash of goods. After Sarah opened the first jar and caught wind of the rancid odor coming from the salmon inside, she immediately rounded up the other mason jars without dates written on them and threw them away. When she was done, the group was left with a few jars of pickled beets, a jar of pickled cucumbers, and several jars of almost tasteless applesauce that only Ben seems to enjoy eating. The only form of protein they have actually came from the house next door, where Rachel and Matt found a couple of boxes of dry pasta in an otherwise cleaned-out home. As appetizing as 'pickled beet and apple pasta' sounds, even those few ingredients are beginning to run out — and without a proper amount of protein, reaching the sandy shores of Ocean City or Copalis on foot might prove to be more difficult than they realize.

Aside from a few stray animals passing through the area, the neighborhood has been remarkably quiet — except for one person. Matt was the first to see him, standing on the far side of the parking lot and watching their house closely, with a long beard that hangs down to his stomach. After seeing him again, Larry stood on the front porch and took a couple of shots at him with the .30-06 rifle they took from the bank, but the man took cover before he could zero in on him, and he's maintained an even greater distance ever since.

"He's out there again," Matt says, watching out the front window as the first morning light illuminates the street enough to see the man standing several houses down from them.

"He's always out there," Christine replies from the chair next to him. "It's what the Watchers do — they watch."

"Do you think he'll follow us when we leave?"

"Yeah, he'll follow us — until we eventually kill him."

"Is Amanda a Watcher?" he asks, in almost a whisper.

"No, I don't think there's a name for whatever she is — but she's definitely not one of them."

"Are you guys about ready?" Curtis asks both of them, picking up a bag from the floor and swinging it over his shoulder.

"Yeah, we've been ready for a while."

"How is Ben's foot? I asked him and he just shrugged."

"I think it's okay — he doesn't wanna leave the house though, he's afraid of that guy out there."

"We'll keep an eye on him. If he gets too close, we'll take him out."

After you cross over one of the bridges in Hoquiam, there are two possible routes that lead to the beach. One of them is Highway 109, which runs along the northern side of Grays Harbor — and the other is Ocean Beach Road, which takes you further inland and to higher elevations than the other route. Either way they decide to go, the walk is still somewhere around twenty-five miles according to the map, which is a good eight or nine hours when members of your group are only halfway healed up from their injuries.

When they reach the bottom of the hill and turn toward the west, passing by the smoldering ruins of the county hospital, Curtis instinctively looks behind him to where he last saw Amanda — but this time he only sees an empty road and burned out cars, and a plume of smoke in the distance that's even bigger today than when he saw it from the roof of the hospital a few days prior.

"Stick to the sidewalks, everybody," Curtis says, waving the boys off of the asphalt roadway and onto the concrete pathway instead.

"Why?" Matt asks, stepping onto the curb next to his father.

"The road looks like it's caved in up ahead, and the concrete is reinforced," he answers, pointing up ahead where a few large sinkholes have developed in the middle of the street. "The fire must have burned something under the surface."

The farther west they walk, the more extensive the damage from the fire becomes, with most of the buildings completely burned to the

214

ground as they approach the river that separates the two cities. They can see charred bones next to the highway, half buried beneath inches of fine ash that covers the ground. Crows and hawks are scattered through all of it, picking off the last bits of flesh before it rots away entirely. They can see other animal tracks as well, like raccoons, possum, dogs — and humans, all of them barefoot. The footprints left by the animals have virtually no straight lines at all, unlike what you would expect from a person — they wander around in twists and turns with no rhyme or reason as to the pattern. Alongside of them, however, are what look like dozens of human prints, and any irregularity to the animal signs pale when compared to the chaos and randomness of the infected. From the shifting piles of ash that are constantly moving from the wind off the harbor, they can only assume that all of these were likely created sometime in the last several hours, otherwise any trace of them would've been destroyed by now.

"At least there's no child footprints," Sarah says, noticing that most of them head north, where there's still quite a few houses sitting against the hill with no apparent damage done to them.

"Like a little girl?" Larry asks.

"Something like that."

"Is this the north or south bridge we're coming up to?" Rachel asks from the front, stopping in her tracks as she looks straight ahead.

"The north — why?" Larry replies.

"I don't see it."

"Maybe we're not close enough to it."

"No, she's right," Curtis says. "That bridge is ugly enough to see a mile away." He turns to the left and looks downstream, where another narrower bridge should be sitting right next to them, near the harbor. "I don't see that one either."

At one time, either bridge could be easily concealed behind the commercial buildings and homes in the area — but there are no structures left, and the large concrete foundation of the southern bridge can still be seen rising into the air. The group walks down to the riverbank, where the slow-moving Hoquiam river ends its short run into the harbor — and they can see their first clear glimpse of the city of Hoquiam across it, although all that's left is the outline of foundations where its buildings once stood. The steel structure of the bridge is still protruding above the surface of the river, and they can look upstream and see that the same is true for the northern bridge as well.

"What do we do now?" Rachel asks.

"We swim or find a boat." Larry answers back, looking up and down the river for any sign of the latter.

"I don't know how to swim," Christine says.

"Then I guess we'll have to find a boat."

"There must be one upstream somewhere," Sarah says, as she begins walking on a road that heads north, against the flow of the river.

They continue along the stream, past the ruined northern bridge, until they come to a bend in the river where the expanse of civilization suddenly ends, leaving nothing but burned wilderness ahead of them. Down on the shore, where a small house and outbuildings once stood, they can see a wooden dock with two small boats tied to it. One of them is made out of fiberglass, and is slightly larger than the second one, with an outboard engine hanging off the back of it. The other is an aluminum row boat that's full of dents and scratches, but seems to be in good shape otherwise.

"I don't know if I really trust the engine on the fiberglass one, so I guess that means we'll probably be making two trips with the smaller one," Larry says, as he looks over both boats for any supplies that might have been left onboard.

216

"Do you see him, Matt?" Curtis asks, looking at his son.

"See who?" Sarah asks.

"Yeah, I saw him a minute ago," Matt answers him, pointing downstream in the direction of the last bridge. "He's behind that car over there."

"Are we still being followed?" Sarah asks Curtis.

"Apparently — I can't see shit over there," he replies, squinting as he looks south. "Has anybody ever seen these things swim?"

"Yeah, I have," Christine says. "As long as the water is calm, they don't have any trouble at all."

"Well, the engine is seized on the fiberglass one anyway, so I guess we're taking the row boat," Larry says. "Who's gonna be the first three to cross with me?"

"Sarah and the boys are," Curtis says quickly, sounding as if the topic isn't up for debate.

"We don't know what's on the other side," Sarah responds.

"Everything is burned on the other side — you can practically see the ocean," he replies, obviously exaggerating, but the other side is remarkably visible.

Sarah looks back down the road and sees some movement in the distance — then she sees a man running quickly from one car to another, his movements quick and agile. After watching him for a moment, she sees him move again, only this time with something else shadowing his every movement. "We're not gonna make it to the beach at this rate — we're gonna have to find someplace to stay the night before the sun goes down."

"We still have plenty of daylight left," Curtis says. "Once we get past this it'll go a lot faster."

"I know, but there's two of them following us now," she says, watching a second man follow behind the other. "The first safe place we find on the other side, we're staying the night."

After making both trips across the river, with each of them taking turns manning the oars across the high-flowing stream, they pull the boat up onto the shore on the western side and hide it beneath a pile of twisted metal roofing — the last remaining material of what used to be a home. Although they have no plans to ever return to the area, they also have no idea of whether the northern coast is better or worse than what they've seen elsewhere.

Shortly before they set off down the highway, headed toward the southern route that runs along the harbor, they could see the two men in the distance as they scrambled from one vehicle to the next, each of them pushing and shoving as they fought to stay hidden from sight. Although the entire group was anxious to separate themselves from the watchers, and knew that this was their greatest opportunity to do so, they couldn't help but watch as one of them brutally murdered the other, then tossed his body into the river before disappearing into the brush beside the riverbank. It wasn't the act itself that they found so captivating, it was the almost elegant way that he did it that fascinated them — as if his body were moving in fast-forward. His victim was fast, much more so than most of the infected, but clearly not fast enough to stop the beating that he endured.

The damage from the fire continues through most of Hoquiam, taking with it almost every home and commercial building clear to the high school on the far side of town. The devastation is immense, and despite keeping a close eye out for anything that might prove useful, the group leaves the city limits with only the few supplies they came with.

As they reach the wildlife sanctuary, where the harbor disappears behind a large section of tidal grasslands and muddy channels, the

fatigue from walking begins to catch up with most of the group —
especially after seeing no sign of their follower on the straight stretch
of road to Hoquiam.

"I'm wearing down, guys," Larry says, wheezing as they climb a
slight incline where the road turns north and away from the water.

"We're not even a third of the way there, Larry," Curtis tells him,
although his own legs and back are beginning to seize up as well. "I
figured we'd at least make it halfway before nightfall."

"What is that, another five miles? I don't think I can make it that far
— not after all of that damn rowing."

Sarah ignores the comment about rowing and starts looking at the
map for any possible residential areas nearby. She rowed most of the
way across the river on the first trip over, but she also knows that she
wasn't injured when she did it. "There's a place called Grays Harbor
City just up the road — has anybody ever been there?"

"I've been by there plenty of times," Rachel says. "You can't really
see much from the highway though."

"It's another mile or so up the road, do you think you can make it
that far?" Sarah asks Larry.

"Yeah, I'll be fine — I'm just running out of air."

Nestled in amongst the trees, and only a stone's throw from the
heavily bird-infested marshes of the harbor, Grays Harbor City turns
out to be much smaller than the ambitious name implies. Consisting
of several winding roads on both sides of the highway, the sprawling
community is spread out through thick forests and around small
creeks, where dozens of houses look untouched from the ravages of
the past few months.

One house looks especially well cared for, with stone siding and
vines growing neatly around the doors and windows of the first floor.
It looks as though it was only abandoned a short while ago, and sits by
itself in the middle of a large clearing, with a creek that runs across

the driveway and underneath a small wooden bridge. The only real sign that it's been abandoned is the overgrown grass in the lawn, and the unpruned fruit trees along the highway.

"Matt, keep watching the road — we still don't know if that guy is following us," Curtis says, as they approach the front door with their weapons drawn. He reaches out and turns the handle, and the door swings open against the loud protests of the rusty hinges. "I'm not sure if unlocked is a good thing or not," he says, stepping inside and smelling the familiar scent of dampness. Although the inside of the home doesn't look quite as pristine as the outside, with small patches of mildew on some of the walls and ceiling — it still doesn't appear to be ransacked or damaged in any way, and it quickly becomes apparent that they're likely the first people to walk across the threshold since the outbreak began.

"This doesn't look half bad," Sarah tells Curtis, as they both walk into the kitchen and see containers of flour and sugar still sitting on the countertop.

"There must be two dozen doors and windows on this floor alone though. It's gonna be a bitch to watch every opening," Curtis replies. With Christine and the boys waiting in the living room, he sees Larry and Rachel coming down the stairs after searching the second floor. "Was anybody upstairs?"

"Nope," Larry answers. "There's just an empty master bedroom and an office up there."

"I think that's probably where we're spending the night, we can keep an eye on the staircase a lot easier than all of these windows."

"We did find this though," Rachel says, handing Curtis a handwritten note.

"What is it?" Curtis asks.

"A suicide note."

"And you didn't find a body?" Sarah asks.

"No, we didn't."

CHAPTER 28

GRAYS HARBOR CITY: APRIL 6TH

Still half asleep, Rachel opens her eyes to almost complete darkness, feeling a cold breeze blowing right through the blanket that she's lying under. She looks across the room in the direction of the cold air, and after a few moments of her eyes adjusting to the light level, she finally sees the outline of the bedroom window, and the curtains flapping gently in the wind.

"Larry, are you awake?" she calls out quietly, remembering that he was sleeping on the floor when she went to sleep.

"I'm awake," comes a voice from right beside her.

Although startled at first, Rachel turns her head and sees Christine lying next to her. "Did you open the window?"

"No, it's freezing in here," Christine responds, pulling the blanket up over her nose.

"It must've been Larry..."

"Larry is always cold."

Rachel feels around on the nightstand beside her and finds the flashlight she left there, then shines it around the room, seeing the casement window swung wide open, and wet, muddy footprints leading from the window sill to the other side of the room.

"Shit!" She grabs the blanket and throws it to one side, then swings her legs over the side of the bed and quickly closes the window. "Christine, get up, somebody's been in here."

Seeing Larry still lying on the floor, with the footprints only inches from his body, she leans over and starts shaking him. "Larry, wake up!" she says, still semi-whispering. Finally, after punching him in the arm, she sees his eyes open and glance around the room, his face still a mask of confusion. "We need to stay quiet, but there's somebody in the house, and I'm not sure where Curtis and Sarah are."

All three of them are still wearing their clothing, including the sidearm pistol that accompanies them everywhere they go, day or night — but when Larry reaches down to his side to draw his out, he discovers an empty holster where his gun used to be. Noticing his predicament, Rachel pulls another one out of her bag and hands it to him, then follows the footprints with her flashlight to the open doorway and into the hall. With Larry and Christine following her, and the two boys still sound asleep in the large walk-in closet, she steps out into the hallway carefully, hearing the steady rainfall on the roof, and the gusty winds in the trees from the storm that's passing through. At the far end of the hall, sitting next to the staircase and facing the other direction, are Curtis and Sarah — but the rest of the corridor is entirely empty.

"Go warn them, I'll stand guard here," Larry tells Rachel, as he stands next to the only other door on this floor — a second bedroom that's been converted into a home office.

As Rachel sneaks past the office, she notices that there's no sign of any footprints past it — although they have been slowly fading away since she left the bedroom. She crouches down and then makes three quick clicks with her tongue — a signal that one of them is approaching in secrecy.

"Have you guys seen anybody?" she whispers.

"No, why?" Curtis asks her.

"The window in the bedroom was open when I woke up, and there's muddy footprints right behind you."

"Are the kids okay?" Sarah asks, suddenly alarmed.

"They're fine, they're still asleep, but whoever it is might still be in the office."

Curtis sees Larry waiting down the hallway, but as he stands up and takes a few steps in his direction, they all hear the creaking hinges from the front entrance downstairs, and the sound of the wind as it blows into the house and up the staircase. "Larry, check the office, make sure we're alone up here..." With a ninety-degree turn at the bottom, none of them can see the living room downstairs, even with a lantern illuminating the last few steps — but they can hear slow-moving footsteps on the hardwood flooring below them. Curtis aims his gun at the bottom landing as the noises become louder, watching as the flickering propane flame dances around in the breeze.

"Whoever comes up those steps, you need to shoot them," Sarah says quietly, standing right beside him with her own weapon drawn.

"You should go back and stay with the kids, just in case," he replies, feeling anxious about their two sons with only Rachel and a scared sixteen year old watching over them. After she disappears down the dark hallway, he hears Larry come out of the office and stand next to him.

"The office was clear, they must have gone back out the window."

"How the hell did they get up there?"

"The roof of the back deck comes right up to it."

"Shit, I should have thought of that."

"I think they might have snagged my gun too — I'm sure I had it on me when I went to sleep."

The footsteps, still moving incredibly slow, stop right before reaching the landing — and a beam of light suddenly appears, gradually working its way up the wall toward Curtis and Larry's location. They both back up as the beam flashes over the chairs that Curtis and Sarah were sitting in only minutes before — then it disappears completely, and the footsteps continue once again, this time heading toward the back of the house.

224

"Are they leaving?" Larry asks.

"It doesn't sound like it — they aren't heading back to the door."

Seeing Rachel exit the bedroom to join them, Larry looks down at Curtis' gun and notices that he has it gripped in his left hand, which doesn't really surprise him considering the damage that Amanda did to his other wrist. "Let me and Rachel take this one — you can back us up from the top of the stairs," Larry says, glancing over at Rachel to get her approval, which he does.

"I'm perfectly fine," Curtis answers back.

"How many rounds have you shot with that hand?"

"Probably not enough."

"Just hang back here, we'll take care of it." As Larry sneaks back down the hallway and listens at the top of the stairs, he feels a pull on his coat, and he turns around to see Rachel leaned in closely.

"Are you sure this is a good idea? Maybe we should wait until light to check it out..."

"They're not waiting that long — these things strike fast when they decide it's time. Just keep track of where I am, and shoot anything else that moves."

He steps down off of the first step and hears a slight creak from the wood underneath the carpet, but the rest of the way down he stays completely silent, hearing more footsteps from the living room as another door opens up. As he turns the corner on the landing and creeps into the living room, he just catches a glimpse of a figure vanishing through a doorway — a door that was locked when they first arrived at the house.

"Let me go first," Rachel says, stepping beside him. "I won't make as much noise across the floor."

He steps aside and waits for her to take the lead, then watches the front entrance that's still wide-open and waiting for anybody to walk through. There's several sounds of footsteps coming from the other

225

door, sounding as if someone is descending down another flight of stairs and into a basement — then a loud sound of metal crashing against the floor echoes throughout the house, and Rachel begins firing her gun rapidly at the doorway, stopping only when the pistol runs out of ammunition. Seeing her back away and lower her weapon, Larry stands in front of her and sees a flashlight sitting on the basement floor below, part of it shining on a person sprawled out on the bottom tread.

"Larry, watch out!" Rachel screams at the top of her lungs, pointing behind him toward the kitchen, where another man is aiming a gun right at his head.

Larry instinctively grabs for the pistol as the first shot is fired, dropping his own gun in the process, and sending the bullet into the front wall behind them — then as he wrestles the man to the floor, another shot rings out and hits the sleeve on his coat, but just barely misses his flesh. The man eventually drops the gun when Rachel starts stomping on his hand, but he still manages to scramble to his feet and pull a knife out of his pocket. For a moment, all three of them just stay still, with the man standing over a defenseless Larry, and with Rachel holding an unloaded pistol in her hand — but then another shot is heard, followed by several more, and they see the man slowly crumple to the ground as Sarah steps down from the staircase landing and into the living room.

Larry immediately scrambles to his feet and finds his gun, then looks down into the basement where the man is still lying in the same spot — this time with blood pooling up on the floor next to him.

"Are you sure he's dead?" Sarah asks from behind him, looking at the man she just shot.

"Yeah, they both are," Larry answers, still looking down at the basement. "Rachel, why don't you go check on the others — tell them we're fine."

226

"Shouldn't we all go upstairs?" Sarah asks, as Rachel exits the room. "I didn't want her to see this."

"See what?" Larry steps aside and shines his flashlight down the staircase, where she sees the man lying dead on the floor, surrounded by a stockpile of survival supplies. "Do you think he was healthy?"

"We've never seen the infected store anything like this." He steps just inside the room and looks around at the rest of the basement, making sure that nobody is hiding in a corner somewhere, then he walks to the front entrance and closes the exterior door. "I'm gonna find something to cover him up. If she asks, he had bruises all over his body — okay?"

"Yeah, okay. What about the other guy?"

Larry stands over him with the light, and they both cringe when they see the grotesque condition of his face. You can only scarcely tell what he looked like before the infection — his darkened eyes and gangrenous wounds effectively concealing those features from them. What they can tell, however, is that this is definitely the same man that's been following them since Aberdeen — they recognize the long beard, which he clearly had for some time before the outbreak.

"Is this what happens to all of them?" Sarah asks.

"The unlucky ones I suppose."

"You've seen others like this?"

"Yeah, even worse." He pulls a blanket from the back of the couch and throws it over the man, then reaches down and picks up his stolen gun from the floor. "Here, give this back to Rachel, it came from her pack," he says, handing the other pistol to Sarah. "You should try to get some sleep before morning, we really shouldn't stay here another night."

Waiting for her to leave the room, he grabs a rug off of the floor and then heads down the staircase and into the basement, where he finds a homemade calender on the wall with some the dates crossed

227

out. The last day marked was March 21st, which could mean that this is either the 20th, 21st or the 22nd, — or possibly none of them if the man was delusional. The group lost track of the date over the winter months, when the endless days of non-stop rain and wind merged each day into the next — but they do know for certain that they're in the month of March, so the timing seems about right.

The man didn't have any weapons, only a flashlight and a wallet — the latter of which contains a photograph of a family, including a husband, wife, and three kids. While there are no clues as to what happened to the others, he does find it rather strange that the man wasn't armed with some sort of defense, and it makes him wonder whether this area might actually be relatively safe. Unless he was a prepper beforehand, no sensible person would ever stockpile the amount of food he sees on the shelves in front of him, because no single person, or even small family, could possibly consume all of it before it spoiled. Wheat, for example, will last practically forever when left whole — but when you grind it into flour, you reduce its potential shelf life to a matter of months. On the floor, under a neatly organized shelf of commercially canned fruits and vegetables, sits multiple sacks of flour, of all different sizes and brands — much like the rest of the inventory. To Larry, it appears as though Mr. William Pirkola lived through the viral outbreak — then spent the last several months of his life gathering all of the food items in the neighborhood. The fact that he was taken out in a case of mistaken identity is certainly tragic, but that's not an uncommon thing these days. Every house they pass by, and every car, business, or pile of bones they come across, they all have a tragic story behind them — and the only difference between this story and all of the others, is that they've been here to witness the conclusion of his.

There was much debate of whether to stay longer in the Pirkola house, considering the amount of food and clean water that was available — but in the end, none of them truly felt safe behind those walls, or any of the other houses in the area for that matter. The location was just too close to the cities of Aberdeen and Hoquiam, and too far away from the easy harvest of shellfish along the sandy beaches of the Pacific. The next morning, they gathered what supplies would fit into two wheelbarrows, and set off down the highway once again, all of them determined to reach their destination by sunset.

By the time they reach the coast, where the highway turns to the north and heads into the Olympic Peninsula, the sun has only started to peak in the overcast sky overhead. The only lengthy stop they made was where the picturesque Humptulips river crossed beneath the road, dumping vast amounts of water into the harbor right before it flows into the ocean. It's also home to countless salmon that breed just a short distance upstream, although none of them could see any while they were there.

Over the last several miles, after passing by several individual houses and a few small communities, they still haven't seen any sign of life anywhere — infected or otherwise. Even the road is vacant, with no cars or scattered bones along the way.

"What's that way?" Matt asks his father, pointing at a road that heads south toward the opening of the harbor. The two of them are walking together side-by-side, each pushing a wheelbarrow as the others walk slightly ahead of them.

"That's Ocean Shores," Curtis answers.

"It looks like there's smoke coming from it."

"It might be from Westport on the other side — they sit across the bar from one another," he says, glancing back at the thin wisp of smoke that's moving quickly in the stiff wind. He can't really tell where it's coming from exactly, but from this angle it appears that Matt could be right — it certainly looks like it's coming from Ocean Shores.

"It might be healthy people, like us," Matt says, still looking back at the long road behind them.

"Yeah, it could be. If they're still around in a few months, we might have to check it out."

"Do you really think it's safer where we're going? I mean, truthfully?"

"I don't know, son — but there were fewer people over here even before the virus hit, so it stands to reason there'll be fewer infected." He points at a house they're coming up to, taking the boy's attention off of the town behind them. "The driveways are a good sign too."

"Why is that?"

"They all have cars parked out front, and the houses look like they've been empty for years. You know what that means?"

"That the people are dead?"

"It sounds horrible, but I think it's a good thing."

In many ways, this section of coastal highway looks similar to the roadway between Westport and Grayland, with thick stands of pine, alder, and Douglas fir trees on both sides of the pavement, and very few places where the ocean is actually visible. Although they've remained dry for their entire walk up to this point, the skies suddenly open up as they reach the southern edge of Copalis Beach — a town that seems every bit as empty and deserted as the other places they've seen throughout the day.

Most of the structures that they can see from the highway are small rental cabins and seasonal homes, none of which were likely to have visitors when the virus struck nearly seven months ago. They're also the reason the group chose to come to this location, because the permanent population is so incredibly small. Having said that, it's the larger homes that the group is most interested in checking out, houses that might be stocked with essentials, like food and water, and possibly even weapons — but these are also the places that pose the most danger. The infected are an obvious cause for concern, especially the kind that they found living in Grayland — but even those that are healthy present a substantial risk.

After crossing over the Copalis river, and past several vacant campgrounds, they eventually come to a large, two-story house on the outskirts of town. It has visibility on all sides, and shutters on the windows that are already secured into place, something that gives them all pauses as they approach the front door.

"Should we knock?" Larry asks, noticing the two cars that parked under a carport next to the house.

"Go ahead, it probably wouldn't hurt," Curtis says, as the group huddles together underneath the roof of the porch, trying to stay out of the downpour of rain.

He knocks on the door, then patiently waits for a response — feeling strangely awkward at the same time. After a few seconds he knocks again, then he wiggles the door handle quietly and finds that it's locked.

"Larry, I don't think anyone is gonna answer — there's a dead cat on the window sill," Sarah says, looking inside at what appears to be a living room.

The front door has a small, oval window with textured glass in the middle of it, which Larry quickly breaks out with a rock from a flower bed. He then reaches in and opens the door, and is surprised to be met with the smell of fresh air coming from inside the home. Their first impression is certainly mixed, with miscellaneous trash and clothing thrown onto the floor, and open cans of food and dirty dishes stacked everywhere in the kitchen — the smell of which is being washed away by the open windows and door beside the kitchen table.

It takes Sarah a few minutes to take everything in, as they try to decide whether the place looked like this before — but then she picks up an open can from the countertop and looks inside. "This chili has been opened recently — probably within the last day or so." She looks at some of the other cans, and sees a mixture of old and new scattered around the room. "Somebody is living here."

"There's some graves in the backyard," Larry says, standing in front of the back door and looking out at two mounds of soil, each with a crudely made cross on them. "They look pretty new."

He turns and looks down a hallway beside the kitchen, an area they haven't checked yet, and sees at least three open doors down the length of it. As he places his hand onto his pistol and takes a couple of steps forward, someone jumps out of the last room and fires a few shots directly at him, then runs down to the end of the hall and disappears around a corner.

"He's running across the backyard!" Curtis yells, aiming his gun through the open door.

"Wait, hold your fire!" Larry says, placing his own gun back into the holster. "The little asshole just has a BB gun."

"Did he hit you?"

"Yeah, but I think they lodged in my coat."

"How old is he?" Rachel asks.

"I don't know, a little older than Matt maybe." Outside, hiding behind a fence at the edge of the dunes, he can see the boy crouched down and staring back at him. "Wait here, I'm gonna check that room out."

"Be careful, he might not be alone," Rachel warns.

As Larry walks slowly down the hallway and aims his gun into the first room, he hears something from further down the corridor, like someone sniffling. He checks each of the rooms as he passes by, with

Curtis right behind him, but when he quickly moves into the last doorway and aims his gun inside, he almost drops the revolver onto the floor. A girl, who can't be any older than seven or eight, is standing in the middle of the room and clutching a blanket with both arms, her eyes filled with terror as she stares at Larry and Curtis.

"Was that your brother back there?" Larry says softly, as he holsters his gun and drops down onto one knee. After the girl shows absolutely no reaction, he looks at both Rachel and Sarah and waves at them to come down the hallway.

"I'll watch the boy," Curtis says, returning to the kitchen.

Sarah steps in front of Larry and enters the room slowly, causing the girl to back up against the far wall. "It's okay, we're not gonna hurt you..."

"Does she look sick?" Larry asks, from outside the room.

"No, she looks fine — she's just scared," she says, sitting down on the floor just inside of the room. "Do you have a name? My name is Sarah..." The girl says nothing at first, but even after a few minutes of just sitting there, Sarah can see her anxiety start to lessen little by little.

"Tina..." the girl says, almost whispering the name.

"That's a pretty name, Tina — and what's your brother's name?"

"His name is Albert."

"Are you two hungry by any chance? We have plenty of food..."

Tina nods her head. "I am, but Albert won't eat anything."

"Why is that?"

"He's sick."

CHAPTER 29
COPALIS BEACH: SEPTEMBER 15TH

Sarah is looking out at the surf, watching as her two sons attempt to catch their first fish from straight out of the ocean. This isn't their first attempt — she's lost track of how many times they've been out here getting cold and soaked to the bone, all to catch something that's relatively easy to find in the stream beside their house. Still though, she's impressed at their determination to accomplish something that isn't easy — knowing that sooner rather than later, they're going to face a situation where even the most basic of necessities will seem impossible or out of reach.

It's been over six months since they've seen a human being outside of their group, and while the warmer months of summer provided them with greater comfort and a chance to settle into their new homes, their experiments in gardening and beekeeping have been nothing short of disastrous. They knew that raising vegetables along the coast would be difficult, especially so close to the beach itself — but they really had no idea how many hurdles to expect. The cold, wet weather of spring was their first problem, not allowing the seeds to properly germinate — then once it did actually warm up, the insects and fungus annihilated much of what was left. Their only saving grace was the variety of mature fruit trees and berries throughout the neighborhood, which provided them with just enough food to supplement the canned goods they've stockpiled, a supply that was stressed with so many people depending on it. With the warm weather now slowly diminishing, however, and replaced with the brisk nights of mid-September, Sarah worries about the coming months of winter, which seem to last forever in this harsh environment of endless rain and wind.

The local sustenance that they've all been enjoying, including fruit, seafood, and small game — is starting to show signs of mildew and rot without the proper refrigeration or canning necessary to preserve it, and the bitter reality of survival without modern conveniences is finally starting to sink in.

It was only a few weeks ago that they finally decided to split their group into two neighboring houses — the Lockwood family in one — and Larry, Rachel, and Christine in the other. The hardest thing was deciding where to place Tina, but in the end she made the choice for them, and informed Sarah that she would be living with them. The fact that Matt and Ben are so close to her brother's age was probably a factor, but as the weeks and months passed by, she talked less and less about the boy who once meant so much to her.

Tina was right about Albert being sick, but it wasn't exactly in the way that they imagined it would be. He didn't have the virus, since he had no bruising or congestion to speak of, and exhibited no strange behavior. He was simply wasting away, little by little, from a disease that was never figured out by any of them, and never responded to the medication they tried. The information that could be found in the homes around the area didn't exactly help, since medical books and encyclopedias disappeared years before the outbreak began, and were replaced with an Internet that no longer existed. The health clinic on the outskirts of Ocean Shores provided them with medicine and emergency supplies — but it too had little in the way of printed literature. He died in early May, at the age of only fifteen. Curtis speculated that it might have been some form of childhood cancer that took him, or possibly another long-lasting form of the virus that killed their parents months before — but in the end, none of them really knew what happened, and the memories of her family were beginning to slowly disappear from Tina's young mind.

As much as Sarah worries about their future food supply, she's also grateful that the horrors of their past seem to be gone, at least for the time being. The constant stress of being overrun by the infected had all of them at their breaking point, and most of them still find themselves waking up in the middle of the night from a panic attack, or hearing a knocking sound that doesn't actually exist. Over the past several weeks, their days mostly consist of cutting firewood for the coming winter, and trying to figure out how to ration food and toiletries to make them last as long as possible — but they also keep an eye out for other things as well, sometimes in secrecy for fear of looking foolish. Among them, only Rachel has given up on the survival of humanity. The others still look for contrails in the sky, or boats on the water, or listen to their hand-crank radio as they fall asleep at night. They've waited months for a sign — but so far, they haven't seen or heard anything that gives them even the slightest bit of hope.

"Have they caught anything?"

Sarah turns around and sees Curtis walking down the path toward her, carrying a pair of binoculars in his hand as he sits down beside her on the sand dune.

"No, nothing yet. It's probably mussels for dinner again tonight," she says, looking back at the ocean where Matt and Ben are still casting into the incoming tide.

"We'll go back to the river again tomorrow — we should be able to snag whatever the hell is sitting under the bridge."

"I think they're steelhead."

"Well, whatever they are, they'll look better in the bottom of a frying pan."

"Do you remember what we were doing exactly a year ago today?"

"Yeah, we were packing the truck for the drive north, right?"

"Not in a million years did I ever think it would get this bad."

"It could be a lot worse — we could still be in Grayland, or Westport."

"Have you thought about the fact that Matt and Ben's best and only prospects for marriage would be a little girl, a bratty teenager, and a grieving widow that's older than we are?"

"I hadn't really thought about that, no," Curtis says, laughing at the idea of it.

They both sit in silence for a while, listening to the perpetual rushing of the ocean current as it moves further inland against the setting sun. Sarah glances down the beach, where she can see several houses lined up along the shore, and where every night at this time she half-expects to see lights come on from inside the homes as the sunlight disappears from the sky. She looks back at the ocean, and sees a flash of light suddenly appear in the fog ahead of them, then it disappears again after a few short bursts.

"Did you see that?" she asks, pointing slightly to the south.

"No, what was it?"

"It looked like a..." She's interrupted by another series of dim flashes, only this time red instead of white. "There, did you see that?"

"Yeah, it's the lighthouse..." Curtis says, dumbfounded.

"Which lighthouse?"

"The one in Westport."

EPILOGUE
WESTPORT: SEPTEMBER 15TH

Closing the door of the lighthouse behind him, Aaron turns around and faces the pine trees that are blowing in the breeze, then begins his nightly routine of walking along the pathway through the dunes and onto the streets of Westport.

Although it's been weeks since he's seen another person, and several months since he's seen more than one at the same time, he still stands in the shadows every evening and watches closely for any sign of movement between the park and his new home. After the smoke appeared in the south, he saw crowds of the infected following the highway out of town, with just a few stragglers left behind — most of them too injured or weak to move very far. Since then, he's had the town mostly to himself, seeing only a dozen or so of them returning after the fires settled down sometime in April.

Hearing a couple of dogs barking in the distance, he places his hand into his pocket and grabs onto a pistol, then relaxes when he finally realizes that they're only coyotes. Twice in the last week alone, he's faced a growing pack of wild dogs that have settled in Westport over the summer. In that short span of time they've managed to wipe out virtually every cat and rabbit in the area, and the scarcer their food supply becomes, the more willing they are to take on bigger prey — like himself. Still feeling spooked, he begins jogging the last two blocks to his house, and is relieved when he turns the final corner and sees an empty road between him and the front door.

After the infected left, he could choose any house in town that he wanted — but most of them had already been trashed and picked over by the time he started searching them. One was the Regency Hotel, a place he'd only seen from the outside while passing by in a car, despite living in town his entire life. He spent one night there, attempting to sleep in a room that looked untouched and perfect — but he woke up in the middle of the night, hearing strange noises and slamming doors echoing down the long corridors. When he left the next morning, he was surprised to find the doors still locked, and figured that the people who kept him up all night must have been there since he arrived.

There were only a handful of houses that had been unoccupied from the beginning, and the one he chose to live in was the closest to the beach. It's an older, single-story ranch house that had been deserted since the beginning of the evacuation. His parents actually knew the owners, and he found their car sitting in the middle of the road not far from the hotel — and what was left of their bodies still lying in the front seats.

Sliding the key into the lock, he turns the handle and steps inside, locking the door behind him as he takes his coat off and starts to place it on the hook — but then he freezes, and simply stares straight ahead when he sees another coat hanging in its place. Feeling his heart pounding, he reaches inside of his pocket and fumbles around for his gun, then hears a voice coming from the living room behind him.

"Don't bother with the gun..."

Still holding the coat in his hands, he spins around slowly, and sees his sister sitting in a chair next to the fireplace, which has already been lit. She has a gun in her hand that's aimed in his direction, and a knife in the other hand that's resting on the chair cushion.

"I thought you were dead, Aaron," Amanda says, her voice cold and without emotion. "I thought you were still lying in our basement, starving to death..."

"No, I got out," he says, stammering as he looks at the back door in the kitchen.

"Aren't you glad to see me?"

"Yeah, of course I am," Aaron answers back, his voice shaking with fear.

"I feel bad for what I did to Dad, I really do. I even feel bad about Diane — but I'll give you a choice I never gave them."

"What choice is that?"

"Do you want your death to be quick — or slow?"

ACKNOWLEDGMENTS

I'd like to thank everybody again for continuing to support this series, your words of encouragement (and sometimes nagging) have really meant a lot.

My next book, which I've already started, is titled 'The Regency', which tells the story of the hotel that was featured in 'Westport'. A few people have asked me whether it's based on a real-life place, or completely made up — and I suppose the honest answer is both. There was a grand hotel in Cohassett Beach before WWII, and they would actually pick people up at the docks and transport them by stagecoach to the front entrance. It all was quite fancy for the Grays Harbor area, but there were investors at that time that were convinced that Westport could be a place where people of high society could vacation and spend their money. Needless to say, things didn't work out in the way they'd planned. That real-life place, which didn't survive for very long after the war, was the inspiration behind my own fictional hotel.

After an additional stand-alone book later in 2019, book 4 of the Grays Harbor Series should be ready for publication sometime in early 2020.

As always, you can find updates on my website, jamesbierce.com, along with information on where you can find my books for sale.

Thanks again for reading — and be sure to tell your friends about it (unless you didn't like it, in which case silence would seem the appropriate response)

Sincerely,
James Bierce

Made in the USA
Monee, IL
06 January 2020